WHISKERS OF THE LION

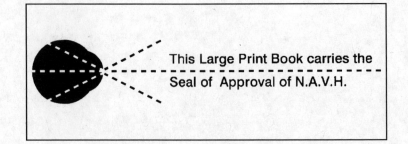

This Large Print Book carries the
Seal of Approval of N.A.V.H.

For Noah, Grant, and Pierce,
who have shown us
the magic in life that is possible
only with grandchildren.

AN AMISH-COUNTRY MYSTERY

WHISKERS OF THE LION

P. L. GAUS

THORNDIKE PRESS
A part of Gale, Cengage Learning

GALE
CENGAGE Learning®

Farmington Hills, Mich • San Francisco • New York • Waterville, Maine
Meriden, Conn • Mason, Ohio • Chicago

GALE
CENGAGE Learning®

Thorndike Press® Large Print Mystery.
The text of this Large Print edition is unabridged.
Other aspects of the book may vary from the original edition.
Set in 16 pt. Plantin.

LIBRARY OF CONGRESS CATALOGING-IN-PUBLICATION DATA

Gaus, Paul L.
    Whiskers of the lion : an Amish-country mystery / by P. L. Gaus. — Large print edition.
        pages cm. — (Thorndike Press large print mystery)
    ISBN 978-1-4104-7774-3 (hardcover) — ISBN 1-4104-7774-6 (hardcover)
    1. Amish—Fiction. 2. Large type books. I. Title.
PS3557.A9517W48 2015b
813'.54—dc23   2015014958

Published in 2015 by arrangement with Plume, an imprint of Penguin Publishing Group, a division of Penguin Random House LLC

Printed in Mexico
1 2 3 4 5 6 7 19 18 17 16 15

PREFACE AND ACKNOWLEDGMENTS

The theme of this novel is taken from the Scriptures, but Sheriff Robertson's story arose from a modern song, "Pacing the Cage," written several years ago by the Canadian musician Bruce Cockburn. I particularly like the version sung by Jimmy Buffett on his 1999 CD, *Beach House on the Moon.* As I wrote the novel, and as the sheriff's story unfolded for me, I found myself listening to this song often. I greatly admire both the writer and the singer. Cockburn wrote (and Buffett sang) about the inside of the cage. I have written about the outside.

I am especially and continually grateful to my wife, Madonna, for reading my novels with a critical eye, and for her insights on this one in particular. I also thank my two older grandsons, Noah McKee and Grant McKee, for their enjoyable and enthusiastic discussions with me on the content and

7

direction of the story's ending chapters. They are very insightful young men.

Next, I wish to thank the editors at Plume, and especially Denise Roy, senior editor, who has believed steadfastly in this series and whose support has been of great encouragement to me personally and of great benefit to me as a writer. I am also most grateful for the fine work of Mary Pomponio, publicity manager at Plume. Many thanks are due also to my agent, Jenny Bent, for her critical and useful comments on the manuscript.

I finally thank Steve and Dawn Tilson and Kate Clements for an engaging evening of literary discussions, which helped me to discover the title for this novel.

Have I not commanded you? Be strong and courageous. Do not be terrified; do not be discouraged, for the Lord your God will be with you wherever you go.
— JOSHUA 1:9

1

Wednesday, August 17
4:50 A.M.

Stan Armbruster had been a Holmes County deputy sheriff long enough to know that even the best day could skip sideways on you like a ricochet. With the instincts of all patrol officers, he had ridden his entire career knowing that the positive could flip to the negative with the single bark of a gun. A bark as arresting and irreversible as the clang of a bell.

But Stan Armbruster wasn't going to ride in patrol cruisers any more. He was done with that. Done with the uniforms and done with the heavy-duty belts of gear. Now he'd wear a suit with a simple leather badge case hung from his suit pocket. He'd trade the big 9 mm pistol for the diminutive .38 revolver of a detective.

Armbruster stood in his new suit in front of the closet-door mirror in his trailer home and liked what he was seeing. He liked it so much that he found it easy to dismiss his patrol officer's instincts for the negative. Found it easy to dismiss thoughts of gunshots, ricochets, and clanging bells. Found it easy to be positive, because his first day as a probationary detective would surely prove to be the best day of his life.

Armbruster fished in the side pocket of his suit coat and took out his new flip case of business cards. He fanned the short stack of cards, then closed the case and dropped it confidently back into his pocket. Then he finished the knot in his tie, cinched it under his chin, and studied his new image in the mirror. Hair black, growing out long enough to sustain a part. Complexion fair, with a ready smile, offset by a dark blue suit with a sophisticated charcoal pinstripe. White dress shirt with a roomy collar and a red power tie. A new look for a newly minted detective. He was done with crew cuts, uniforms, patrol cruisers, and rental trailers. He smiled at himself and turned for the front door.

There he smiled, too, at the photo on the wall of his partner, Detective Pat Lance. Maybe, he dreamed, this would be the day he would tell her. Maybe this would be the day he'd ask her out. If not today, then soon. Because it just wouldn't do for her to learn, before he had a chance to explain himself, that he kept a picture of her at his door.

Outside, August's moist heat painted Armbruster's cool skin with cloying humidity. Runoff from the overnight rains dripped from wet branches hanging heavy and low. The last cloudburst had just finished with the racket of close thunder. Runoff clattered from the trailer's metal roof into the gutters and downspouts. As he locked up, a vaporous negativity again brushed the margins of his thoughts — Fannie Helmuth, missing since April, probably already dead.

But OK, Stan, *be positive.* They'd find Fannie Helmuth soon enough, safe after all, in some remote Amish colony a thousand miles away.

Then again, maybe not. Maybe she really was dead. Fannie Helmuth. The locus of Sheriff Robertson's summer-long obsession.

Settling in behind the wheel of his red Corolla, Armbruster shook his head. Stop this, he thought. Just *stop* it. The sheriff will never change. Giant Bruce Robertson — impulsive, insistent, and impossible. As big as a Barcalounger, with the personality of a tank commander.

So do your job, Stan. Hit it early and have

another report on Robertson's desk before the man makes it down to the jail. Go out to their farm and wake up the Dents if you have to. Ask them again. Not that they'll ever tell you anything. Not that they'll ever admit they know where their Howie has been hiding with Fannie Helmuth.

Armbruster started his car, turned on the air conditioner, and drove down the lane toward the blacktop of County Road 189. At Ohio 83 in Holmesville, he turned south toward Millersburg. At Courthouse Square in Millersburg, he joined truck traffic climbing eastward up US 62. Outside town and down in the next valley, he turned south on Ohio 557. After the long curve at the roadside tourist stands, he angled right to climb a wooded hill on an unmarked gravel lane. When he crested the hill, Armbruster parked on the hill in front of Miller's Bakery and set the brake because of the sloping grade. He got out in the dark and walked past a line of black buggies, the familiar country fragrances of fresh road apples and wet horsehair ushering him up to the door. Aromas like this outside a bakery? Armbruster thought. Only in Amish country.

Inside, Armbruster stopped to let his eyes adjust to the white-hot glow of the Amish gas mantles spaced at intervals across the

12

low ceiling. Morning sales had long been under way, and a mother in a black bonnet and shawl was paying for pastries at the cash register. Her three young daughters, also in black shawls, pulled close to the hem of her long olive dress when they saw Armbruster enter through the screened door.

At the front of the salesroom, a white-bearded grandfather in Amish-blue work denims was stacking loaves of bread into his wicker basket. He gave Armbruster a reserved nod of his head. Two Amish lads in black denim suits stood beside a low table at the rear of the salesroom. They were pouring coffee for themselves from a steel thermos into Styrofoam cups. They ignored Armbruster with the practiced aloofness of religious separatists, mixed with the disdain of all teenagers, making private jokes at the expense of their elders.

From the back, one of the older Miller girls carried a wide aluminum tray of pies out of the kitchen and said to Armbruster, "Sticky bun, again?"

Armbruster smiled, "Maple cinnamon today, Edna."

The girl set her tray down, brushed flour from her hands, and turned back toward the pastry case. Over her shoulder, she asked, "You're not on patrol?"

"New job," Armbruster said and stepped up to the front of the case. "The biggest one, there at the corner," he pointed. "It's a celebration."

The girl teased the corner bun away from the rest, dropped the bun into a white pastry box, closed the lid, and handed the box across the top of the case to Armbruster. "I can take your money."

Armbruster handed her five dollars. "Keep the change."

Back in his Corolla, Armbruster put the pastry box on the passenger's seat and drove down off the hill to turn right again on Ohio 557. In the quiet little burg of Charm, he parked beside the Roadside Amish Restaurant and went inside as the first dim hint of sunrise was giving vague outline to the congestion of old rooftops in town. He took a seat in a booth by the front windows and ordered the farmer's special — eggs over easy, bacon, sausage, hash browns, orange juice, toast with butter, and coffee. When he had finished his celebration breakfast, the sun was coming up stronger on a day that Stan Armbruster planned never to forget. Outside, the heat of an August morning was already starting to build.

■ ■ ■ ■

From Ohio 557, Armbruster made the sharp turn onto County Road 70, to climb the blacktopped lane up toward Troyer's Ridge. Overnight rains had left the pavement wet and puddled, and the Corolla's tires hissed and splashed as Armbruster leveled out to turn north through a stand of timber on narrow Township 369.

This would be Armbruster's second visit to the Dent farm this week. The sheriff had ordered the visits at least three times a week. Drive the narrow blacktop and gravel lanes north of Charm, out into the middle of pastureland nowhere, and ask the Dents again. Ask a thousand times if you have to, Robertson had insisted. Find Howie Dent. Whatever it takes. Because that's where we'll find Fannie Helmuth.

Armbruster crested the rise south of the one-room Troyer's Ridge schoolhouse, and he turned his Corolla right onto Township 371 toward the Dent farm, which would be at the second lane after the turn. But first, Armbruster came to the long drive leading back to the deserted Jonas Helmuth farm, and as he passed the drive, the corner of his eye caught a patch of yellow off to his left.

15

He stopped twenty yards beyond the gravel, backed up, and looked toward the main house some seventy yards down the drive. There sat the yellow VW bug.

In that single glimpse of yellow, Stan Armbruster's celebration came to a halt. He flashed the thought of a bullet striking a bell — a ricochet. His grand breakfast was a distant memory. The maple cinnamon bun lay forgotten on the passenger's seat beside him.

This was going to be Howie Dent's yellow VW. Armbruster considered the radio, but as he pulled to a stop behind the VW, he saw that the doors were standing ajar. An odd assortment of items had been tossed out onto the gravel on either side of the car.

Armbruster shoved his gear shifter into park and shouted out the window, "Howie Dent?" He got nothing but lifeless silence in response. He shut his engine off, climbed out, walked a circuit around the VW, and made a mental catalog of the puzzling items scattered on the wet ground beside the car.

There was an old red backpack, soaked from the overnight rains, zippers pulled open, apparently empty. Armbruster picked it up and felt inside the pockets. Nothing there.

In addition to the red backpack, there was

a small travel pack of tissues floating in a muddy puddle outside the passenger's door. There were also the contents of a typical glove compartment strewn across the gravel nearby — a tire gauge, a metal penlight, a bottle of aspirin, and napkins and straws from fast-food restaurants.

As he mounted the wooden steps leading up to the front porch, Armbruster again called, "Howie Dent?" He tried the door and found it unlocked. Heading inside, he called, "Howie?" and stepped farther into the front hallway. Deserted since April, the empty house sounded cavernous. "Where are you, Dent?"

In the parlor, the long Amish-purple drapes hung like sentinels, in straight pleats of plain cloth guarding either side of the glass. Morning light sparkled the dust that stirred into the stale air as he paced around the empty room. As he walked down the long hallway to the kitchen, Armbruster's footfalls on the hardwood floor punctuated his steps and gave him grade school memories of tapping a hollow wood block for music. It reminded him of the simple tunes of his childhood. The trouble was, it wasn't the pleasant tune of a grade school melody that was playing right then in his mind. It was something more frenetic.

Something more akin to distress. Maybe Led Zeppelin in manic high pitch, Armbruster thought, or a wrenching guitar solo by Carlos Santana.

Armbruster continued to search inside. Like the rest of the house, the kitchen hadn't been used in months. Drawers and cabinets stood open and vacant, just as the Helmuths had left them when they had packed up last April and cleared out abruptly for Kentucky.

At the back porch, Armbruster climbed down the short run of block steps to the outside and hurried across the muddy yard to the tall barn at the back of the property. With each step, he felt his polished shoes sinking into the ruination of the muddy drive, but he dismissed this in his urgency to find Dent. A lightning strike broke suddenly into a clap of thunder over the pastures to the east, and a hard wall of rain fell instantly down, soaking his hair and the shoulders of his blue suit coat just before he managed to duck into the cover of the barn.

Ten paces in, Armbruster could smell dried manure and pungent, moldering hay. The barn was obviously deserted, but he called out for Dent again. A flight of purple martins shot loose in the rafters.

Armbruster stood inside the wide doors

18

of the barn and watched a gloomy wall of gray rain hammer the gravel of the drive as if it were an anvil, eradicating his footprints in the span of only minutes. Erasing tracks that might have been made there. Then, as suddenly as it had started, the rain stopped.

Distrusting the break in rain, Armbruster hurried out onto the drive again and turned right toward the little Daadihaus. There, too, he searched inside for Dent. But he found only the gloom of an abandoned home.

Outside, a light rain had started to fall again. Not bothering to run, Armbruster crossed the drive to go back inside the main house. There he searched briefly upstairs. Most of the bedroom furniture had been taken away when the Helmuths, the extended family of Fannie's brother Jonas, had caravanned to their new land in Kentucky. In the second-floor bathroom, he tried the faucet in the sink, but it was dry.

So the well water tanks in the attic were empty, Armbruster muttered. Of course. They would have disconnected the windmill when they left. Again he felt the abandonment. Even the water had deserted the pipes.

Down on the first floor, on the screened back porch, Armbruster took an old rag from a Shaker peg and sat on a wicker chair to wipe the mud from his new Florsheims. Standing again, he turned in place to remember his last time in the house. He and Ricky Niell had guarded the Jonas Helmuth family while Robertson hunted the county roads for Teresa Molina's gray Buick, which had been described by Fannie Helmuth and identified among others registered in northern Ohio by after-market tire prints that Armbruster had molded from the muddy edge of the Helmuths' driveway.

Armbruster remembered that day. He had guarded the rear of the house from this very porch. Down the interior stairs, the family had taken shelter in the basement.

Armbruster crossed back through the kitchen to the top of the basement steps. Using the handrail, he eased down the steps in the dark until his feet found the dirt floor of the basement. He could see only the dim shape of an eight-by-eight upright post, and he reached out for it, caught his suit on a protruding nail, pulled back, and heard the expensive fabric of his sleeve take a short rip. He groaned in self-reproach, fingered the tear, and climbed back up the steps, angry with himself for the vanity of his new attire. In better light, he inspected the tear in the sleeve, rolled his eyes, and muttered a scolding invective at himself. Then he pulled off his ruined suit coat and tossed it in a heap onto the kitchen counter.

A battered red kerosene lantern was hanging beside the back porch door. Armbruster found matches in a kitchen drawer, lifted the globe to light the wick of the lantern, set the globe back into place, and turned again for the basement steps. Lantern in one hand, railing in the other, he descended.

The lantern's flame threw a troubled glow of yellow light onto the basement's dirt floor and gave dim outline to the posts and walls. On the far wall ahead of him, there were wood shelves for canning jars. The shelves were empty. Against the wall to his left there was a stack of empty wooden crates and pallets, held in store perhaps for firewood. To his right, clotheslines hung lifelessly from hooks in the braces. His eyes adjusted more to the lantern's anemic glow, and Armbruster saw worn leather tack and harnesses, pegged to the wall beyond the weary clotheslines. And it was only then that he noticed the faint odor of urine, mixed strangely with something sweet. Maybe alcohol.

Armbruster took another anxious circuit around the front portion of the basement, then turned to the back part behind the step risers. A boarded partition nailed to the risers partly divided the front half of the basement from the back. He rounded the corner of the partition and saw a vague and disturbingly upright form strapped to the far side of another eight-by-eight post. He turned the wick of the lantern higher and advanced. The question, *Howie?* caught in his throat, and he asked aloud, "Who's there?"

No movement. No sound. He stepped forward and came around to the other side of the post. He took a nervous step in place, and something sounding like plastic cracked under the sole of his shoe. He lifted the lantern to eye level, advanced two steps, and was startled by the swollen, bloodied face of Howie Dent.

There in the basement, in the lantern's pale light, Probationary Detective Stan Armbruster stared with shock at the pale death mask of a man who had died badly after hideous torture. He stared slack-jawed at the evidence that Fannie Helmuth might now be dead as well. He stared with an addled mind at the proof that was written in Howie Dent's ashen face. The proof of both the beginning and the end of Armbruster's new career, over and done with in this morning's single clang of a metaphorical bell.

The big celebration breakfast rumbled in Armbruster's gut like corked fury. He set the lantern down on the dirt floor and circled back to the steps fighting a vomit reflex. With one hand clamped over his mouth and the other hand pulling himself along the railing, he labored up the steps. Running then, and losing control of his stomach as he crossed the kitchen linoleum, he spewed vomit onto his shirt and tie, and hurtled himself on unsteady legs down the back steps. Outside Armbruster doubled over onto his hands and knees and felt a wet chill soak into the expensive fabric of his new suit pants as he heaved the rest of his breakfast onto the grass of the back lawn.

Then, with his legs rubbery and his mind struggling to make sense of a useless tangle of grotesque images and fragmented thoughts, Armbruster got himself somehow back to his Corolla. He sat behind the wheel, pulled the microphone off the dash hook, and clamped the fingers of both trembling hands over the switch to radio in. "Armbruster! Over."

He eased back in the driver's seat, groaned from the gut, and drifted among ragged thoughts. He was alone. He wasn't sure how the new temp dispatcher would handle him. He was defeated. She had started just yesterday. He was finished. Adele "Just Call Me Del" Markely. Brought over from the Mansfield Highway Patrol to handle communications while Ellie Troyer-Niell was bedridden during a difficult third trimester with twins. Ricky Niell was home with Ellie, taking paternity leave. Mind wandering, Armbruster realized that he didn't know if Del Markely had responded to his radio call.

"Base, this is Armbruster. OK?"

"Go ahead," Markely responded evenly.

"Howie Dent is dead. Helmuth farm. Need the captain. Medical Examiner. Everybody. Over."

"What's that twenty, Armbruster?"

"Helmuth farm. North of Charm."

"I'm gonna need more than that, Armbruster."

"The sheriff knows where it is, Del! Just send everybody out here!"

Exhausted by shock and emotion, Armbruster switched off and pulled himself out of his car. Leaning against the front fender like a derelict hobo, he felt his stomach heave again, this time dry, and he bent over at the waist to wait it out. Then he sank to his knees, turned himself around, flopped down with his legs out straight, arms limp at his sides, back resting against the front wheel, with cold wet mud soaking into the seat of his new suit pants.

"A new suit, Stan?" he whispered to himself. "Really? Get a grip! What happened here? THINK."

Fannie Helmuth had disappeared in Charlotte with Howie Dent in April. On a bus run from Sugarcreek to Sarasota.

Robertson had been manic since then to find them. Best hope, that Fannie Helmuth and Howie Dent were hiding in one of the remote Amish colonies that were scattered across America. Second-best hope, that knowing the danger to Fannie, they'd never try to come home. Not without the sheriff's help.

But now they *had* come home. At least Howie Dent had.

It had all started with the murder of Ruth Zook, an Amish girl vacationing in Sarasota's Pinecraft colony. Murdered by the Teresa Molina drug gang. For refusing to deliver a suitcase of drugs that she had been coerced into carrying on the bus ride home to Ohio.

Her friend Fannie Helmuth had then gone to the sheriff to say that she had earlier brought home a suitcase, too, one that she now suspected had also held drugs. She had

25

carried the suitcase for a woman in an old gray Buick. Teresa Molina.

Then the sheriff's sending Ricky Niell on the chase to Florida, hunting the Molinas. And a shootout in Sarasota/Bradenton's eastern outskirts. Killing Dewey Molina, cousin to Teresa. And Teresa Molina and the rest of her crew? Vanished like smoke on the wind.

So Fannie Helmuth had fled the sheriff's protection. With Howie Dent's help. And Ricky Niell had tracked them as far as the bus depot in Memphis.

Thus you were assigned the Dent watch, Stan, Armbruster chastised himself grimly. Show up three times a week and ask Richard and Susan Dent if they've heard yet from their son. Two days ago, they had answered again in the negative. Now their son was dead.

So here you sit, Stan, Armbruster thought, laughing nervously. New suit ruined, and you *failed* Howie Dent. Celebration breakfast spewed across the lawn, and you *failed* Fannie Helmuth. Promotion to detective now a total loss, and you *failed* your first day on the job.

And the whole happy gang is headed right here to your position.

And what position is that, Stan?

The unwitting victim of a ricochet.

Fumbling uselessly with the quandary of unringing a bell.

Butt down in the mud.

On the worst day of your life.

2

After Armbruster's call, Holmes County's captain of detectives, Bobby Newell, was first to arrive at the Helmuth farm. Newell had planned this as a personal day, and when the call had come in from dispatcher Del Markely, he had been standing on the second tee, dressed in blue-and-white-checkered Loudmouth golf pants, a matching knit golf shirt, and a white visor. He changed out of his golf shoes before leaving the parking lot at the country club, and he drove for Troyer's Ridge still dressed in the rest of his golf clothes.

A short fifteen yards into the Helmuth drive, Newell parked, switched on the flashers of his sedan, and climbed out. He saw Armbruster standing beside his Corolla in front of the yellow VW farther down the drive, and Newell raised his voice. "Tire

28

tracks, Stan? Footprints? What?" He tossed his golf visor in through the open window and waited for an answer.

Armbruster shook his head, called back, "All washed out in the rains," and waved Captain Newell forward. Once Newell had reached his position, Stan added, "If anything was ever out here to see, I've already tracked over it. Then the rain washed it out."

"You've been inside?"

"Everywhere. He's in the basement."

"You sure it's Dent?"

Armbruster nodded. "I've been staring at his driver's license photo for the last four months. He's a mess, Captain, but it's Dent."

"Is Fannie here, too?"

"No."

"You sure, Armbruster? I mean dead certain?"

"Pretty sure, Captain. Before I found Dent, I had gone through the whole place."

Newell rubbed with frustration at the small black patches of hair over his ears, and then he ran a palm nervously over his bald pate. "We've got to be sure about her, Stan."

At the front end of the long drive, the medical examiner's van turned in and stopped. Melissa Taggert stepped out at the driver's door and called down the drive, "OK to move up?"

Newell waved her forward, and Taggert pulled the van around the captain's sedan. Behind her, a cruiser pulled in and stopped, and Pat Lance got out in her customary blue pantsuit. Newell waved her forward, too, and Pat came ahead on foot while Taggert parked her ME's van beside the back corner of the house. As Pat Lance was walking up to Armbruster's Corolla, Taggert called back, "Where is he, Stan?"

Grimly, Armbruster shook his head. "In the basement."

Joining the others beside the Corolla, Taggert next asked, "OK, who has been inside?"

Armbruster gave a chastened shrug of his shoulders. "Only me, but I tracked it up, Missy. Went up and down the basement steps at least twice with muddy shoes."

Missy Taggert turned back to her assistant, who was just opening the rear doors of the van. "Booties and gloves for now," she called out. "We'll dust and photograph everything going down the steps. But nobody goes down to the basement floor until I clear it."

The assistant pulled boxes and a camera

bag out of the van and disappeared around the back corner, heading for the rear porch door.

Armbruster shook off dejection. "I wasn't careful, Missy. You'll find my prints on the railing and in the kitchen. Everywhere, really. And muddy footprints, too. I thought I'd find Dent in the house somewhere. Never thought he'd be dead."

Intending encouragement, Missy said, "Maybe we'll find what we need with the body."

Melissa Taggert, Missy to her friends, had first held the elected position of Holmes County Coroner. Then, because of her medical and forensics credentials from Ohio State University, among others, she had been appointed Holmes County Medical Examiner. On duty, she dressed perpetually in either green or blue scrubs, and she managed not only the county morgue in the basement of Millersburg's little Joel Pomerene Memorial Hospital, but also forensic investigations out of a lab she had built and equipped there with the aid of her husband, Sheriff Bruce Robertson. A little younger than her big husband, and considerably slimmer, she still had a fair and youthful complexion and moderately long brown hair that had been naturally curly since she was a child.

She studied the chagrin written into Stan Armbruster's expression and said, "You found him, Stan. That's a good thing. Otherwise, he might have rotted there for weeks."

Seeming too distracted to notice her attempt at kindness, Armbruster said only, "I need a change of clothes. Need to clean up."

"OK," Taggert said, "but what am I going to find in the basement? Tell me that much before you go."

"It's dark," Armbruster said. "I left a kerosene lantern down there, but you'll need flashlights to see anything clearly."

"Or lights on a stand," Taggert said to Newell. "With a generator."

The captain nodded a command to Pat Lance, and Lance said, "Right. Lights and a generator." She stepped off to the side to make a call.

Then Captain Newell pressed Armbruster. "Tell us what you saw, Stan. All of it."

"I got a good look at his face. He's bound to an upright post behind the steps. Strapped in place with rope or something. Maybe tape. And I held the lantern right up to his face. I lost it, Captain."

"Then how can you be sure Fannie

Helmuth isn't down there, too?" Newell advanced. The muscles in his neck and jaw were bunching into knots. His arms were flexing and his fingers were clenching and opening as if he'd just finished a workout with his free weights and needed to dump tension from his muscles. Newell seemed to notice the tension he was broadcasting, so easing his tone, he said, "Relax, Stan. Just tell us what you know."

Armbruster hesitated. "I didn't see her, Captain. Fannie, I mean. Doesn't mean she isn't here."

Newell nervously adjusted his thick black glasses, pulled Pat Lance along the drive toward the back corner of the house, and called over his shoulder, "Where's the lantern, Stan?"

Armbruster shouted at their backs, "In the basement, right at his feet," and he leaned unsteadily against the front fender of his Corolla.

Taggert ran after Lance and the captain, caught up with them on the back steps, and said, "Wait. Booties and gloves."

At the back of the van, the three put gloves on their hands. Taggert pulled three flashlights out of a drawer, and once they were standing on the linoleum floor of the kitchen, they put booties over their shoes.

Then Captain Newell led Lance and Taggert down the basement steps.

They first searched forward from the base of the steps to the far wall with its canning shelves. Then they worked down the left side of the basement, turning over pallets and crates to look under them for a second body. Once at the back corner, they could see the body of Howie Dent strapped to the post under the steps. He was illuminated by the erratic, yellow glow of the flame that Armbruster had left burning in the kerosene lantern at Dent's feet.

Newell held the lantern up to Dent's face as Taggert approached with her flashlight. She paused and then took a step forward for a better look, and she felt something crunch under her foot. She backed carefully away, pointing with her flashlight to debris on the basement's dirt floor. Back at the base of the steps, she directed Lance and the captain to search the other corners of the basement, and once they were certain that Fannie Helmuth wasn't there, she led them back up the steps, saying, "We won't go back to the body until we've rigged the lights." Then she went outside to her van.

In the kitchen, Captain Newell pulled Detective Lance aside. "How much of him did you see, Pat?"

"Enough," she said. "He was tortured. I've never seen anything like that. Looked to me like his whole body was one vast carpet of blisters."

"I saw punctures in the skin," Captain Newell said. "Like needle marks at the centers of swollen blisters."

Missy came back inside with her ME's bag. "That's an ugly way to die," she said. "I mean strapped in place like that. How long until I'll have those lights?"

"I called," Detective Lance said. "It won't be long."

3

Wednesday, August 17
11:15 A.M.

Well beyond the bounds of propriety, and significantly past all pretense to the contrary, Sheriff Bruce Robertson was indignant. Also irate, and why try to hide it? He wanted them all to know — his wife, the medical examiner; his captain of detectives; and all the patrol captains. His three detectives, and all the deputies inside and outside the jail. Everyone for miles around for that matter, Amish and English alike. The whole state of Ohio, if need be. Because murder in Holmes County was one thing, but torture/murder was quite another.

The sheriff's deepest instincts told him to charge into the investigation of this murder, but his intellect told him to wait. It told him to let his new detective bureau take the lead, and with mounting difficulty, Robertson was struggling to obey his intellect. So outside on the Helmuths' driveway, as Bobby Newell's and Missy Taggert's investigations crept forward in the farmhouse, the heavy sheriff paced beside his blue Crown Victoria, relegated to the role of an observer.

Truly, it galled Robertson to have to watch from a distance. Scuffing at the gravel of the drive, the sheriff heard himself growl, and he recognized the agitation that this morning of disengagement was causing him. He marched back to his Crown Vic, bent over to the glove compartment, and pulled out his bottle of Ativan. This was his latest prescription. Something new to address his long summer's anxiety over the failed search for Fannie Helmuth. Years before, he had taken Ativan in combination with an anti-depressant. That was before he had married Melissa Taggert.

But Missy had been a blessing to him, and he hadn't needed the Ativan so much. In the years since their marriage, he had tapered off the medicine. Now, with Fannie Helmuth missing, everything had changed, and Missy had insisted that he start taking the Ativan again. For his anxiety. And a regimen of aspirin for the chest pains.

Still, the last four months had been harder on Robertson than anything he could remember, and although he grumbled about having to take the Ativan, the truth was that it cooled him out when he most needed to remain calm. He crunched one small white tablet between his back teeth, took a long pull from a bottle of water, and slammed the door on his Crown Vic, all the while watching the back corner of the house for movement.

After long and anxious minutes, the sheriff finally saw Bobby Newell come around the corner of the house, walking slowly as he made notes in a spiral pad. The captain was still dressed in his checkered golf outfit. Robertson marched immediately up to him and spouted, "Bobby, I need to get down there."

Newell looked up from his notepad and shook his head. "No, Sheriff. We're still processing evidence."

"Does Missy know that I want to see the body?"

"You're not the only one, Sheriff. She's telling everyone 'no.' She's not ready."

"Then she can send somebody up here with a report!"

The sheriff got no reply from Captain Newell other than a slow shake of his head, so as Newell returned his attention to his notepad, Robertson struggled alone to frame the argument that would get him into the basement. The argument that Missy could accept.

But Missy had said no, and Robertson knew his wife better than anyone did. There might as well be an iron gate bolted across the door to the basement steps. Nobody but Taggert and her people was going down to the body. Not until she was ready. Robertson clamped down on his ire and started again to pace on the drive. When it was apparent to Newell that Robertson would have nothing further to say, the captain returned to the kitchen at the back of the house, leaving Robertson alone again with his thoughts.

A short while later, tires crunched in the gravel behind the sheriff, and Robertson turned to see his chief deputy, Dan Wilsher, pull in behind the sheriff's Crown Vic. Wilsher climbed out into the August heat, pulled off his gray suit coat, and asked Robertson, "Why are you out here on the driveway?"

Exasperated, Robertson huffed, "Missy says I'll contaminate the scene."

A sympathetic smile drifted across Wilsher's face. He tossed his suit coat onto the driver's seat of his car and loosened his tie. With his belly straining against his belt more than last year, Wilsher smoothed his shirt in front and took his first look at the scene outside. There was the main house — two and a half stories of white-sided solidity. There was the tall barn — painted tobacco red and faded in weathered places to rust brown. There was the little Daadihaus to the rear — an Amish tradition for farmers who had raised their families and then retired. And there was the yellow VW with its doors standing open — parked like an abandoned wreck, near the front corner of the house.

Wilsher frowned and rubbed at a nervous tic on the back of his neck. "You sure that's Howie Dent's yellow bug, Bruce?"

"Yes," Robertson muttered. "The plates match."

"It looks like somebody pulled it apart," Wilsher said. "And tossed its contents out onto the driveway."

"They did. Stan Armbruster insisted that he needed something to do. He has just cataloged and photographed everything that was in it."

"Is Armbruster still here?"

"Went home to change. He's still *wobbly,* as Bobby puts it."

Wilsher ignored the indignant tone of the sheriff. "OK, Bruce, do we know for certain who is dead down in the basement? Who it is that Missy is looking at?"

"It's more like 'what it is' that Missy's looking at."

"But is it Howie Dent?"

"Missy won't say for sure."

"Do we have a wallet, fingerprints, anything like that?"

"Haven't found a wallet. And Missy told Bobby it'll take some time for the swelling to go down. Can't get prints just yet."

"Once she gets him to the morgue, she can use dental records," Wilsher said.

"Missy says that's gonna take a while."

Then, wondering why the Ativan wasn't helping, Robertson held an uncomfortable silence beside Wilsher and rode the strong pulse in his temples. Gauging his level of anxiety to be increasing, Robertson stepped back to his sedan, crunched a second tablet of Ativan, and carried his water bottle back, to stand again beside his chief deputy. "That's Howie Dent's VW," he complained to Wilsher. "And if it's really Howie Dent in the basement, then Fannie Helmuth is already dead."

"You didn't find her here, did you?" Wilsher asked.

"Doesn't mean she isn't dead."

"OK, Bruce. But if this really is Dent, his parents could identify the body. It's the best

ID we could get."

Robertson shook his head. "He was tortured, so Missy has ruled them out for an ID. She wants Mike Branden to identify the body."

"Why Mike Branden?"

"Howie Dent was Branden's student a few years ago. She figures that if Mike can give us a more reliable identification, then that spares the Dents."

"More reliable than what?" Wilsher asked.

"Armbruster. He's the only one who's sure that it's Dent."

"You'd think the Dents would be here, waiting or something," Wilsher said. "Keeping vigil."

"Here and gone already," Robertson said. "I had a deputy take them back to their farm. It's the next one over."

"How bad is it in the basement, Bruce? Really."

Robertson kicked hard at the gravel under his feet and stared angrily at the deserted farmhouse. "Missy says he was tortured with a syringe. Other than that, she really hasn't told me much."

Wilsher acknowledged the sheriff's display of anger with a silent and awkward nod of his head. He rubbed at the nervous twinge on the back of his neck and said, "I've called in all the patrol captains, Sheriff. I've got everybody I can spare out looking for Fannie Helmuth."

Robertson's eyes drifted to the skyline, and there was distance in his gaze. "I should have found her a long time ago, Dan."

Wilsher stiffened. "This is not our fault, Sheriff."

Robertson wheeled around to face his chief deputy. "It's somebody's fault, Dan!"

"Yes, but not *our* fault," Wilsher said evenly, taking Robertson's heat and trying to quench it with reason. "Dent should never have come back here, Bruce. Not before you had the Molina crew in custody."

Robertson took an aggressive step forward to reply, but at the end of the long drive, Professor Michael Branden pulled his small white pickup onto the gravel lane. Once he had parked, the professor came up to Robertson directly. "Any sign of Fannie?"

Robertson growled out, "No!"

Long familiar with the sheriff's intensity, Branden said only, "OK, Bruce. Where's the body?"

Robertson led the professor up to the back steps and handed him nitrile gloves and paper booties. Raising his voice over the portable generator, Robertson said, "Missy's still working on him. In the basement."

Branden gloved himself and pulled the booties over his sandals. "I was in a meeting with the new college president. She's not happy with my status as a reserve deputy."

"She's been there a year," Robertson said. "You'd think she'd be used to it by now."

"I was on sabbatical, Bruce, and we only just met. She thinks I should have come back to campus sooner."

"When did you get back?" Robertson asked as he led the professor up the steps.

"Couple of days ago."

"When will classes start?"

Branden said, "Week and a half."

Robertson turned back to face the professor. "Tell her you're mine until then, Mike."

"I don't think she'll appreciate that."

The professor was wearing jeans and a green and white Millersburg College T-shirt. His full gray beard, trimmed close and carefully edged, made sharp contrast with his new Florida tan. His hair was still mostly brown, but it was bleached lighter from the Florida sun. It was long, parted, and combed, and it showed a little more gray at the temples than Robertson remembered from before the professor's sabbatical.

Inside the kitchen, the sheriff took Branden to the top of the basement steps. There he called down to his wife. "Mike Branden's here, Missy. I'm sending him down to give us a better ID."

Branden stepped around the generator's electrical cables that fed down the steps, and he descended into the basement that Missy had flooded with light.

When Branden came back up, the sheriff thought he looked pale under his tan. Outside, Branden stripped off his gloves and booties and leaned back against the house. The fumes of the gasoline generator soon made him nauseated, so he rounded the corner and stood in the narrow line of noon shade between the driveway and the house.

Robertson followed Branden without comment, and the professor took a minute to speak. "Bruce, it's Howie Dent," Branden said eventually. "I'm certain of that. I'm also certain that if you let his parents see him like that, they'll never get over it."

Robertson punched a fist into his palm. "We should have prevented this!"

"What would you have done, Bruce? Maintained county-wide roadblocks for the last four months?"

"I don't know," Robertson answered. "This weighs on me, Mike. It weighs on me hard."

"Well, it shouldn't," Branden said.

Robertson had nothing to say. Head

down, he glowered silently at the gravel of the drive.

"That's Howie's VW, right?" Branden asked.

Robertson tipped a nod.

Branden continued. "But I thought he left it parked in the lot in Sugarcreek when he and Fannie Helmuth got on that bus to Sarasota."

"He did," Robertson said. "I impounded it for a couple of weeks, right after they disappeared. Then I sent it back to the Dents."

"OK, but when did *Howie* get it?"

"Don't know."

"But you sent it back to the Dents?"

Robertson straightened up a bit. "A couple of months ago."

"Has it been at their farm all this time?"

"Yes," Robertson said, heading immediately for his Crown Vic. He pulled the door open, sat behind the wheel, and said, "Mike, you're right. If Howie had come home for his car, they should have called me right away."

Branden leaned in at the window. "Maybe the Dents haven't been telling you everything they know about their son."

Robertson cranked the engine of his Crown Vic to life. More exasperated than at any other time that morning, he said to the professor, "Get in, Mike. While Missy finishes up here, I've got some new questions for Richard and Susan Dent."

4

In uniform, Deputy Ryan Baker ushered Sheriff Robertson and Professor Branden into the Dents' living room. Richard and Susan Dent, looking haggard and worn, came immediately forward from their kitchen. Susan Dent, thin, short, and frail, paused in the archway wringing her hands silently, as if her not asking about her son carried the power to deny his death. Richard Dent, stout and authoritative, addressed Robertson directly. "Is it really our Howie, Sheriff?"

Robertson walked past Richard Dent and took Susan's arm to escort her to a seat on the sofa. She cried out, "No!" as he seated her, seeming to deflate with the sheriff's gentle and telling gesture, losing all the stubborn hope she had managed to sustain as she had waited for official news of her son's death to arrive.

Only when Robertson had attended to her did he turn back to Richard. "Yes, Mr. Dent, I'm sorry. We think it is your son."

Richard took the news with mechanical woodenness. Stubbornly, he asked, "How do you know?"

"We've had his photo for four months, Mr. Dent. Our Detective Armbruster identified him from that. And the professor, here, knew your son well."

Branden held out his hand to Dent. "I am Mike Branden, Mr. Dent. Howie was my student. I am sorry for your loss."

Stunned by the professor's words, Mrs. Dent whispered from the sofa, "He liked you, Professor. Are you certain it's Howie?"

"Yes, Mrs. Dent," Branden said. He sat on the edge of the sofa beside her. "He doesn't look good right now, but I'm certain that it's Howie."

Susan Dent held her head in her hands and wept. Robertson waited a discreet moment and then said to Richard, "Mr. Dent, can you tell us if Howie has a doctor in Millersburg? Or a dentist?"

"Why?" Susan asked, standing abruptly. Branden stood beside her, worried that she might fold.

Robertson turned back to face her. "We

would want dental X-rays, Mrs. Dent. For comparison."

"So, you're not really certain," Richard Dent asserted. "You're just guessing."

Branden shook his head but didn't speak. Robertson said to Richard, "We just want to be thorough, Mr. Dent."

Susan stepped toward the sheriff and pleaded, "I want to see him."

"Susan, really," Richard said, sounding reproachful.

"Please, Richard," she answered him. "We need to see him. Then we'll know."

"Mrs. Dent," Robertson said. "You shouldn't see him right now. Not like this."

Susan Dent retreated and sank again onto the sofa. Branden moved some newspaper clippings off the sofa and onto the coffee table so that he could sit beside her.

Robertson motioned Richard Dent to a soft chair at the end of the coffee table and asked, "Please, Mr. Dent. Can you take a seat?" Over his shoulder, he asked Baker, "Ryan, can you get the Dents some water?" and Baker stepped back to the kitchen.

Richard Dent dropped wearily into the chair, and Robertson pulled a wooden chair in from the dining room table. By the time they were all seated, Baker returned with two glasses of water, and Robertson directed

Baker back outside, saying, "Get pizzas and drinks out to the Helmuths' farm, Ryan." Baker pulled his phone and went out through the door to make his calls from the front porch.

Susan Dent stared blankly at her glass of water. Richard Dent set his glass on a side table and pressed the sheriff, "When can we see him?"

"Maybe tomorrow," Robertson said.

"Because he'll look better by then?" Susan whispered.

"I think so," Robertson said. "The ME says there are some puncture wounds and a lot of swelling."

"Is he just lying in that basement?" Richard demanded.

"No, Mr. Dent," Branden said. "He was strapped to a post. He's standing upright."

"Did he die that way?" Dent demanded of the professor.

"Yes, I think so," Branden said. "I think he died there, and they just left him."

Susan groaned and sank back against the sofa cushions. She dropped her glass of water, and it spilled across her dress. She seemed to take no notice of it. She pushed forward slowly as if caught in a dream. She took the newspaper clippings from the coffee table, and she sat clutching them to her breast as if they held something precious to her. As if there were something in them that was more fragile even than her tenuous hold on reality.

Richard Dent then addressed Robertson. "Who's gonna decide when we can see our son, Sheriff?"

Robertson moved to the edge of his chair. "Mr. Dent," he asked, "do you know where Fannie Helmuth is?"

"No. Is this about her?"

"I think you know it is, Mr. Dent."

"Well, we don't know where she is."

"Were Fannie and Howie *involved*?" Robertson asked.

"You mean like lovers?"

"Yes."

"Howie was sweet on her when they were younger. But she made it plain that he'd have to convert to Amish. So, no. They weren't *involved.*"

"But they were good friends."

"Very good friends, Sheriff. Maybe more special than lovers would be. Seems to me that's what got Howie killed. So I want to know. Was our son tortured?"

"Yes, Mr. Dent," Robertson said carefully. "We think he was."

Next to Branden on the sofa, Susan Dent groaned mournfully with her eyes closed.

She clamped her newspaper clippings to her breast, rocking in place as if she were holding an ailing child.

Richard Dent ignored her and asked Robertson, "Why? Why would someone kill him like that?"

"You know they've been hunting for Fannie, Mr. Dent. I've explained this to you many times since April. They'd kill her, too, if they could find her."

"Your Deputy Armbruster has pestered us all summer," Dent complained. "Like we'd somehow *magically* be able to tell you where to find them."

"I thought you might have gotten a letter or a phone call."

"Well, we haven't."

Robertson pressed forward carefully. "I'm not trying to make you angry, Richard, but I think your son was tortured so that he would tell them where Fannie is."

Dent closed his eyes and shook his head. As if drained of all strength, he whispered, "They were best friends. He would never have told them where she is. He never would have told them. So that's the reason he's dead."

Professor Branden returned from the kitchen with a new glass of water for Mrs. Dent. He set it on the coffee table in front of her, and he sat at the opposite end of the coffee table from Richard Dent. Catching Robertson's eye, he asked Dent, "When did Howie get his car, Mr. Dent?"

Sullenly, Dent muttered, "Night before last. Monday night some time."

"But was it evening or night?" Branden asked.

"Night. We were asleep."

"Did he wake you up?"

"No. We just saw that his car was gone the next morning."

"Why did you assume that he was the one who had taken it?"

"Who else?"

Branden shrugged, and Robertson said, "You might have thought it was stolen, Mr. Dent."

Dent shook his head with certainty. "He came inside and got his spare keys from the back porch."

Robertson stood. "Anyone could have taken the keys, Richard."

Again Dent shook his head. He stood and led the men through the kitchen and out to the back porch. Behind a battered hutch with tall shelves that held canned goods and old magazines, he reached in with his hand and said, "See for yourselves. Other than us, Howie is the only person who knew where we hid the spare keys."

Robertson took Dent's place beside the hutch and felt blindly behind the shelves. "A nail for the keys," he said to Branden, and he withdrew his hand.

Back in the living room, the three men stopped near the front door. Taking a sterner tone, Robertson asked Dent, "If you knew yesterday morning that your son had come for his car in the night, why didn't you report that to us immediately?"

"Why?" Dent huffed. "It's his car."

"Because we would have gone out looking for him," Robertson said with a mix of consternation and surprise.

Still clutching her clippings, Susan Dent stood up from the couch. "What? What about looking?"

Robertson turned to her. "If you had told us Howie was back in Holmes County, we would have looked for him, Mrs. Dent. Maybe we could have found him first."

Stricken, Susan Dent looked first to Robertson and then to her husband. With tears spilling out onto her cheeks, she shrieked at Richard, "We killed our own son!" and then she stabbed a finger at him and cried out, "You should have told them!"

Fighting a rush of anger, Richard Dent turned on the sheriff. "Just what makes you think you could have found Howie before these people did? You haven't been able to find anyone. You've had four months!"

"We could have tried," Robertson said. "We might have had a chance, here. If we had known he had come home."

Overwhelmed with grief, Susan doubled at the waist and dropped her clippings onto the carpet. Richard Dent went to her, but she pushed him away and sank to her knees. He looked impotently to Branden and then to Robertson, and said, "These clippings are from the *Budget.*" He tried to lift his wife to her feet.

She refused his efforts, choosing instead to lie weeping on the carpet between the sofa and the coffee table. Richard stood with a bewildered vacancy in his eyes and muttered, "She thinks she sees messages in the *Budget.*"

When they drove back toward the Helmuth farm, Robertson and Branden left Deputy Baker to tend to Mr. and Mrs. Dent. Branden briefly read some of the clippings as Robertson drove, and he said to the sheriff, "What have you tried, Bruce? To locate these two."

"Nothing that worked," Robertson said as he pulled into the Helmuth drive.

56

"But what?" Branden insisted.

Rolling toward the house, Robertson answered, "Greyhound bus records, credit cards, Howie's phone records. Plus road patrols in Holmes County, places they might go, like motels and restaurants. And Ricky made a couple of trips down to Memphis, to try to trace them after they got off the bus from Charlotte."

As Robertson pulled up at the back of the house, Branden asked, "Do you have a likeness of Fannie?"

Robertson and Branden got out, and Robertson said over the top of his Crown Vic, "We put together a composite sketch. It looks just like her."

Branden followed Robertson to the back door, where the cables from the gasoline generator snaked up the steps into the house. Robertson hesitated there as if perplexed.

So they could talk above the growl of the generator, Branden pulled the sheriff back twenty yards toward the barn and said, "We're going to have to do better, Bruce. Finding Fannie Helmuth has got to be the first priority, now."

Robertson kicked angrily at the gravel where they stood and said, "I should have anticipated this, Mike."

57

"And what would you have done?" Branden asked. "Shown their pictures to everyone who enters Holmes County?"

"Something like that."

"No. This is on the Dents, Bruce."

Robertson glowered pent-up frustration at his friend. "It's on me, Mike! I have to take the weight, here."

Branden smiled a degree of concession, and Robertson spun away from him to walk off several paces toward the tall red barn. Branden followed and said, "OK, Bruce, you take the weight. But listen. Just listen."

Robertson stopped and turned back on the wet gravel to face the professor with a menacing scowl, looking for all the world as if what he needed most right then was a purging fistfight.

The skies were overcast again, and a light rain began to fall. Robertson held to his exposed position, refusing to surrender any ground to Branden's attempts at encouragement.

Branden held up a warding palm, stepped five more paces to gain shelter inside the barn, and turned back toward Robertson. "You've been on this for four months, Sheriff. How'd *they* find him in a single day?"

Some of the antagonism bled out of

Robertson's gaze. He joined Branden inside the barn, and the rain fell harder outside. "What do you mean?" the sheriff asked over the clatter of the rain on the barn's metal roof.

Branden stepped closer. "Could the Molina crew have known exactly what day out of the last four months to come back here looking for Dent?"

"Too much of a coincidence," Robertson sputtered.

"OK," Branden continued. "Could the Molina crew have been here all along, looking for Dent right beside you? In your county, Bruce? Right under your nose, and you didn't notice them?"

"We'd have noticed," Robertson allowed as he lumbered out of his wet suit coat. "Somebody would have noticed them."

Branden nodded. "And could the Molina crew have camped unnoticed out here at the farm, anticipating that this was the one place where Howie would eventually show up?"

Robertson started pacing a circle inside the barn, thinking new thoughts. To let the sheriff think, Branden stood to the side. When Robertson stopped pacing, Branden asked, "Do you see it?"

Robertson punched his palm. He faced

Branden briefly and then with a smile, as if he were experiencing a degree of optimism for the first time that morning, he turned in place to face the big house.

When he turned back to the professor, he was purposefully composed. "OK, Mike. This changes it all around. I need to tell Missy. She might find something along these lines anyway, but I need to tell her while she's still processing the basement."

Then the sheriff marched across the gravel in the rain and climbed the block steps leading into the back of the house.

Before Robertson disappeared inside, Branden called after him from the barn. "Bruce, I'm going to read more of those clippings."

5

Wednesday, August 17
2:05 P.M.

It was cool in the Helmuths' kitchen, and once Robertson had closed the door to the back porch, it was also quiet enough to talk over the noise of the generator outside. Still in his golfing outfit, Captain Newell stood near the sink reviewing photographs on the back of a Nikon camera. He had been filling out the voucher slips for each new memory card of photos. Next to his elbow, on the green Formica countertop, there were three bags with memory cards already organized. To fill so many cards with data, Robertson realized, Newell's team must have photographed every minute aspect of the farm's circumstance and condition. Every corner, in every room, in all of the buildings.

Robertson stood beside Newell to watch a few photo images on the Nikon's LCD display, and when Newell clicked out of the review, the sheriff asked, "Is there any sign of Fannie? Anything to indicate that she came here with Dent?"

Bobby Newell shook his head. "Nothing, Sheriff. And we've been through everything out here."

Robertson leaned back against the counter. To no one in particular, he said, "Where is she?" Then he said to the captain, "If she came here with him, Bobby, she's probably already dead. Or if he told them where to find her, she's probably already dead."

Newell set the Nikon carefully on the counter and turned to face the sheriff. "There's no trace of her here, Bruce. And Missy says there's very little to go on, down in the basement. We don't have any reason to think she came here with Dent, and you shouldn't assume the worst."

"You've been down to the basement?"

"Yes, with Pat Lance. Taking photos."

"Mike says he looks like he died hard."

Newell nodded. "You wouldn't believe."

Frustrated, Robertson stepped to the top of the basement steps and called down to his wife. "Missy, I need to come down there."

"Five minutes," she called back, and the

sheriff turned away from the steps. To Newell, he said, "Where's Pat Lance?"

"I set her up with a team to search again through the little Daadihaus."

"You've been through all of the main house?"

"Of course."

Robertson acknowledged that with an arch of his brow and stood in place to think.

Newell returned his attention to the camera equipment and finished his record keeping concerning the memory cards. When he turned around, Robertson was staring out the window over the kitchen sink. Newell asked, "Are we doing anything about food?" and Robertson said, "Baker's on it."

From the basement, Missy called up. "OK, Bruce. You can come down."

Robertson eyed Newell and asked, "You done with photos now, Bobby?"

"Yes, but Pat will have more from the Daadihaus."

"OK," Robertson said, "Mike's got a theory. I need to see if it lines up with what Missy has found down there. But while I do that, maybe you could check on Mike. He's reading clippings from the Sugarcreek *Budget.*"

"Why?" Newell asked.

63

As he took the steps to the basement, Robertson called back, "Susan Dent thinks there are messages for her in the letters."

At the bottom of the basement steps, Robertson turned left toward floodlights that shined from atop tripods to illuminate the back corner behind the steps. Missy was standing in the middle of the light, waiting alone. At her feet, the body of Howie Dent was laid out straight on a black rubber body bag. His clothes were in tatters, and his exposed skin was a battleground of swollen puncture wounds. Robertson stopped at the edge of the light and stared. After a long and difficult hesitation, he said, "I've never seen anything like that."

Missy said, "First, I want to show you what I found down here." She pulled her husband into the corner where she had positioned a folding aluminum table on which she had laid out her evidence — bagged, sorted, and cataloged. She let the sheriff study the items. She waited for him to speak.

"Missy," the sheriff said eventually, "you've got to be kidding."

"I wish I were," Taggert said, "but this is how he died."

On the table, Taggert had arranged

evidence bags in groups. One set of bags on the left held soft yellow latex gloves of the type that an emergency room doctor would use. Next to that were five bags, each containing either a 3 ml or a 5 ml plastic syringe with bloody, inch-long needles attached to the tips. Robertson sorted through the bags and noticed that one of the needles had been snapped off at the base. He held up the bag with a silent question in his eyes, and Missy answered, "I found the broken needle buried deep in his cheek, just under his right eye."

Robertson returned the evidence bag to the table and moved on to the next items. In separate bags, there were bottles of Amish folk remedies. One was labeled CHILD CALMER and another was labeled TINCTURE OF IODINE. In a bag larger than the others, there was a flattened tube that had held BLEIB-RUHIG, FOR CALM HORSES. Robertson inspected the label and read the ingredients — dextrose, ethyl alcohol, ground limestone, potassium sorbate, sodium bentonite, sodium benzoate, sodium saccharin, thiamine hydrochloride, and finally, water and xanthan gum. When Robertson put the bag with the tube down, he stepped back from the table and said, "These are mostly empty."

Missy turned her husband around to face the body of Howie Dent. "They shot it all under his skin, Bruce. They injected it while he was strapped to that post, and then I think they rubbed it in, so that it would hurt even more."

Robertson shook his head and knelt beside the body. He looked first at the welt under Dent's right eye, and then he studied the arms, torso, legs, and scalp.

Dent's clothes had been shredded to expose his skin, and in the centers of ugly swollen patches, there were puncture wounds that had bled trails of red into the tatters of his clothes. Some of the swollen patches were fairly round in shape, and some were oblong, as if the needles had been sunk laterally under the skin and then withdrawn slowly, while the plunger was depressed, to deliver a line of chemical, for the most brutal effect. Once he had seen enough, Robertson pushed up and stepped back. He didn't speak. Missy let him absorb the impact of the brutality, and then she said, "While he was still alive, Bruce, his skin would have felt like it was on fire. Not flames, but like a deep chemical burn. They might as well have cut him a thousand times and swabbed all the wounds with acid."

Wearily, Robertson rubbed his sockets

with the flats of his fingers. He shook his head and said, "He'd have told them anything they wanted to know, Missy."

Missy smiled. "I'm not so sure."

"Why in the world not?"

"Because I think he died of a heart attack."

"During the torture?"

"Yes," Taggert said. "I think one of these injections might have hit a vein. The poison could have gone right to his heart."

"Then Fannie still has a chance," Robertson said with a measure of satisfaction. "There's a chance he didn't talk."

"I think so," Missy said. "Everything down here tells me that they worked on him right up until that last injection. When he died, I think they dropped everything and walked out of here. He died suddenly, and they couldn't do anything about it."

"Is that why he smells like urine?"

Missy nodded. "His bladder released when he died."

"Does Bobby Newell know this?" Robertson asked.

"I've told only you," Missy said. "I just now finished with my preliminary exam. And I'll have to wait for his autopsy. But I think I'm right."

Robertson thought, frowned, and rubbed

at his temples. "Maybe they got what they wanted from him, Missy, and they injected that vein on purpose. To finish him."

"I'll know more once I conduct his autopsy," Taggert said.

The sheriff turned back to the evidence table. He made a brief study of the bagged items again and said, "This was all bought locally. Maybe in a harness shop. Or a health food store."

"I think so," Missy said. "Harness shop, tack shop, or something like that. Really, Bruce, anywhere in Amish country."

"Then it fits," Robertson said with cautious satisfaction.

Missy waited for an explanation, and Robertson said, "Mike has a theory. That it wasn't the Molina outfit that did this."

"But that's who would have been looking for him," Taggert argued.

"I know. But it's improbable that they'd find Dent here so easily. So quickly."

"I'd hate to think we had someone living locally who could do this sort of thing," Missy said.

"It has to have been someone local, Missy. The Molinas can't have put this all together that fast. Anyway, that's Mike's theory."

"That's the angle that I couldn't figure," Missy said. "I mean, how could they find him so quickly?"

"You have something that fits?"

Missy nodded. "There's nothing wet down here, Bruce. Everything is dry, even his clothes. They didn't bring him down here during the rains last night or yesterday afternoon."

"It started raining yesterday around noon," Robertson said. "And it rained most of the night."

"I know," Missy said. "So they had to have brought Dent down here before that."

"I don't know," the sheriff said. "He might have been staying inside the house. Maybe he wouldn't have been out in the rain, anyway."

"Bobby says there's no evidence of that, Bruce. He doesn't think anyone was staying here. All he found was where Stan Armbruster tracked through the house this morning."

Shaking his head, Robertson started for the stairs. At the base of the steps, he stopped, turned back, and asked, "You about done here?"

"Yes. The next step is to get him up the steps and into town."

"I'll send some people down to help carry him up," the sheriff said. "But I want to talk to Branden and Armbruster. Also, to my

69

captain. Because between taking his car sometime Monday night and the start of the rain around noon yesterday, Howie Dent went somewhere local — the wrong somewhere local — and that's what got him killed."

6

Wednesday, August 17
3:15 P.M.

When Sheriff Robertson rounded the corner outside the Helmuth house, he found Professor Branden leaning back against the hood of his white truck reading newsprint, and at the end of the drive Robertson saw Stan Armbruster's red Corolla turn right onto Township 371. Robertson approached Branden and asked, "Armbruster made it back?"

"Just now."

"Then where's he going?"

Branden held up the clipping he had been reading and said, "To get more of these. In Sugarcreek."

"Really, Mike? The *Budget*?"

"Stan's going to check, but read this," the professor said as he handed the clipping to the sheriff.

Robertson read from the top:

Centreville, MI
North District

July 18 — We had hot weather the past two weeks and it was hard on the field corn. Then we got an all-day soaker on Saturday and we are all grateful for the cooler weather.

Gardens here are doing very well. The sweet corn will be ready soon and we'll start digging up potatoes tomorrow. Some of us are picking purple hull peas and the produce markets have plenty of fruit. Especially peaches are coming in strong here and we are busy with canning them.

Sunday Gemie was at Wayne Hostetlers' by Henry Schrock. Next to be at Vernon Kropfs' and service to be by Leland Yoder. Visitors at Hostetlers' were the Toby Eichers, Sam B. Grabers, and Min. Melvin Troyers. Absent at Hostetlers' were the Linus Gingeriches who were visiting in Bronson. The flu is going around and several other absences were noted as well.

Some special baby news from this neighborhood is a son born to Chester and Leona Kauffman and a niece born in Boonville MO. for John and Emma

Mast. That brings their total to 52, nephews included.

Returned from the West Country bus tour were the Levi Millers and Joe Shetlers. A group is looking into hiring a bus to make the trip to the Jake Schwartz and Anna Bontrager wedding in Mt. Hope, OH. come September. John Coblentzes were to Vista, Colo. to visit her brother Roy after he was kicked by one of his horses and life-lined to Denver, Colo. Going to Wisconsin to see the Andy Wengerds were the Josiah Shetlers with newest daughter Amy and two other children Ben and Mary while the older sons keep duties up around the farm.

Neighbors Albert and Lizzie Kuhns are getting ready for the wedding of their eldest girl Annie, on September 22nd. Her boyfriend is John, son of Andy and Verna Miller of Shipshewana. They were published on July 17th.

Our guests from OH. wish their families to know that they are fine though weary of moving around so much. Maybe they can stay. A Daadi-haus was made available to them at the Daniel Gingeriches, woman to sleep in the bedroom, man to take a cot on the screened back porch at nights until winter sets.

— IVAN MILLER

Robertson looked up doubtfully, and Branden said, "That could be Fannie Helmuth and Howie Dent. The 'Our guests from Ohio.' In Centreville, Michigan."

Robertson shrugged out a measure of skepticism and asked, "The other clippings?"

"Stan took them to Sugarcreek. He has an idea how to search them."

"Maybe the *Budget* already has a database," Robertson said. "You know, maybe they keep a database of all the letters that are sent in."

Branden shook his head. "We called, and they don't. But Stan says he has it covered."

"If that's Fannie and Howie mentioned so openly in this letter, then they've pretty much told everyone where they were."

Branden smiled. "Right. Everyone who reads the *Budget.* But do you think Teresa Molina is smart enough to do that?"

Robertson pulled his tie loose under his chin. He turned anxiously in place to survey the scene outside at the farmhouse. He waved an arm over the whole of it and grumbled, "We're wrapping up, Mike. We've got nothing solid here, and I should have anticipated that they'd put messages in the *Budget*."

"We're going to read all the *Budget* letters since April," Branden said. "And we know Dent's killer is probably someone local. So that's not nothing, Sheriff."

Hands planted stubbornly on his hips, Robertson frowned and shook his head. "He was tortured, Mike, and it's my fault. I should have figured the *Budget* angle sooner, and OK — maybe it is someone local. But otherwise, we've got nothing."

"You're wrong, but OK."

Robertson responded with a disaffected growl and Branden added, "So what are you going to do?"

"Can you talk to the Dents again?"

"Sure, in the morning. They need some time right now."

"Then I'm going back to wait on Missy's autopsy report. There's nothing more I can do out here."

"Stan's work with the letters might give us something," Branden said. "Maybe later tonight."

Robertson huffed, "Long shot, Mike. Besides, if Teresa Molina has half a brain, she's already found Fannie Helmuth anyway."

"Well, she's not that smart, Bruce. And she's not going to read an Amish newspaper. People like her don't read the *Budget*. I doubt she even knows it exists."

Robertson glowered into empty space. Eventually he said, "Tortured and murdered, Mike. If he gave them Fannie's location, she's already dead. And if she's dead because I couldn't find her, I'm gonna have to resign."

"Stop talking nonsense," Branden said softly. "You're not thinking straight."

Robertson leveled his eyes at his friend. "I am thinking straight, Mike. If they've killed Fannie, I'll resign."

7

Wednesday, August 17
3:30 P.M.

With the white box from Miller's Bakery
still on his passenger's seat, Stan Armbruster drove his red Corolla to Sugarcreek
on Ohio 39 from the west. As he came into
town, he passed the red-brick Mennonite
church on his left. He slowed around the
sharp bend at the edge of town and
continued past the sprawling Amish flea
market on the right, where cars, vans, and
buses were scrimmaging for parking spots
beside the cluster of old buildings. Slowing
further, Armbruster angled gently right onto
West Main St. and drove several blocks
through an older residential neighborhood
into the small downtown business district.
At Factory Street, he turned left to follow
the railroad yard, and soon after the turn,
he pulled in at the plant and business of-
fices of the *Budget.* His new suit lay in a

crumpled heap on his bedroom floor. He was dressed now in brown loafers, tan slacks, and a yellow button shirt, a change of clothes that he thought was appropriate, considering the disaster of his morning. He got out, looped his badge case over his belt, and locked up. Here he hoped to redeem himself with his plans to search all of the letters that had been sent by Amish scribes into the *Budget* since April.

Inside, Armbruster spoke to the lady at the counter. While she took notes, he explained which back issues he wanted to buy, and then she took her notes down the hall. When the lady came back, she had an old ten-ream copy paper box stacked full of newspapers. When she lifted it up onto her counter, she asked, "This for the sheriff?"

Armbruster nodded and pulled his wallet out, but the lady said, "No charge."

"Thanks."

"That's a lot of letters," she said tapping the side of the box. "We get them from all over the world."

"I just need the ones from the States," Armbruster said.

"They're all mixed in," the lady said.

"And you don't have a database?" Armbruster asked. "You don't keep any digital copies?"

"No," she said. "These Amish scribes write by hand, mostly. They mail their letters to us on the Mondays after their Sunday services. Some of the letters are typed these days, but mostly they're still handwritten."

"What about when you set type for the paper each week?" Armbruster asked. "That's digital now, isn't it?"

"Yes, but we erase the files to make way for next week's letters. We don't save a copy."

"That'd be easy enough to do," Armbruster lamented. "To save copies I mean."

"We don't." The lady shrugged. "Sorry."

"OK, thanks," Armbruster said. He carried the box out to his trunk. He climbed in behind the wheel of the hot car, started his engine, cranked the air conditioner to max, and called Rachel Ramsayer's cell phone.

Rachel served as IT chief for the sheriff. She had spent the spring and summer months upgrading computers and modernizing software and databases. She had also created a Web site for the sheriff's department. She was a dwarf woman from Atlanta, the daughter of Caleb Troyer — a friend since kindergarten to both Mike Branden and Bruce Robertson. Cal Troyer was the pastor at Millersburg Christian Church, and his daughter Rachel had moved to town only recently. Because of her relationship to Cal Troyer and because of her extraordinary expertise with all things digitized, she had been accepted as IT chief in the sheriff's department almost immediately. She answered Armbruster's call on the first ring.

"It's Stan," Armbruster said over the chatter of the Corolla's interior fan. "I've got the *Budget*s."

"How many letters?" Rachel asked.

"I'm guessing hundreds," Armbruster said. "It's a boxful. It'll take hours to scan them all."

"Did you ask again about a database?"

"No luck. They start over each week. They don't save the files."

"Have you got today's issue?"

Armbruster thumbed the papers and said, "It's the top one."

"OK," Rachel said. "You'll fold and scan, and I'll devise a strategy to search the results. It's going be a long night."

Armbruster put his gearshift in reverse. "Like anybody's actually slept through the night since April."

8

After an administrative stop at the jail, Bruce Robertson climbed the steps to the back porch of his Victorian house and pushed inside to a spacious and modern kitchen of stainless appliances and white quartz countertops. He called out to his wife and got no response. He changed into house slippers, pulled a Diet Pepsi from the refrigerator, and carried it into the parlor to sit on the sofa in front of the cold fireplace.

When the phone rang, the sheriff had no idea how long he had been sitting there. The Diet Pepsi sat unopened on the coffee table. He answered the call, "Bruce," and Missy asked, "You cooking anything for dinner?"

"Nope."

"Go out?"

"Where?"

81

"I'll think about that. I'll be home in thirty minutes."

The sheriff was still immobile on the sofa when Missy walked into the parlor. She saw the unopened can of Diet Pepsi, picked it up to gauge its temperature, and carried it back into the kitchen. When she returned, she had a cold Diet Pepsi for her husband. She set it on the table next to his elbow, and she climbed the stairs to change out of her scrubs. When she rejoined her husband, taking a seat beside him, his eyes held a fixed gaze on an inward thought. She reached around him, opened the Diet Pepsi can, and handed it to him. When she gave his hand a nudge, he drank and seemed to regain the present.

Recognizing his brooding mood, she asked, "How long have you been sitting here?" and he answered, "Don't know. Couple of minutes."

"Your Pepsi was warm."

Robertson cast a frown toward the fireplace and closed his eyes. "Been thinking."

"About what?"

The sheriff turned to look at Missy. "Retirement."

Missy nodded with a chagrined smile. She

82

recognized the hollow tone in his voice. He had been sliding in this direction since early summer, when it had become obvious that Fannie Helmuth would not be easily found. "You think you're done with law enforcement?" she asked. "Because I don't."

Robertson shook his head and stared again at the sooty bricks inside the fireplace. "I should have found her by now, Missy. Maybe a younger sheriff would have."

"You don't really believe that," Missy said.

Robertson stood to pace in front of the fireplace. He made two passes, kicked an old coal back onto the grate, set his Diet Pepsi on the end table, and dropped back onto the sofa beside Missy. "Missy, Mike thinks there may have been messages that we missed in the *Budget.* If it's true, then it's my fault that Howie Dent is dead."

"I'm not going to listen to this," Missy said sternly. "You've had your whole department in turmoil since the day Fannie walked out of your jail, and if anyone *could* have found her, it would have been you and your people who did it. Well, you didn't find her because she didn't want to be found."

"And if she gets dead because I failed?" the sheriff said, turning with weary eyes to face his wife.

Missy stood up in front of him. "Mike said

you'd been talking this nonsense."

"He called you?"

"Of course."

"What'd he say?"

"That you'd been talking about resigning. Which is nonsense."

The sheriff stood with a self-disgusted "Harrumph," and carried his Diet Pepsi back into the kitchen. He poured the rest of the Diet Pepsi into the sink, crushed the can, and cast it into the recycling bin.

Missy followed him into the kitchen and said, "We're going to the Brandens' house for pizza."

"Maybe we could stay in tonight."

"Not a chance in the world, Sheriff. And you're not resigning."

"Oh? Why's that?"

"Because I'm not ready to retire, and I don't have the patience to break in some new kid as sheriff." She fished her keys out of a bowl on the kitchen table and said again, "Pizza at the Brandens'. Then maybe we'll check in with Rachel and Stan at the jail."

Robertson followed her out through the back door. "You talked to Rachel?"

"No, Bruce, to Stan. He says the *Budget* letters are going to give us something we can use."

"Why'd you call him?"

"He called me at the lab."

"I didn't get a call."

"Bruce, really. After the kind of day he's had, do you think he'd call you at home?"

"He should have."

"Well, he didn't," Missy said while locking up. On the steps of the back porch, she added, "He's embarrassed, Bruce. He contaminated a crime scene, and he knew I'd see you tonight. So he asked me to tell you that the *Budget*s might be useful after all."

"He can't have read them all by now," Robertson said and opened the driver's door on the Crown Vic. He got in with Missy, and while she buckled herself into the passenger's seat, he backed up into the graveled alley behind their house.

"He's scanning them," Missy said. "Rachel's scanners have optical character recognition. They're scanning the scribes' letters to make digital files, and they're searching the digital files for specific phrases and key words. It's impressive, and you need to pay Stan a compliment. He could use a boost."

9

Wednesday, August 17
9:30 P.M.

At the boxy red-brick jail on Courthouse Square in the center of Millersburg, Rachel Ramsayer's corner desk in the first-floor squad room had been custom built for her because as a dwarf woman of Amish descent, she was only four feet three inches tall. Her desk therefore sat lower to the floor than average, as did her computer consoles, bookshelves, monitors, copier/scanner/fax, and phones. Even her power and data outlets had been custom installed at the proper height for her. The same was true of her light switches, phone jacks, floor lamps, and file cabinets. It was Rachel's special den, suited to Rachel's special size, and it was well insulated from the rest of the large and busy squad room by soundproofing partitions of average height, so that with an excellent degree of privacy behind her tall partitions, she commanded an elaborate IT hub for the sheriff department's data centers, servers, networks, and systems. Only the communications consoles at the jail's front entrance had more elaborate equipment.

From her hub, Rachel programmed, monitored, and maintained all of the department's digital and wireless concerns. It was a system that Rachel had designed and built herself, and it had taken her over a year to accomplish it. More than any other person — and where everyone else had relented — she had dragged the obstreperous sheriff into the twenty-first century by demonstrating to him the power of the digital age, and tonight her accomplishments were proving of greater value to the department than the resolutely twentieth-century Sheriff Robertson could have imagined when Rachel first had laid her IT plans before him for approval.

Now she sat at her desk searching digital files that were coming in from scanners run by Stan Armbruster on the far side of the squad room, and by Pat Lance in Captain Newell's office on the second floor. At her computer, Rachel had created separate folders for each of the scanners, and as Armbruster and Lance scanned the scribes' letters published in the *Budget,* the files automatically accumulated in Rachel's two new folders, with file names indicating city location and date of publication.

While the initial files accumulated, Rachel had developed a search strategy that employed Boolean operators, finding instances where words such as *friends* OR *visitors* OR *guests* were combined using the AND operator with descriptors such as *Ohio* OR *Buckeye* OR *Holmes.* In this way she was able to identify text segments in which scribes had written about friends/visitors/ guests in conjunction with the words *Ohio/ Buckeye/Holmes.* With the early samples, she had learned to include *Millersburg* and *Charm* among her location descriptors. Whenever these methods flagged a passage, Rachel printed the passage and marked it with a place/date indicator.

When Bruce Robertson and Missy Taggert entered the squad room after pizza with the Brandens, Rachel had three passages to show them, all found by her search strategy in letters from the *Budget* between the middle of April and the beginning of May.

While Missy checked on Armbruster at his scanner, Robertson threaded his way across the crowded squad room to Rachel's far-right corner hub. He peered in over the top of Rachel's partitions and started to ask a question. Rachel held up a hand, typed briefly, and then took the three passages from a tray on her desk to hand them to the sheriff. When Robertson took the pages, she said over her shoulder, "I've got another one running right now, but see what you think so far," and she returned her attention to her monitor and keyboard.

Robertson retrieved a metal chair from one of the squad room's long tables. He brought it back to sit at the opening to Rachel's IT den, and he sat there to read the first letter's excerpt. Rachel had identified it as coming from Whiteville, Tennessee, for the April 27 edition of the *Budget:*

Guests from Ohio by way of Memphis surprised us yesterday at services and may stay only a while.

Robertson started again to ask Rachel a question, but she stopped him with a shake of her head. As she continued to work, the sheriff turned his attention to the second excerpt:

Paris, TN, May 4
Our Ohio travelers stayed only two nights at the John Troyers and want their

families in Charm to know that they are
well.

Robertson then read the third excerpt Rachel had given him:

Cub Run, KY, May 11
Two friends from Ohio traveled through
after services yesterday at Daniel Brocks
and report to Holmes County that they are
well but weary.

When Robertson looked up from the
page, Rachel was waiting for him. He asked,
"Where are these places?" and she pointed
to a large wall-mounted monitor above her
desk. There she had posted an electronic
map of the center states, and on it, red
digital pins marked the towns of Memphis,
Whiteville, Paris, and Cub Run.

Robertson smiled. "They're traveling from
one colony to the next."

"Yes, if it's really them," Rachel agreed.
"But chances are it is."

Robertson passed a palm over the bristles
of his flattop haircut and blew a breathy
whistle. "Rachel, if this is them, they're right
here in these letters. Right out in the open."

"It's only three letters from this spring,"
Rachel said. "We'll get more, if there are

any, but it'll take most of the night. And if you weren't looking for it, these references to them wouldn't register like they do with us. We know what we're looking for. I don't think Teresa Molina will ever get this, even if she did read a *Budget* once in a while. My guess is that she doesn't have a clue."

Robertson paused with a thought and then asked, "Are you scanning them in sequence?"

Rachel nodded. "Starting with April."

"Why not go straight for the recent ones?"

"Because I'm finding it necessary to revise the search strategy as we go along. Before I got that second one, I wasn't using *travelers*. Then the third one gave me *friends*. It's going to evolve and expand with each new letter. So by the time we have scanned them all, I may have to adjust the search parameters. Maybe use *couple* AND *Charm* NOT *Saskatchewan*. Like that."

"All night, you say?"

"It's just the three of us — me and Pat and Stan. Everyone else is working to find Fannie."

"Chief Wilsher put double shifts into the deputy rotations," Robertson commented.

"It has been a little crazy around here," Rachel laughed. "But we've got the two scanners running. Still, it'll be morning before we're done."

Robertson stood. "Can you send me that map during the night? As you update it?"

"I'll put it on the FTP server, Sheriff. You can log in anytime from home."

On the other side of the room, Missy was helping Stan Armbruster fold newsprint for his scanner. Robertson came forward and asked, "Can you do that, Stan, and talk a little, too?"

Without interrupting his rhythm, Armbruster said, "Sure. It's not a thinking job."

"Then tell me what was in the yellow VW, Stan. Howie Dent's things, I mean."

Armbruster laid newsprint on the flatbed scanner, closed the lid, chose PREVIEW SCAN, and turned to answer the sheriff. "The only personal item was his old red backpack. And it was empty."

Armbruster's preview scan finished quickly. He turned back to use his mouse to select one specific letter from the page, and then he initiated a full scan.

Robertson waited and asked, "No other personal items, then?"

"Nothing," Armbruster said, turning around to the sheriff again. "No keys, no wallet, no phone. Neither in the car, nor on the body."

Armbruster looked to Missy, who confirmed, "There wasn't anything, Bruce. Nothing in the basement and nothing on the body."

"Luggage or toiletries?" Robertson asked Armbruster.

Armbruster shook his head. The scan finished and he used the mouse again to select another letter in the scan area. After he selected SCAN, he turned again to Robertson. "No watch, no glasses, no prescriptions. He didn't have papers, receipts, or books."

"Bills, Stan? Maps? There had to be something."

"There wasn't, Sheriff."

"Kids these days always have a tablet," Missy said. "Or some game."

"Sorry," Armbruster said. "He didn't have anything like that."

"Then it was all taken," Robertson concluded.

Armbruster nodded his agreement. "Whoever killed him took everything he had."

Before pushing out through the back door of the jail, the sheriff hesitated and asked Missy to wait at the end of the hall. He went back into the squad room and pulled Armbruster out into the long hallway, saying, "Stan, about this morning."

Anticipating what was coming, Armbruster shrank a little in stature. But Robertson shook his head and said, "No, that's not it, Stan."

"I know I ruined a crime scene, Sheriff."

"No, you *found* a crime scene," Robertson said. "And as soon as you knew it *was* a crime scene, you cleared out and called in."

"Mud, fingerprints, and vomit, Sheriff. I fouled the scene."

"I don't disagree," Robertson said. "But the next time, Stan? Before you discover a murder scene? Don't eat such a large breakfast."

Looking puzzled, Armbruster seemed to bend at the shoulders, as if struggling under a new burden.

In the squad room, Armbruster crossed back to Rachel's corner and asked, "What's wrong with the sheriff?"

Rachel looked up. "I didn't know there was anything wrong."

Armbruster furled his brow and said, "It's weird. And I don't like it."

"What?"

"I ruined his crime scene today."

"So?"

"So, he's not angry."

"And you're complaining?"

"This is *Robertson.*"

Rachel smiled. "You just have to know how to handle him."

"I've mostly dealt with Wilsher. And now Captain Newell."

"You have to handle Robertson."

"Nobody just *handles* Robertson."

"Ellie always does."

"What are you talking about?"

"She started here over fifteen years ago as a dispatcher, and she's handled him from her first day on the job."

Armbruster gave a perplexed shrug of his shoulders. "OK, what do you think of this temp dispatcher?"

Rachel smiled confidently. "Del knows what she's doing."

"Are you talking about doing her job, or about handling Robertson?"

"They're the same thing, Stan. That's what I've been telling you."

Armbruster walked slowly back to his scanner. He pondered what Rachel had said to him about *handling* the sheriff, but he could not imagine any such thing. He didn't think he could ever muster the nerve to do it.

Once back at his scanner, he took up

another page of the newspaper and began to fold it for a scan. As he worked, he thought again of Pat Lance, working a second scanner in Captain Newell's office. He considered climbing the steps to see her. Maybe just to say hello. Then he thought again of the gruff sheriff, and the notion of asking Lance out on a date seemed preposterous.

10

Missy was nearly asleep when Bruce rolled over in bed to face her. "He thought I was going to tear into him, Missy."

She opened her eyes and resettled her head against her pillow. "Who?"

"Stan Armbruster. He thought I was going to rip into him for tracking through my crime scene."

Rubbing her eyes with the heels of her palms, Missy asked, "How do you know?"

"I could see it, Missy. He expected it."

Missy propped herself up on an elbow to face her husband. "Maybe you should have, Bruce."

"What are you talking about?"

"Maybe he needed you to berate him."

Robertson rolled onto his back and stared in the dark toward the ceiling. "He was looking for it."

"So why didn't you?" Missy asked, lying back on her pillow.

"I don't know. Things are different now."

Missy sorted through her thoughts and then said, "You've been yapping too much about resigning."

"Yapping?"

"Yapping. Barking. It's all nonsense."

"What are you talking about?"

"They all feed off your strength, Bruce. They're each stronger because they know you demand it from them."

"Privately, Missy? I don't feel like I've got the right to demand anything these days."

"That's the problem."

"It just doesn't seem right."

"Why in the world not?"

"Because I haven't been able to find Fannie. Because I can't protect her from Teresa Molina. Because another Amish girl is going to be murdered on my watch, and right now there isn't anything I can do to stop it. I can't protect her."

"Maybe Fannie doesn't want you to protect her."

"Well, she ought to!" the sheriff shouted out. He pushed angrily off the bed and paced in front of the dresser.

Missy watched him wordlessly. Eventually he stopped pacing and said, "I'm sorry."

"You shouldn't apologize."

"Why not?"

"Because you're *Sheriff Bruce Robertson.*"

"So?"

Missy propped her pillow against the headboard, sat up, and said, "You're Bruce Robertson, and everybody needs you to stay that way. Now, especially. You've pushed everybody to the limit hunting for Fannie this whole summer, and now is not the time they can afford to see you showing doubt."

The sheriff sat on the edge of the bed with his back to Missy and held his gaze on the carpet. "You're not making any sense," he complained.

"What do you value most, Bruce?" Missy asked. "Don't think about it, just say it."

"Loyalty, steadfastness, duty, honor. Competence. Determination."

"That's who they need you to be, Bruce. That's why Armbruster needs you to hold him accountable."

"He was disappointed, Missy."

"I know, Sheriff. I know."

After Missy had fallen asleep, the sheriff eased out of bed, carried his robe and slippers into the hall, and quietly closed the door. He pulled his robe on and tied it, then he got into his slippers.

In Missy's front-room study on the first floor of their old Victorian home, with yellow porch lights illuminating the curtains behind the chair, he started the desktop computer and waited impatiently for it to come to life, wondering how Howie Dent had made it home to Millersburg. From wherever he had been. Without a car.

That's the puzzle that had kept him awake. He didn't know where Howie Dent had been staying for the last four months, and it caused him to understand that he also didn't know how Howie Dent had gotten himself home.

Once the computer had paced through its initializations, he used it to pull up Rachel's electronic map. When it was loaded on his screen, he saw a total of six red pins. There were the original three, plus a pin for Memphis, the origin. The two new pins marked Horse Cave, Kentucky, on May 9 and Grabill, Indiana, on May 30.

With the map still on the screen, Robertson wandered into the parlor and stood to gaze out the front window at the dark street below the long slope of their front lawn. He stood there for a while, watching for the occasional car passing by, and he wondered about the things Missy had told him. He wondered how all the qualities he cared most about would survive a crisis of confidence. How they would survive the loss of Fannie Helmuth.

He knew Missy had been right to challenge him about the qualities of character that mattered most to him. The qualities of character that had always underpinned him. The qualities that had always underpinned his entire department. Not because any one person was so strong. But because he simply had demanded it from everyone. But since Howie Dent had been murdered, he had been wondering privately if he had the right to demand so much of anyone.

Missy had also been right to challenge him on the matter of his threatening to resign. He had said it, he knew that. He had threatened it. But standing at the dark window, looking out at the silent street in front of his house, Robertson had no idea where that kind of talk had come from. He only knew that since Fannie had fled his protection, he had felt increasingly like an old circus lion, reduced to pacing the cage. A caged lion whose tone in full roar no longer broadcast anything fearsome. A lion made impotent by a loss of self-assurance.

Still he knew that, regarding duty and honor, a man was reliable only insofar as he was relentless. And relentless was something he still was willing to be. Relentless in his dedication to duty. Relentless, regardless of how he felt, in his dedication to finding and preserving Fannie Helmuth. The trouble was — and he was learning this for perhaps the first time in his life — it all required self-assurance. Confidence.

Without that, relentless devotion to duty was just bravado made laughable by incompetence. And incompetence was the last thing Bruce Robertson was willing to tolerate in himself. He'd rather be dead than be found pacing the cage. He'd rather resign.

Robertson stirred, stretched, and turned back toward the study. At the desk computer, he minimized Rachel's map and ran a Bing search for Greyhound bus routes. On a site that gave a nationwide map of bus routes, it seemed at first to the sheriff that Howie Dent could have traveled home from just about any location in the States. On a bus, he could have gotten back to Ohio from just about anywhere. But when Robertson drew in closer to Ohio, he also found that none of the bus routes would have brought Dent closer to Holmes County than Akron to the north or Mansfield to the west. Giving no thought to the time, the sheriff phoned Bobby Newell, and giving Newell no time to say anything more than a sleepy "Hello?" Robertson asked his captain, "Bobby, how'd Dent get back to Holmes County?"

"What?"

"It's Bruce. The bus routes would get him no closer than Akron or Mansfield. So how did he get the rest of the way home?"

"Dunno, Sheriff. What time is it?"

Robertson looked at his watch and said, "Sorry. I'm up. Checking bus routes into Ohio. And nothing by Greyhound comes closer to Holmes County than Akron or Mansfield."

"OK."

"Question is, Bobby, how did he get the rest of the way home?"

Still sleepy, Newell answered, "Maybe he didn't come by Greyhound. Maybe he had a ride."

Robertson paused on an answer and then said, "He used Greyhound before, Bobby. If he did that again, he'd still have to get a ride into Holmes County."

"Maybe he called a friend?"

"Or took a cab."

"We can check that," Newell said. "Cabs and maybe limo services."

"OK, are you coming in early?"

"I am now."

"Sorry. I wasn't sleeping. But I got this idea, so I checked on Greyhound routes."

"Give me an hour, Sheriff. I'll start checking cabs and limo services once I get into the jail."

The sheriff pushed his chair away from the desk, wandered into the kitchen, and poured milk into a bowl of cereal. He carried it into the parlor and sat to eat it in an upholstered chair in the corner by the front window.

When he woke up, he was lying on the divan, and he had dreamed of an angry lion pacing its cage. He was a boy. There was a strangely familiar lion tamer inviting him to draw closer to the cage. Taunting him to put his face close to the bars. Taunting him to let the whiskers of the lion brush against his cheek when the animal lunged at the bars to bite. Above the cage was a large red scroll, written in bold, old-world script:

Fear the Roar
Trust the Bite

The sheriff knuckled his eyes and stood beside the divan. Most of his dream had fled from him, but he clearly remembered the lion and the sign. It was a nightmare he had suffered often as a child. He got himself moving toward the window, and there on the end table beside the corner chair was his half-eaten bowl of cereal. He checked his watch. Two hours had passed.

Stiff in the neck and rubbing at a vague pain in his lower back, Robertson bent side to side tentatively to stretch, and then he walked slowly to the study. He eased himself carefully into the desk chair, and he refreshed the map that Rachel had been assembling in the night. As the map was redrawing on his screen, he rubbed at his back and swiveled around to look out the window behind him.

The yellow security lights on the porch had switched off, and gray morning light was starting to announce the dawn. He checked his watch again because he couldn't remember the time — five thirty. He wheeled his chair around and parted the curtains. There was more traffic on the street out front. Cars, light trucks — the morning routine was under way.

Turning back to his computer, the sheriff saw new pins on Rachel's map. There was Montgomery, Michigan, on June 15. Bronson, Michigan, on June 27. Montgomery, Michigan again, on July 4. And another Bronson, Michigan, on July 18.

Robertson reached for the desk phone and

called Rachel's cell. When she answered, he said directly, "Bronson and Montgomery are repeats, Rachel. They've stopped moving."

"I know, Sheriff," Rachel said in stride, as if he were still standing in the squad room, looking in over her partitions.

"That's dangerous," he added.

"I know. The letter from Bronson said they were thinking about Middlefield."

"That's too close to home," Robertson complained. "They weren't being smart about this."

"Really, Sheriff, they could have been anywhere. All we have are these newspaper snapshots — locations on certain dates."

"Have you finished with all of the *Budget*s?"

"Yes," Rachel said. "The last pin is Middlefield. I was posting that one when you called."

"Have you gotten any sleep?" Robertson asked.

"Not really. I'm not sure I can."

"Me neither. But you should."

Rachel chortled. "Right, Sheriff."

"Really."

"Maybe when Fannie Helmuth is safe."

The sheriff stood at the desk and held a long pause. He sighed, turned to face the gray light at the window, and thought.

Rachel asked, "You still there?"

Robertson stirred and asked, "OK, when is that last one, Rachel? What date?"

"Thought you'd fallen asleep on me, Sheriff. It was in last week's *Budget*. It's our last pin. It comes from a rather vague reference, but I think it's Fannie and Howie. It was written and mailed before Howie Dent was murdered."

"You say it's a vague reference?"

"Yes. If I hadn't done the earlier dates first, I wouldn't have caught it. It just mentions 'a couple from Charm by way of Michigan,' and says that they might stay at the scribe's house for a while."

"OK, then I need to read the letters, Rachel. Can you send a file? Something I can print?"

"Sure, right away."

"Where are Stan and Pat?"

"They've both gone home to sleep."

"You, too, I hope."

"As soon as I send you this file. Then what?"

"It's barely daylight," Robertson said. "But someone needs to go to Middlefield."

"Armbruster and Lance are exhausted."

"Then I'm going up to the college heights," Robertson said. "Gonna see what time a professor still on sabbatical gets himself out of bed."

11

From Courthouse Square, Sheriff Robertson drove his Crown Vic up the village's steep hill on East Jackson Street and circled through the sculptured stone archway onto the campus of Millersburg College. After skirting the first quadrangle of historic academic buildings, he turned off campus onto the Brandens' street, which terminated near the eastern cliffs of town in a cul-de-sac only one block from campus. He rounded three-fourths of the circle and parked the Crown Vic at the curb in front of the Brandens' brick colonial.

When he climbed out of his air-conditioned sedan, August heat and humidity embraced him like the vapor from a steam room. Overhead, the morning sun had begun to burn through the dense cover of gray that had lingered since yesterday's storms. Beside the car, Robertson pulled his tie loose and struggled out of his sport coat. He folded the coat on the driver's seat, closed the door, and locked up. As he lumbered up the short walkway to the Brandens' front stoop, he was already starting to perspire. After he had rung the bell, the sheriff took out his handkerchief to wipe his brow, and he stepped back from the pad to study the front windows for light inside.

When Professor Branden opened the front door, he smiled a wordless greeting to the sheriff, waved Robertson inside, and retreated down the center hallway toward the kitchen at the back of the house. Robertson stepped inside, closed the front door, and followed the professor.

Professor Branden was dressed in brown leather slippers, soft blue cotton pajama bottoms, and a well-worn green and white Millersburg College T-shirt. He hadn't yet brushed his hair, and the sheriff considered some flippant remark about absent-minded academic bed hair. But in the kitchen, Caroline Branden was seated at the table, and in her presence Robertson found his instinct to tease the disheveled professor quickly assigned to a vague memory.

Caroline's long auburn hair was pinned in a loose bun. Her recent Florida tan looked elegant against the rich jade color of her robe. She smiled a greeting as the sheriff came in, and she asked if he would like coffee. Robertson answered happily that he would, and Caroline rose and inquired, "Breakfast, too?"

Robertson smiled wanly, took a mug of coffee from her, and said, "I guess I could eat."

Caroline pointed him to a chair at the kitchen table and remarked, "Bruce, you look pale. Like something's kept you up all night."

As Robertson sat, he traced the elaborate wood grain in the curly maple top of the table. Seeming distracted, he remarked, "Jonah Miller made this table, the way I remember it."

Mike Branden sat beside the sheriff with his own mug of coffee, and he said, "His father the bishop gave it to us after we brought his grandson home." He threw a look over to Caroline, and she shrugged her shoulders, with concern about the sheriff mixing into her expression.

"Old Bishop Eli Miller," Robertson mumbled, not noticing their exchange.

Caroline carried three plates to the table and nudged her husband. "You're cooking eggs?"

Branden rose at the suggestion, took a skillet down from the ceiling rack, and asked, "How many pieces of toast?"

Caroline shook her head. "Just orange juice for me."

Robertson said, "I could eat a couple," and he took his first sip of coffee. Then he groaned, set his mug down, pushed up from the table, and said, "I forgot the letters."

The sheriff disappeared down the hallway, went out to his car, and came back inside holding pages he had printed from Rachel's search. When he sat back down at the table opposite Caroline, he handed the pages across to her and said, "We think we know how to find Fannie Helmuth."

Caroline held up the pages with a silent query, and Robertson said, "They're excerpts from the *Budget.* They were published in the last four months, after Fannie Helmuth and Howie Dent disappeared. After they took that Greyhound bus to Memphis. So Memphis is the first place in their sequence."

As he was cracking eggs into a mixing bowl at the stove, the professor asked Robertson, "Are those from Stan and Rachel's work?" Again he caught a glance from Caroline.

"And Pat Lance," Robertson said, and he

explained how the letters had been identified.

Branden finished cracking eggs, came back to the table, and sat next to his wife. Together they read Rachel's excerpts.

1. Memphis — assumed to be the origination.
2. Whiteville, TN, published April 27
   Guests from Ohio by way of Memphis surprised us yesterday at services and may stay only a while.
3. Paris, TN, published May 4
   Our Ohio travelers stayed only two nights at the John Troyers and want their families in Charm to know that they are well.
4. Cub Run, KY, published May 11
   Two friends from Ohio traveled through here after services yesterday at Daniel Brock's and report to Holmes County that they are well but weary.
5. Horse Cave, KY, published May 18
   Our guests say to their families that they are fine though weary of traveling and may stay a while.
6. Grabill, IN, published June 1
   Our Ohio guests stayed three nights.

No new news for their families near Charm.

7. Montgomery, MI, published June 15
   Guests from Ohio seemed exhausted by travel but insist they are fine. They may be able to stay with us for a while.
8. Bronson, MI, published June 29
   Our friends from Ohio stayed four days to rest. They are considering the location.
9. Montgomery, MI, published July 6
   Our guests from down south of Wooster returned here to look at a trailer rental. Stayed four nights.
10. Bronson, MI, published July 20
    Our friends returned unsure about the Montgomery location. Will try the Middlefield area next.
11. Middlefield, OH, published August 10
    Travelers here are exhausted and have been shown hospitality closer to home by this scribe.

When they had finished reading the Middlefield entry, Caroline placed the pages on the table and said, "Whatever you're paying your people, Bruce, it's not enough."

Robertson reached across the table, tapped the pages, and said, "Look at the last page."

Rachel's last page was a map of the center states, with red digital pins marking each letter's location. Rachel had given the head of each marker its proper number in sequence, identifying the route Fannie and Howie had apparently taken in their travels.

Caroline handed the first pages back to Robertson, and she placed the map page on the table between them. She pointed to the Middlefield marker and said, "That was published over a week ago, Bruce."

"I know," Robertson acknowledged. "It's a long shot."

Branden asked, "Do you think she's still there?"

"Not if she knows that Howie Dent is dead," the sheriff answered sourly.

The professor returned to the stove and started cooking the eggs. Turning briefly from the stove, he asked, "What do you want, Bruce? Why are you here?"

After a deep breath and sigh, with his palms raised as if asking a question, Robertson said, "Mike, I was hoping you could go up there today. To Middlefield, I mean. I want you to find Fannie Helmuth for me."

Branden gave his eggs a last scramble and

carried the skillet to the table. He divided the eggs onto the three plates and walked back to the stove saying, "What makes you think she'll talk to me?"

Robertson answered, "It's a long shot, Mike, but it's the only shot I've got."

Branden put two pieces of toast down and pulled a pitcher of orange juice out of the refrigerator. Caroline reached around to the counter behind her to get three juice glasses, and after she set them on the table, the professor filled them. Then he set the pitcher on the table and sat next to his wife, across from the sheriff.

Caroline started on her eggs and said, "Bruce, I think Michael would only alarm her. She doesn't know him at all."

"That's why I figured Mike for this," Robertson said. "He can clean up almost Amish in five minutes. Just wear that suit of Amish clothes from the old Jonah Miller case. It'll put her at ease."

Branden laughed. "That was almost fifteen years ago."

"What about your detective bureau?" Caroline asked.

"All of my people are pulling doubles. They're looking for Fannie here, on the off chance that she came home with Dent. So I really need someone to try to find her up in

Middlefield."

"Bruce," Caroline said, "it shouldn't be just Michael who goes to find her."

Robertson put hopefulness into his tone. "Perhaps you could go with him, Caroline?"

"I don't know," Caroline said. "I've been spending days with Ellie. I'm worried about her pregnancy. Twins, and there's some trouble."

Robertson cranked a smile into a question. "Isn't Ricky home with her most of the time?"

"Yes, but sometimes he needs to go out."

"We can cover it, Caroline."

"She's at risk for a miscarriage," Caroline said. She glanced with an old sorrow at her husband. In a near whisper, with her sight turned to the tabletop, she added, "I know too much about miscarriages, Bruce."

"It's not too far to Middlefield," the professor remarked softly. He pulled Caroline's hand into his lap. "An Amish or Mennonite couple would be less alarming to Fannie than a single strange man. And talking to a woman would be less threatening to her."

Caroline sighed and considered her memories as she stared at her plate. She took her hand back from her husband. She glanced to Robertson, then to her husband,

and back to Robertson. "OK, Bruce, is this just to talk with her? Just to find out where she is?"

"Yes," Robertson said, "but also to convince her to come into protective custody. To make certain that she can't be harmed, while Teresa Molina is still at large."

"One day?" Caroline asked. "Are we talking about just one day?"

"Yes," Robertson said. "First to find out if she really is in Middlefield. And then to put me in touch with her."

"You think she'll run?" Caroline asked.

"She did once before," the sheriff replied. "I need another chance with her. And I think she should hear about Howie Dent from someone like you. If she doesn't already know."

"One day, Bruce," Caroline said. "One day, and then I need to be back here to take care of Ellie. I couldn't live with myself if she were to miscarry while I was chasing around northern Ohio, trying to find someone who may not even be there."

As Robertson was leaving through the front door, Caroline hooked her husband's elbow and whispered, "Find out what's wrong with him."

Branden hesitated, but she pushed him gently out the door behind the sheriff. Standing on the front stoop in his pajamas, Branden waited until Caroline had closed the front door. "Why does Caroline think you're worried about something?"

The sheriff turned back on the front walkway and said, "I didn't sleep last night, Mike. That's probably all it is."

"What else, Bruce? Normally you'd just have called me about something like this. Or maybe had me come down to the jail."

"We're spread thin, Mike. If I could, I'd go up there myself. But my detectives are exhausted from last night's work. All my deputies are working the local angles. I can't use Ricky, because he's taking paternity leave. And if Fannie Helmuth really is still in Middlefield, then she hasn't got a clue about how much danger she's in."

"We can go, Bruce," Branden assured him. "We'll be there by early afternoon."

Robertson tipped an appreciative nod and held to his place on the walkway.

The professor stepped off the stoop and said, "Caroline's right. What is it?"

"Apart from torture and murder?" Robertson asked, laughing unconvincingly.

"Something more," Branden pressed.

Embarrassed, Robertson said only, "Like

I said, Mike, I didn't sleep much last night."

"So, tell me why."

Robertson shrugged. "I had my lion dream again."

"That old dream from the circus? We were just kids."

Robertson shifted nervously. "I can't believe you don't remember that lion."

"Sorry," Branden said. "It was always just a circus to me."

"There was a lion tamer," Robertson remembered. "Or maybe he was one of the animal handlers. I realize in the dream that I'm supposed to know him, but he's always at the periphery."

"Always the same man?"

"Yes, and there's always that looped whip in his hand. He raps the whip handle across the bars, and that makes the lion roar. But I can't make out who the man is. The trainer."

"Is there always the same sign on the cage?" Branden asked. "Fear the roar, or something?"

Robertson nodded. "He gets me to come close to the bars, Mike. I can't remember how he did that. But he raps his whip handle on the bars, right next to my face, and the lion jumps at me. Its whiskers brush my cheek through the bars."

"You've been having this dream for years,"

Branden said.

"I know."

"Do you really think it happened? We were what, about eight or nine?"

"I don't know," Robertson said, shaking his head and rolling his shoulders to pull himself loose from frustration. "I can't see the man. I always wake up wanting to know who the man is."

"It's just a dream," Branden said, wondering what hesitation he was seeing in his friend. Wondering if Robertson was troubled by something more than a bad dream. "It's just a childhood nightmare," he said to the sheriff.

"You ever feel a lion's whiskers on your cheek, Mike?"

"No, Sheriff." Branden smiled. "I think that's your special torment."

Robertson drew a deep breath and turned for his car. Over his shoulder, he said, "Stop at the jail before you go, Mike. Del Markely will have a folder for you at the front counter. Photos, descriptions, that sort of thing."

"Descriptions?" Branden asked.

"We have that sketch and description of Fannie. I told you about it out at the Helmuth farm yesterday. Plus there are driver's license photos of both Teresa

Molina and Jodie Tapp."

"We met Jodie Tapp in Florida, Bruce," Branden said. "With Ricky Niell, last April. She can't be involved in any of this."

"You've been saying that all summer, Mike. And you only met her that once."

"She was just a Mennonite waitress who got caught up in all of this, Bruce. Just like Fannie. Just like Ruth Zook."

"Right, Mike," Robertson said. "And Ruth Zook is dead. Fannie's been hiding since April. So what if Jodie Tapp is looking for Fannie, just like Teresa Molina is?"

Branden considered that, shook his head, and said nothing.

"You're not seeing this, Mike," Robertson complained. "If Jodie Tapp really was part of the Molina crew, then she's been looking for Fannie all this time, too."

"She's Mennonite," Branden said. "Maybe you're just being paranoid because you had your lion dream again."

At his car door, Robertson shook his head and spoke sternly over the top of the Crown Vic. "You find Fannie, Mike. Then maybe I won't have any more nightmares."

"OK," Branden relented. "Anyone else I should know about?"

"Just Teresa Molina and Jodie Tapp," Robertson said. "They're the ones you should worry about. And I'm telling you, Jodie Tapp is hunting for Fannie Helmuth. Every instinct I have is warning me that Jodie Tapp is part of the Molina crew."

"Jodie Tapp cannot be part of this, Bruce."

"I'm just saying."

In far northeast Ohio, Fannie Helmuth's cell phone rang as she was riding in a black Amish buggy with her new fiancé, Reuben Gingerich. She fished her phone out of her apron pocket, checked the display, and said to Reuben, "It's Jodie again."

Reuben held a stern expression as Fannie answered the call. "Hi, Jodie. You OK?"

"Sure," Jodie Tapp said. "I guess. You?"

"We're fine."

"You with Reuben?"

"Yes. We're out buying groceries."

"Do you have a good town, Fannie? A good place for groceries?"

"I suppose so. You?"

"I'm in Columbus now, Fannie. I keep moving around."

"Us, too."

"Do you have good weather there?"

"It's hot. And we've had a lot of rain lately."

Jodie paused as if thinking and then said, "We can never go back, Fannie. They'll never stop looking for us."

"I know."

"I wish I could see you, Fannie."

"I know, but Howie doesn't think we should tell anyone where we are."

"Probably not."

"Are you finding work?" Fannie asked.

"Waitress," Jodie said. "I'll always be a waitress. How about you?"

"Reuben has money. We want to start a family, settle down."

"You can't, Fannie. Not until they find Teresa Molina."

"I know."

"I don't want you to tell me where you are, Fannie, but I need to know that you're safe. And in a good place. Maybe somewhere out in the country, with lots of Amish people."

"We have a lot of farms here," Fannie said.

"With Amish people?"

"Yes."

"That's good. Are you still with Howie, too?"

"Yes, but he went home to get his car."

The buggy rattled as its right wheels caught the gravel berm, and Jodie said, "Sounds like you're in a buggy. Once Howie gets his car, he can drive you anywhere."

"We'll probably go back to Michigan."

"Is that where Reuben is from?"

"Yes."

"A lot of Amish there?"

"Oh yes. Plenty."

"Wouldn't that be a long drive for you?"

"No, not really. Are you going to stay in Columbus?"

"No. I move around. You should, too."

Reuben reined back and steered his buggy horse around a cluster of potholes in the blacktop. Fannie sighed. "I'm tired of moving, Jodie."

"I know, but you can't trust anyone, Fannie."

"I can trust Howie and Reuben."

"Sure. You're lucky in that."

"Do you have anyone? In Columbus?"

"No."

"Then I wish I could see you, Jodie."

"We can't risk it. You stay with Reuben. Get a ride from Howie to some faraway place. Never tell any *English* where you are."

"What about you?"

"I'll be fine."

"Will you call again?"

"As often as you like. And you can always call me. You know that."

"Thank you, Jodie. Thank you for being my friend."

"Sure. Take care."

"You, too."

"Bye."

"Bye, Jodie."

Reuben turned onto a gravel drive, and the scratching chatter of his buggy wheels mixed with the hollow and rhythmic footfalls of the horse. A frown knitted Reuben's brow. "Are you sure you can trust her, Fannie?"

"Yes, Reuben. As much as I trust Howie."

"Tell me again how she knows your number."

"I called her. From Memphis. As soon as we got our new phones."

"Why does she want to see you so badly?"

"She's lonely, Reuben. So am I."

Reuben stopped the buggy behind a farmhouse and asked, "Doesn't Howie say that we can't really trust anyone?"

Fannie took up a bag of groceries and stepped down from the buggy. "Jodie says the same thing. And she's never asked me to tell her where I am."

Reuben wrapped the reins around the brake lever and climbed down with a second bag of groceries. "Is that why you trust her? Because she never asks where we are?"

"Yes, but she's also my friend, Reuben. I don't have any reason not to trust her.

Besides, she's hiding from Teresa Molina, too."

"And you met Jodie in Florida?"

Fannie stepped around the nose of the horse and started for the back door of the farmhouse. "Yes. We were waitresses together in Sarasota. In the Pinecraft vacation colony."

Reuben followed her toward the door. "Has Howie ever met her?"

"No."

"Then why does he say you can't trust her?"

Fannie started up the steps, and Reuben followed. "It's not Jodie, Reuben. Howie doesn't want me to trust anyone, really."

Reuben waited while Fannie pulled the back door open. "That's probably the best policy."

Inside, Fannie placed her groceries on the kitchen counter and turned to take Reuben's bag, saying, "OK, Reuben. But when this is all over, I'm going to find her. I'm going to find Jodie and give her a long hug."

12

Inside the main entrance to the jail, while she listened to a radio call, Del Markely greeted the Brandens with a cordial wave from behind the sheriff department's front counter. She stood before a battery of communications equipment and computer monitors, and she wore a headset of padded earphones, with a microphone boom curling around her cheek. As the Brandens came across the small lobby, Del held up an index finger and focused her attention on her call. Once she had dispatched a unit, she held out a big hand. "You must be the professor."

Branden stepped to the counter and shook her hand. Then he moved aside and said, "This is my wife, Caroline."

With easy good humor, Markely stuck her hand out over the counter again, and Caroline came forward to take her hand, too.

Markely settled one of the headphone cups behind an ear and said, "I'm Del Markely, taking over for Ellie until her children are born. I have to listen while we talk. The headphones help me get it all."

Del Markely was a solid older woman with coarse graying hair that was swept back tightly against her scalp to accommodate the headphones. At the back of her head, her hair was roped off into a long and frizzy ponytail. Her face was rugged and severe, as masculine as a WWE referee's. Her eyes carried an inclination toward natural and unassuming mirth, as if confidence and playfulness had long ago settled together in her personality, without any apparent contradiction. Wearing her headset, she could have been mistaken for the pit boss of an Indy Car race crew, or equally, for the director of a Broadway musical.

Smiling, the professor tipped his head down the old pine-paneled hallway toward Robertson's office and said, "Do you have the sheriff figured out yet?"

Markely returned his smile. "We get along." She didn't say anything more.

Branden noted her restraint. "He wants us to look for a girl up in Middlefield."

"Fannie Helmuth," Del said. She pulled a

129

manila envelope out of a drawer under the counter. When she handed it across to the professor, she added, "Captain Newell just finished putting that together for you."

The professor had donned Amish attire — blue denim trousers with side-slit pockets; brown leather work boots, which were nicked and scuffed; a white button shirt with its long sleeves rolled up neatly to his elbows; black cloth suspenders with no belt. His wife was dressed as a demure Mennonite woman in an ankle-length, plain cotton dress of surf-turquoise. Her long auburn hair was pinned in a bun that was covered on top by the requisite disk of white prayer lace.

While the professor opened the envelope and spread photos and sketches on the countertop, Caroline leaned onto the counter and quietly asked Markely, "Is Ellie doing OK today?"

Del arched an eyebrow. "Tricky," she said discreetly. "I mean her pregnancy is tricky right now, Mrs. Branden. But there aren't any new complications, according to Ricky."

"Please, it's just Caroline."

"OK, Caroline then."

Rather than saying anything more to Caroline, Markely said to the professor, "I was supposed to inform Captain Newell when you arrived, Professor. I buzzed him. He'll come down right away."

Branden thanked her, and Markely turned back to her consoles. On the countertop, the professor spread out the contents of the manila envelope. First, there were two different artists' sketches of Fannie Helmuth. Beside them he laid the driver's license photos for Teresa Molina and Jodie Tapp. Caroline picked up the Jodie Tapp license and said, "Michael, this must be an old photo."

"Maybe," the professor said. He examined the license more closely. "It still has ten months until it expires, so it can't be too old."

"OK," Caroline said, "but this is not really what she looks like."

From the hallway to the Brandens' left, Captain Newell came in behind Del's counter. He pushed out through the hinged counter door and asked, "Tapp's license photo is not accurate?"

The professor gathered the pages while Caroline explained. "We remember her hair was different in Florida, Bobby. And she had quite a tan."

"That's all we have," Newell said. "It's the most current photo we have of her."

"Jodie looks rougher than this," Caroline

said. "Salted and windblown, like she's been out in the surf all her life."

"Truth is," Newell said, "we don't know for certain about either of them. Tapp or Molina. They each could have changed their appearance. Their hair especially."

"I'll recognize Jodie, regardless," Caroline said. "We talked with her for a long time in Sarasota last April."

The professor had finished sorting the pages back into the manila envelope, and he said, "Really, Bobby, the sketch of Fannie Helmuth makes her look a lot like Pat Lance."

"She does look like Lance," Newell agreed. "And Pat's German, too."

Caroline agreed. "Pat could pass for Amish, if she dressed the part."

Newell smiled a bit, but said nothing further. He pushed his thick black glasses up on the bridge of his nose and rubbed at the patches of black hair over his ears. He looked to the professor as if he wanted to explain something, but he held his peace. So the professor took Fannie's sketch back out of the envelope, turned it over, and took out a pen. "Bobby, we need an address for the Middlefield scribe who wrote to the *Budget.*"

"I'm still trying to get that," Newell said.

"The editors at the *Budget* didn't want to give it to us."

"Why not?" Branden asked.

"They publish the scribe's name and the church district with each letter. But they have never published any addresses."

"How long before you know for certain?" Branden asked.

"I'll call you," Newell shrugged. "By the time you get to Middlefield, I'll either have it or I won't."

"Can you get a warrant for it?" Branden asked.

"We're trying."

The professor tucked the sketch back into his envelope and changed the subject. "Bobby, what's your read on Bruce these days?"

"You mean that he's worried about Fannie?"

"More," Caroline said, stepping closer. "He's hesitant."

Newell pursed his lips. "I wasn't sure anybody else had noticed."

Del Markely turned around from her consoles and leaned out over the counter. With her hand cupping the padded microphone of her headset, she said, "Deputies are talking a little about this, Captain." Then she turned back to attend to her calls.

133

Newell pulled the Brandens away from the counter and led them toward the front entrance. Whispering as if he were organizing a conspiracy, he said, "We've been pushing everybody too hard this summer. Bruce isn't the only one whose nerves are shot."

Before either of the Brandens could respond, Newell pulled an envelope out of his shirt pocket and handed it to the professor. "It's for Fannie," he said. "From Bruce."

The professor read the inscription on the envelope: "For Fannie Helmuth. Confidential. From Sheriff Robertson." He showed it to his wife. It was written in Robertson's erratic and hasty scrawl.

"Like I said," Newell added, "we've all been pushed a little too hard this summer."

"You have any idea what this says?" Branden asked the captain.

"All I know is that you're not to read it unless Fannie wants you to," Newell said. "The sheriff was fairly specific about that."

Standing stiffly beside one of the west-facing windows in his pine-paneled office, the sheriff watched Stan Armbruster wrestle with an unspoken complaint. When Armbruster had snapped to, Robertson had instantly regretted his tone.

"I'm sorry, Stan," the sheriff said, "but I don't need you to snap to attention like some soldier." They had been talking about Armbruster's finding the body of Howie Dent the day before.

Armbruster turned to say something to the sheriff, but Robertson cut him off with a demand. "When did you call it in, Detective?"

"After I found his body."

"And when should you have called it in?"

"As soon as I noticed that his car had been searched."

Robertson returned slowly to stand behind his desk. "That's all I'm saying, Detective. That's the only mistake you made."

Armbruster's eyes searched the shelves behind the sheriff's desk. He drew a deep breath and said, "I need to do something, Sheriff. Something useful."

Robertson sat heavily behind his desk. "You look as exhausted as I feel, Stan. I can't use you like this."

"Sheriff?"

"Can you sleep?" Robertson inquired.

"No, Sheriff."

"Then can you rest?"

"What?" Armbruster stammered.

"I want you to go home and rest. Lie down. Sleep if you can."

"What?"

"You want to fix this, Detective?"

"You know I do!"

"Then go home, lie down, and try to sleep for four hours. Four hours, Stan, not five."

"And then what?" Armbruster demanded.

Robertson framed an impatient scowl, but he restrained himself. "That's when Rachel is coming back in. That's when I'll need you back here, too."

"OK, why?" Armbruster pressed.

Again, but with increasing difficulty, Robertson held himself in restraint. "Because, Stan, Rachel hasn't been able to sleep, either," he said, careful with his tone. "She's bringing me something I want everyone to look at."

More confused and unsettled than ever, Armbruster asked, "What is it?"

"Building plans, Armbruster. Building plans for the Hotel St. James."

"So you do have a plan?" Armbruster challenged.

"Of course!" Robertson barked.

"You going to tell anyone what it is?"

Robertson rose out of his chair. "That's enough, Detective. You be back here at three o'clock."

As he hesitated at the door, Armbruster asked, "Should I get Pat Lance?"

"No," Robertson said, returning to stand alone at his window. "I've got something different for Lance."

13

Thursday, August 18
10:15 A.M.

In a neighborhood in the south end of Millersburg, shielded behind a hill overlooking traffic in front of the Walmart on Route 62, Cal Troyer's Church of Christ–Christian sat in the center of a wide, sloping lawn. At the front edge of a gravel parking lot, a faded poster was stapled to the bottom of the church's wooden sign. It showed a smiling Jesus in a robe, with long brown hair flowing over his shoulders, as he beckoned for a group of eager children to draw nearer for Vacation Bible School. Summer sun had weeks ago bleached most of the color from the poster. Under the plastic that was supposed to have protected the poster from rain, there were streaks and watermarks where moisture had faded the poster regardless. The hand-lettered dates for the Bible School sessions were from earlier in July.

Robertson parked his blue Crown Vic on the gravel lot in front of the sign and proceeded down the narrow walkway beside the long white building, toward the pastor's office at the back of the church. It was a wood-frame building that Cal himself had helped to build many years earlier. Petunias in a variety of colors were planted along the walkway, and the flower bed was mulched and well tended. To Robertson's right, the lawn on the hillside had been recently mowed and trimmed. At the back corner, a ladder stood against the siding, and a bucket of white paint hung on a metal hook from an upper rung of the ladder. Robertson realized that he couldn't remember a summer when Cal hadn't been painting one part of the building or another.

Robertson reached the end of the walkway and turned left. On the door, Cal's name was printed in small yellow letters. Robertson paused before entering.

Cal had *always* been his friend. At least that was how it seemed now to the sheriff. With Mike Branden, they had come up through the grades together, starting in kindergarten. The relationship between pastor and lawman had not always been smooth, especially on disagreements over how to handle the often inscrutable Amish.

But before he pushed through Cal's door, Robertson reminded himself that, regardless of their differences on issues, Cal Troyer was like Mike Branden in one important way. His friendship had never faltered. On cases where Robertson had needed him the most, Cal Troyer had always come through.

Robertson knocked and entered. Cal was seated behind his desk, writing on a pad. Religious books, pamphlets, and tracts lined the shelves to Cal's right. Framed photos from foreign mission trips lined the wall to his left. On the wall behind him hung a simple cross of rough-hewn timbers, almost as tall as Cal himself. Robertson took a seat in front of the pastor's desk and settled in as best he could amid the religious trappings of the office.

Troyer's white beard and hair were once again trimmed close, almost as close as the sheriff's sixties flattop. In April, when Cal had ministered to Emma Wengerd over her grief at the loss of her adoptive sister Ruth Zook, Cal's hair had been considerably longer.

Cal was short and muscular. His large eyes were set wide on a broad face that was inclined most usually toward a smile. His profession lay behind a pulpit, but he earned his keep as a carpenter, and from years of physical labor, his large hands were rough and his thick fingers were knotted at the knuckles. This time of year, Robertson remembered, it was just as likely to find Cal helping Amish relatives with a harvest as it was to find him in his office. Today, however, the pastor was in, and Robertson was relieved.

Troyer smiled but didn't speak. Robertson nodded a silent and reserved hello. Cal rose and stepped to a corner credenza, where he poured black coffee into two mugs that had been drying upside down on a folded paper towel. Robertson took his mug, smelled the brew, and decided it wasn't too stale. He drank gratefully and set the mug on a coaster on the front corner of the pastor's metal desk.

"Your Bible School sign is a little faded," the sheriff said.

Troyer smiled. "I'm sure you didn't come here to inspect the condition of my sign."

Robertson shrugged and drank more coffee. "I see you cut your hair short. You ever gonna decide on one style?"

A wide grin spread over Troyer's face, but he said nothing.

"Fannie Helmuth," Robertson said, and he shook his head with doubts.

"Something bad to report?" Cal asked.

"Or have you found her?"

"No," Robertson said, "but we found Howie Dent yesterday morning."

"I heard. I've been worried about Fannie."

Robertson recounted the events since Armbruster's finding the Dent body. He took his coffee mug from the desk and stared into it for a long twenty count. Without looking up at Cal, he concluded, "I don't think I can protect her here, Cal."

"Why not?"

"I don't think she'll cooperate."

"Then what's your plan? Or maybe you don't really have one."

"I do. I've got a plan," Robertson said. And he told Cal about the Hotel St. James.

Cal listened, thought, shook his head, and considered what the sheriff had said. He sipped coffee and leaned back in his chair. When he was satisfied that he understood, he rocked forward slowly and set his mug gently on his desk.

All the while, the sheriff watched him intently, waiting for the pastor's assessment. He saw concern and also apprehension pass through Cal's visage. Then he saw a degree of settlement in the pastor's eyes.

Cal's smile acknowledged an appreciation for the sheriff's reasoning. "I don't think she'll stay put for them, Bruce," Cal said.

"Even if she does, I don't think it has any chance of working."

Robertson drove north on the Wooster Road thinking Troyer had been entirely correct. He circled right into the lower parking lot of Joel Pomerene Memorial Hospital. It was perched like a watchtower on one of the hills piled densely beside the north road, where Millersburg was anchored on high ground, overlooking the flatlands of Killbuck Marsh to the west.

Inside the cool and antiseptic basement hallway, Robertson stopped to catch his breath and to gather his resolve for studying the body of Howie Dent. He sat on a bench against the wall and ran a handkerchief over his face. After a moment he pushed heavily up from the bench and continued down the starkly lighted hallway to the single door to Missy Taggert's office. He entered the small room and crossed to press the buzzer at Missy's intercom. From inside her autopsy suite, Missy answered, "Who's there?" and Robertson said, "It's me, Missy. Is there anything in there that I really need to see?"

"One minute," Missy answered. When she came out, she was dressed in green scrubs with a clear plastic apron. A face mask hung loosely around her neck. Her hair was put up under a surgical cap. She had taken off her autopsy gloves, but she still carried them. She dropped them into a biohazard can next to her desk and pulled her husband away from the door, saying, "I have him opened up right now."

"Do I need to look?" Bruce asked stiffly.

"Not really, but what's wrong? This usually doesn't bother you."

"It always *bothers* me, Missy. I just don't have it today."

"Then you don't need to go in there."

Grateful, the sheriff asked, "Do you have anything new for me?"

"I think so," Missy said as she pulled off her apron. She went back into autopsy to hang it up, and then she came back into her office and sat at her desk. "I don't think they wanted him to die just then," she said to her husband. "I think his death was sudden."

"From what I saw of him, Missy, he could not have died soon enough to suit him."

"This may be good news, Bruce. For Fannie. He died instantly of a heart attack. His heart stopped suddenly."

Robertson drew a labored breath and shook his head. "How do you know?"

"It's speculation, of course, but his wounds — from the needles — were not done by a professional. There's evidence of that everywhere. An unsteady hand. Scant knowledge of anatomy. Irregular placement. Hesitations. They just jabbed a spot and shot him full of chemicals."

"So, maybe they were in a hurry."

"I'm sure they were. But on one of the injections, which I think was the final one, they did hit a vein. In his groin. They shot poison straight to his heart."

"And he died instantly?"

"Yes. It was Bleib-Ruhig, Bruce. In order to load it into a syringe, they had to suspend and dissolve it in water. It all went to his heart, and I don't think he had a chance to tell them anything after that."

The sheriff rubbed nervously at the top bristles of his hair. He exhaled vexation mixed with relief. "Missy," he said, "that's the only good news I've had in this case."

"Because you think Teresa Molina still doesn't know where Fannie is?"

"Yes," the sheriff said. "I'm counting on it."

"These are brutal people, Bruce. I mean, burns are the worst cases I see in the morgue. These were *chemical burns,* under his skin."

A shudder rinsed through the sheriff, and he groaned with tension. "At least he's not in any pain now."

"I hope so," Missy said tentatively.

"He's dead," Robertson sputtered. "He can't feel anything."

"I hope so, Bruce," Missy said again.

"I saw his body in that basement, Missy. You're telling me he suffered chemical burns over what, forty percent of his body?"

"Something close to that."

"And you don't think death has put an end to his pain?"

"I don't know what happens after death, Bruce. At least not beyond what I believe by faith. Certainly not in any scientific way."

"Missy," the sheriff said, shaking his head, "if death is not the end of pain, then life is unutterably cruel."

"Hi, Jodie. Are you working now?"

"Yes, but I'm due for a break."

Fannie heard the din of a busy kitchen in the background of Jodie's phone. "Then can you talk? Or should I call you back?"

"No, I can talk. I'm stepping outside."

Fannie heard road noises, as if Jodie were now standing outside at the edge of a busy street. "Are you still in Columbus, Jodie?"

"Yes. I'm working in Worthington. It's a north-end suburb."

"I can hear the traffic."

"I imagine you have a lot of farms there?" Jodie asked.

"It's all farms, mostly. There's one little town."

"Then you can enjoy the quiet."

"Yes."

"That would be good," Jodie said. "You can wear Amish clothes and not get stares from English tourists."

Fannie laughed. "We still get a few of those. Is that a game I hear in the background?"

"The Cleveland Indians. They're pretty good this year, Fannie. We've got the game on the radio in the kitchen. You listen to any games? Because I remember that you said you like the Indians."

"No," Fannie sighed. "It's on the radio all the time, but I haven't been listening. Are you going to stay in Columbus?"

"Probably not. You know how I hate cold winters."

"I don't mind them," Fannie said. "We may get an early one, though. The hummingbirds are thinning out sooner than normal. Going south ahead of schedule, so we may have a hard winter."

"Then I'm out of here," Jodie chimed. "I'll do something like your brother and move south to Kentucky. Maybe even farther south."

"Did I tell you about Jonas?" Fannie asked. "I guess I did."

"Oh yes, Fannie. You said that Jonas moved his entire family to Kentucky, after Ruth Zook was killed."

"I guess I did," Fannie said. "I've always had it in mind to go see him."

"Would that be a long trip?"

"Not in Howie's car. Maybe a long day, down and back."

"You're lucky, Fannie. Anywhere you go, you have Amish. They're all family for you, really."

"Can't you go home, Jodie?"

"No, Fannie. We've talked about this. You know I can't go home until they find Teresa Molina."

"Maybe Howie could drive me to see you, Jodie. When he gets back with his car."

"I'd like that. In the meantime, you stay where you are. Stay hidden, and stay safe."

"I will."

"I have to get back to my tables, Fannie. I'll call you after my shift."

14

Thursday, August 18
12:20 P.M.

While Caroline sat with her laptop on her knees in the passenger's seat beside him, the professor drove northeast out of Holmes County on US 62, and then continued north on US 21. Beyond Massillon, they joined traffic on US 77, and after Akron, they circled east on 271 to skirt the southeast rim of metropolitan Cleveland. As they drove, Caroline had her mobile hot spot open on the dash of their sedan, and she used it to search Internet data-bases and Web sites for the Middlefield community. By the time they had started across the countryside of northeast Ohio on two-lane Ohio 44, she was getting useful information about the Amish businesses in the Middlefield tourist region. On one of the Web sites, she found that the shops and restaurants of Middlefield were indicated on a map, with golden buggy symbols marking the Amish-owned establishments in town.

Near the center of Middlefield, the professor pulled into the parking lot of a historic tavern. Caroline unbuckled her seat belt and turned her laptop so that her husband could better see the monitor. On the screen, she had displayed a map of the town with its buggy symbols marking the numerous Amish establishments. She pointed out one marker near the center of town and said, "That's the biggest one, Michael. It's Miller's Restaurant. On Google Earth, it displays as a very large building. The parking lot holds a hundred cars. Most of the other shops are quite a bit smaller."

Branden backed out of the parking spot, and Caroline rebuckled her seat belt. At the main intersection in Middlefield, Branden turned right and soon found Miller's Restaurant on the left side of the road. He circled into the parking lot, drove down several lanes of parked cars, and finally nosed into a vacant spot in the far back corner of the lot.

The white-sided restaurant building was framed by a wraparound porch with country-scrolled railings as a border. Hickory rocking chairs with tall, elaborate backs were set out on the porch for customers. It was lunchtime, and the rockers were occupied by people waiting for tables inside. A line comprised of English tourists for the most part, with some Amish people, too, had formed at the double front doors. At the side, a single door led into a salesroom set apart from the dining room, and that's where the Brandens entered the building.

The long sales counter with half a dozen cash registers was situated to their left as they entered. Along the wall to their right, there were tall shelves holding dozens of loaves of fresh Amish breads and a variety of pastries. On a display rack just inside the door, there were jars of Mrs. Miller's jams and jellies. Country crafts and trinkets were displayed on stands in the middle of the room. One rack offered personalized ceramic coffee mugs with all the common surnames. Wooden plaques, carved with common prayer phrases and Scripture verses, covered all of the walls. Filling all the remaining corners of the display floor were hard candies in tins, jingle bells on leather straps, bookmarks with Amish scenes, and kitchen gadgets of the type that would prompt an impulsive purchase based on the down-home feeling of centeredness and belonging that few English tourists actually experienced in their daily lives. The offerings were artfully designed and displayed so as to loosen the wallets, purses, and billfolds of visitors who found themselves reasoning that here, more than most places, they enjoyed a profound and metaphysical linkage to a cherished heritage of simpler lives and happier times.

Caroline shook her head and braved a sardonic smile for her husband. "We're here for information, Michael," she said. "That's all."

Branden returned her smile and whispered, "We may have to order a meal."

"Coffee, Michael. And maybe we can share a piece of pie. To be polite."

"But try the sales counter first?" the professor suggested.

Caroline turned back to the bench of cash registers along the far wall. Once she had secured a place in the checkout line, she pulled a postcard from a standing rack and waited beside the professor. They moved forward with the line slowly. When they were next in line to check out, the Brandens were signaled forward by a young girl in an Amish dress and apron. Caroline laid her postcard on the counter, and the girl rang it up without looking at either of the Brandens.

As she was taking money out of her purse, Caroline said, "We were hoping to speak with Abel Mast."

The salesgirl took Caroline's money, but didn't speak.

"He's the scribe for one of the districts here," Caroline added. "We'd like to find him."

The salesgirl handed back change for Caroline's postcard and said, "You're not really Amish, are you?"

The professor eased forward to the counter and said, "No, but we're from Millersburg, and we've come to see Mr. Mast. The scribe."

The girl gave an impatient sigh. "He's from a farm north of here. His niece waits tables here." She shifted nervously in place and eyed the next customer in line. "We're supposed to keep the line moving," she said. "Please."

"You're not really Amish, either," Caroline said.

"No, but the owners like us to dress properly. But please. Get a table and ask for Becky Prayter. She's his niece. She married English, so she won't be in a bonnet. Otherwise, she's dressed like the rest of us."

The Brandens stepped away from the busy sales counter and found the hostess stand near the dining room entrance. A tight cluster of customers was pressing close to the stand, and the hostess was marking and remarking her plastic seating chart to try to advance as many diners to tables as she could manage. Caroline started working her way through the crowd and eventually spoke to the hostess. The professor watched from beside a rack of bread near the back of the line. When Caroline returned to him, she held a brown disk flasher. "Forty minutes," she said. "We can wait outside."

Once outside on the porch, Caroline pulled her cell phone and called Ellie Troyer-Niell. It was Ricky Niell who answered Ellie's phone. He explained that Ellie was resting in bed, and Caroline asked, "How is she today, Ricky? Any more cramping or spotting?"

"No. Nothing new, really. She grumbles about being off her feet, but you know Ellie."

"Is she really staying off her feet?"

"Today she is. She's tired more than usual."

"You going to stay with her all day?"

"Mostly. I need to go out to the pharmacy and the grocery store, but that should only take an hour or so."

"Tell her I said to stay off her feet, Ricky.

Tell her that I'll be back later today. Maybe this evening."

"I will," Ricky said. "She's going to be fine, Caroline."

Caroline responded sternly. "You don't know that. Bad things happen to good people."

"I know. I know. I just meant —"

"Ricky," Caroline interrupted. "You've got to watch her all the time. She has got to stay off her feet."

"We know, Caroline. We're being careful. She's got the bed and the couch. She listens to the radio or watches TV. And she reads. But I always help her move from the bed to the couch and back again. Other than the bathroom, those are her only two places. So we are watching it, Caroline. We are being careful."

"OK, Ricky."

"Really, Caroline. Don't worry so much."

"It's your job to take care of her, Ricky Niell. It's my job to worry."

When their flasher indicated with its circle of red lights that a table was ready for them, the Brandens jostled their way up to the hostess stand, and Caroline handed over the pulsing brown disk with a peevish smile. "Becky Prayter's table, right?" she asked, and the hostess led them into the dining room without responding. At a back corner of the room, adjacent to swinging doors leading in and out of the noisy kitchen, the hostess laid her two menus down on a small table against the wall. "You were in a hurry, right?" she said, as if to apologize for the poor seating.

Caroline pulled a chair out, sat down, and said, "It'll do nicely. I'm not sure we want a meal, anyway." The professor sat across from her.

A middle-aged waitress wearing the nametag BECKY stopped beside their table long enough to set down water glasses and table service. She asked, "Do you know the specials?" and left without an answer. When she returned, she had her pen poised to write an order on her pad, and all she said was a hurried, "OK."

Caroline reached up gently to touch her arm. "Two coffees, please, and a piece of black raspberry pie to share."

Becky didn't bother to write the order on her pad. She stepped away, came back with two cups of coffee, and said, "We seem to have run out of black raspberry."

Caroline flashed an indulgent smile and said, "Becky Prayter, right?"

Becky paused beside the table, and the

156

professor used the pause to say, "We're from Millersburg. We'd like to find your uncle, Abel Mast. He's the district's scribe."

Becky pushed her pen into the hair over her ear and said, "We still have peach, Dutch apple, and peanut butter cream."

"Peach," Caroline said, taking Becky's arm gently again. "Please, how can we find Abel Mast?"

From the back of her order pad, Becky tore a blank page. She wrote on it and handed the note to Caroline. "He answers his phone sometimes. When he's in town, but not when he's at home."

"Can you tell us where he lives?" Branden asked.

"If you can't get him on his phone, I'll draw you a map," Becky said as she turned for the kitchen. "Once the lunch crowd thins out."

Caroline read the phone number and handed the page to her husband. "I think we should try for the map, regardless."

"We can call first," Branden said. "You really want any pie?"

"No," Caroline said, "but leave a twenty on the table for her. If we can't get him on the phone, we'll come back to see her later."

Outside, the professor leaned against one of

157

the wooden posts of the porch railing, and he tapped the phone number for Abel Mast into his cell. Caroline waited beside him, seated in one of the restaurant's hickory rockers.

After three rings, a husky voice answered, "Hello?" and the professor asked, "Is this Abel Mast?"

"Who's this?" the man asked. "Reuben?"

"No," Branden said. "My name is Michael Branden. From Millersburg."

"Do I know you?"

"No. It was your niece who gave me your number. Becky Prayter."

Mast said nothing, so Branden continued. "I'm a friend, Mr. Mast. I read your letter to the *Budget,* and I'd like to talk with you about your houseguest."

Sounding startled, Mast blurted, "Why?" Then he muffled the phone and spoke stridently to someone with him. When he returned to Branden, he said, "How do you know I still have a houseguest?"

"Please, Mr. Mast. I'm up here with my wife, Caroline. From Millersburg. We want to help Fannie, and I have a letter for her from the Holmes County sheriff."

"I don't think she'd want to see you," Mast said.

"Then perhaps you'd be willing to talk to

us, Mr. Mast. We could meet you, and we don't have to do it at your house."

Gruffly, Mast asked, "Where are you?"

"At Miller's Restaurant."

"I can't get there until later this afternoon."

"We can wait, Mr. Mast."

"I can't promise I'll tell you anything about Fannie."

"I know. We just want to help her, Mr. Mast. We know she must be worried."

"You don't know the half of it. Her Howie went home to get his car, and she hasn't heard from him yet."

"Mr. Mast, I need to talk to you about Howie Dent."

"Do you know him?"

"Yes, Mr. Mast. Can you meet us here? Sooner rather than later?"

"I've got business in town. My wife's with me."

"Bring her with you," Branden said. "You can both meet my wife."

"But what about Fannie's Howie?" Abel Mast asked.

"Please, Mr. Mast," Branden said. "Let me tell you about Howie when you get here."

15

Sheriff Robertson stood pensively behind his battered cherry desk and surveyed the large office that had been his post for decades. He let his gaze drift around the room, and he remembered.

His display of law enforcement arm patches, collected over so many years, was framed on the wall to his right. Dan Wilsher had helped him hang the frame.

Against the same wall, just past the office door, Ellie Troyer had long ago set up his coffee credenza, with Ricky Niell's help. Now they were married, expecting twins. Robertson shook his head and wondered if Ellie would agree to come back to work after the children were born.

At the far wall opposite his desk, the tall windows patiently kept their vigil over the Civil War monument on the courthouse

160

lawn. The windows to his left had for decades given a close view of traffic on busy Clay Street, just a half block south of the intersection with Jackson. How many times had he stood at those windows? How many cups of coffee had he shared in his office with friends, colleagues, and citizens?

In front of Robertson's desk were the chairs for visitors. One was a low leather chair that the professor favored. The other two were straight-backed wooden chairs that Robertson had found in the hallway after his election as sheriff. He had moved them into the office even before his cherry desk had been delivered. He would never have predicted that they would serve him so well, considering they were just dusty castoffs when he had pressed them into service on his first day as sheriff.

Overhead was a patchwork of ornate, hand-hammered tin ceiling tiles, the gray squares making an intricate pattern across the span above his head. Robertson knew they had been installed by artisans when the building was first constructed beside the historic sandstone courthouse.

And on all the walls of his office, faded light-pine paneling from the sixties decorated the room. The sheriff before him had put it up. Working loose at some of the corners, the paneling was hopelessly out of date. Ellie had often tried to convince him to remodel. The paneling would be the first thing to go, she had always insisted. But Robertson had never seen the need to change it. He wondered now why he had never considered it. Probably, he thought, for the same reason that he'd never trade this battered desk away. Because there wasn't anything modern that was better. The new age wasn't an answer to anything, he had always thought. But perhaps he had been wrong.

Robertson recognized his melancholy mood for what it was, and he allowed himself to ride the weary sentiments that were distracting him from what he was proposing to do for Fannie Helmuth. He let these sentiments distract him from the consequences of the decisions he had made. Melancholia, it seemed, had its benefits.

Saving his focus for the meeting that would soon take place, Robertson wandered casually out into the hallway and moved slowly down to Del Markely's station behind the front counter. She was making entries on a computer at her desk, still wearing her headset. Robertson cleared his throat, and Del turned to face him. She said, "Just finishing," and tapped several more keys before she stood up.

The sheriff didn't say anything to her. Del let the silence hang. She watched him push out through the swinging counter door into the department's small entrance lobby, and she watched him turn around and push back through the swinging door to stand with her behind the counter.

"They should be here soon," she said. "How long should I ask them to wait?"

Robertson smiled but did not answer.

Del said, "I'll use my judgment," and Robertson nodded his appreciation to her.

"Is my paperwork ready?" he asked, and Markely held up a folder, saying, "Right here, Sheriff."

Robertson arched a brow and returned to his office to wait. When Markely came back later with his visitors, the sheriff was standing at the north windows with his arms folded. Back to the door. Gazing out over the courthouse lawn. Seized with nostalgia. Coasting on his memories as a strategy to be calm. Because it would be better to be placid, for the meetings he had scheduled this afternoon, than to be confrontational.

Del Markely ushered two men in black suits forward to stand at Robertson's desk. "Sheriff," she said, "these are Agents La-Monte Washington and William Parker.

From the FBI office in Cleveland."

Robertson waited for Markely to leave and close the door before he turned around from the windows. He tipped his chin to acknowledge Washington and Parker, and then he took a position standing behind his desk. He waved the two agents into seats in front of his desk. Neither of the agents sat down, so Robertson remained standing, too.

As if they had practiced a precision drill, both agents displayed their badges briefly and then slipped them back into their suit coat pockets. One agent, the taller one, stepped forward and said, "Special Agent Parker. The Cleveland SAC sent us down to take Fannie Helmuth into protective custody."

"And who is Cleveland's Special Agent in Charge these days?" Robertson asked.

"Brenda P. Adams," Parker said. "Of course you already know that, because you've spoken on the phone with her several times."

"Indeed." Robertson smiled. "Have a seat, Agents."

"We'll just be going," Parker said.

"It's not that simple," Robertson said. "Please sit down."

"Really, Sheriff," Parker started.

Robertson interrupted. "Agent Parker.

Please sit down. I need to explain some things to you."

Parker sat, and his partner did likewise. Robertson pulled his desk chair forward, sat down, and rolled in behind his desk. He drummed his thumbs on his desktop, and he frowned as if he had been pondering a difficult decision. With an apologetic smile, he said, "I don't actually have Fannie Helmuth in custody, Agent Parker."

Parker said nothing. His partner took out his cell phone, rose, and stepped into the hallway, tapping a speed dial number as he left.

Parker eased forward on his chair and said, "Sheriff, you said you had her."

"I said I could *deliver* her," Robertson countered. "And I can. I estimate she'll be in your custody by the end of the day. You'll just have to drive a little farther to get to her."

"Just tell us where she is, Sheriff. We're wasting time."

"That's something I want to talk about," Robertson said. "I'll require a transfer-of-custody agreement."

"SAC Adams would never agree to that."

Robertson ignored the objection. "And Agent Parker, I have drafted an agreement for Fannie to sign, stating the terms for her going into your custody. You'll need to sign that, too."

"Look, Robertson, our safe house in Cleveland is expecting her today. We're all set up."

"That's not where you're going to hold her," Robertson said evenly. "It's a stinking, rattletrap hotel room on the wrong side of Cleveland, and it's in a neighborhood I wouldn't visit myself in daylight. You'll have her eating cold pizza and drinking stale pop for a month, and you'll never let her out of her room. She could be there longer than a month, if you can't track down Teresa Molina. So, Agent Parker, I promise you that is one safe house that is never going to happen. Not to Fannie Helmuth."

Agent Washington came back into the office holding his cell phone out for Parker. "The SAC wants your update," he said to his partner.

Parker spoke briefly into the cell phone. "One moment, SAC Adams."

Robertson planted his elbows on his desk and tented his fingers. "Just put that on speaker phone," he said to Parker.

Parker glowered at Robertson, but he placed the phone on the front corner of the sheriff's desk, nonetheless. When he switched it to speaker, Parker said, "You're on my speaker phone, Brenda."

Robertson asked, "Is this SAC Adams?" and Adams replied, "You can't just make this easy, can you, Robertson."

"Adams," Robertson said, "easy is exactly what I'm trying for, here. Easy, that is, for Ms. Helmuth."

"I'm listening," Adams said from the phone.

Robertson said, "It's a hotel near Middlefield, Adams. It's one of the hotels run by Amish people, and the top-floor rooms would be easy to defend. They're all suites. That's where I want you to set up your safe house."

Adams was slow to respond. "An Amish hotel?" she asked eventually. "That's what you want?"

"That's most of it. What I especially do not want is for Ms. Helmuth to be kept in an urban environment. She'll never get any rest. She'd never relax. Not for a minute. But most important, the hotel that I am proposing is close to Middlefield, and I like the cleaning crews that work the rooms."

"Sheriff," Adams huffed over the phone, "we're not going to let any cleaning crews into our safe house."

"They're Amish and Mennonite women from Middlefield," Robertson said. "You're gonna let them come in to clean for Fannie. They're gonna bring her meals from time to time. Maybe they can sit with her for some company. But what you're not going to do is drop Fannie Helmuth into some festering urban stink hole where she'll never see a friendly face again."

"They'll all be searched, Robertson. Everyone who shows up at our doors."

"They'll all be Amish, Adams. Maybe some Mennonite, not that you'll know the difference. You can search them all you want."

"Put Parker on," Adams said curtly.

Washington picked up the phone, switched off the speaker option, and handed the phone to Parker. Agent Parker stepped out into the hallway and closed Robertson's door. When he came back into the office, Parker handed the phone back to Washington and said to Robertson, "You have the transfer-of-custody agreement already drawn up?"

Robertson buzzed his intercom and said, "Del, bring those papers, please."

When he had them from Markely, Robertson spread the two documents out on his desk. "One," he said, "is our transfer agreement. Hotel, meals, visitations — they're all specified. Sign here and here, at the flags."

After taking time to read it carefully, Parker signed the transfer agreement. Then he said, "The second document?"

"That's Fannie's agreement to go into protective custody with the FBI. It also specifies the location and the conditions of her protection."

"Is it a duplicate of the first one?" Parker asked.

"Partly. But it also specifies that Fannie is not going to stay in your custody indefinitely. Once you have arrested Teresa Molina, Fannie is to be allowed to decide for herself when and how she will testify for you. She's to be allowed to go home, if she wants to."

"Why wouldn't she testify?" Parker asked. "That's always been the whole point of this."

"I want her free to decide, Parker. After she has understood all the consequences. And I want to know that you can't force her to testify, if she decides she doesn't want to. Before I tell you where she is, I want the FBI to agree to all of that."

Parker read through the agreement and signed it where indicated. Fannie would also have to sign the document to put it into force. Parker slid the signed documents over to Robertson and said, "OK, Sheriff. Where is she?"

Robertson took up his signed documents, stacked them together in their folder, and said, "I'm not sure just yet, Agent Parker. We're still working on that."

16

Thursday, August 18
2:20 P.M.

Abel Mast arrived at Miller's Restaurant after the lunch crowd had dwindled. He drove his black buggy to the back of the lot and climbed down from his high seat. As his wife got out on the other side, he pulled the reins forward over the head of his dappled mare and tied the horse to the hitching post at the corner of the building.

Together, the Masts walked slowly forward. The Brandens stepped off the porch to greet them. Abel shook hands with the professor, and the women smiled their greetings to each other.

"You're Mr. Branden?" Abel asked. "Michael Branden?"

"Yes," the professor said, "and this is my wife, Caroline."

"You're not really Amish," Mast said. "Why the costume?"

"We thought we'd get a better welcome," Branden said. "We hoped that maybe we wouldn't startle Fannie quite so much."

"She's plenty startled as it is," Mast said. "She's nervous, and she can't seem to relax."

"We want to help her," Caroline said. "The sheriff wants to help her."

"You said you have a letter for her?" Mast asked the professor.

"I do," Branden said. "Could we talk inside?"

"This going to take a while?" Mast asked.

"Maybe, why?"

"I'll just set out some water for my horse."

Mast walked back to his rig and pulled a pail out of the rear cargo bay of the buggy. He filled it from a plastic jug of water and set it down under the nose of his horse.

When he had returned, Branden said, "That's an unusual buggy horse, Mr. Mast."

Mast smiled. "I breed them. Never cared for a plain standardbred."

Inside the restaurant, the four were given a table near the long buffet, where waitresses were cleaning out the chafing dishes that had been used for lunch. Branden offered to buy a late lunch for the Masts, but they declined. So Branden laid Sheriff Robertson's letter to Fannie on the table and said,

"I'm supposed to give that to Fannie. I haven't read it."

Mast stared at the letter as if it were an omen. "Nobody was supposed to know where Fannie is," he said. "How did you find us?"

"Your letter to the *Budget* said you have houseguests."

"They asked me to write that," Mast said with a fatalistic tone. "Now it seems to me that maybe that wasn't such a good idea."

"The sheriff was able to trace their travels," Branden said, "only because other scribes wrote similar things."

"Fannie and Howie wanted their families to know that they were well."

"I don't think it will be a problem," Branden offered. "The people who want to hurt Fannie probably don't even know that the *Budget* exists."

"Still," Mast complained, "you found her easily enough."

"We just want to help her," Caroline said. "The sheriff wants to put her into protective custody."

Mast hesitated. "I don't know. Maybe she should just move on."

"But how long can she hide?" Caroline asked. "Isn't she tired of running?"

Mrs. Mast spoke for the first time. "She's

exhausted, Mrs. Branden. I think she needs someone to help her. We've been waiting to learn something, when Howie Dent gets back."

Caroline looked to her husband and then turned sympathetic eyes back to Mrs. Mast.

Mrs. Mast noticed Caroline's anxiety and asked, "What? What is it?"

The professor said, "We have bad news, Mrs. Mast. We need to tell Fannie. Howie Dent is dead."

Mrs. Mast sat at the restaurant table and cried into her hankie. Abel Mast paced in the aisle making calls on his cell phone. The Brandens waited in their seats, Michael across the table from Mrs. Mast, and Caroline seated beside her, holding her hand.

When Abel sat back down, he shook his head and seemed to have deflated. "I don't think Fannie can handle this right now."

Branden faced him and said, "We can help, Abel."

Mast spoke with a heavy weariness. "I wasn't supposed to tell anyone where she was, Mr. Branden. Now it seems that everybody knows."

"Not everyone," Branden said. "We haven't told anyone, and you probably haven't either."

"But haven't you already called your sheriff? To say that you've found her?"

"No, Mr. Mast. We won't call, either. Unless Fannie agrees to it. We came here just to talk to her and to give her the sheriff's letter. If she doesn't want our help, then we can't really do anything."

"You might tell the sheriff where she is."

"Mr. Mast, she'd be gone by the time he was able to get someone up here."

"You're the only ones who came?"

"Yes."

"What if she doesn't want to talk to you?"

"I hope she will," Branden said. "She needs to know about Howie Dent."

Mast turned pensive. "How did he die?"

"He was murdered, Abel. Probably by the same people Fannie has been so afraid of."

With sorrow cast in his eyes and weariness wrinkling his brow, Mast sat thinking for a long time. He seemed to be wrestling with Fannie's dilemma. When he appeared to have reached a resolution of sorts, he asked, "What do you do, Mr. Branden? What is your profession?"

"I work for the sheriff as a reserve deputy," Branden said. "But I am also a college professor."

"Really," Mast said, surprised. "What do you teach?"

"Civil War history."

"War?"

"Yes, Mr. Mast. The American Civil War."

"Shouldn't you be in class?"

"We don't start for another week or so."

"Then shouldn't you be preparing your subject?"

"I've been a professor for over thirty years, Abel. I ought to be able to make a few cogent remarks without too much preparation."

"I suppose so."

"Abel, are you going to let us talk with Fannie?"

Mast shrugged. "I can't find a reason not to."

"That's good," Branden said. "That's very good."

Mast examined the professor's Amish costume. "You've had these clothes for a while," he said, smiling wanly. "They're a little out of date."

"I didn't think Amish people cared about that sort of thing."

"We don't care," Mast said. "But we notice."

"Do you think Fannie will care?"

Mast shook his head sadly. "Once she knows that her friend has been murdered, I don't expect Fannie will care about much

176

of anything."

"Hi, Fannie. My shift just finished. Have you heard from Howie?"

"No, Jodie. Nothing yet. He'll call."

"I hope so, Fannie. Anyway, I wanted to ask you if you're still sewing your own clothes? Or if you have a good fabric store in town?"

"There's one. It's decent, I suppose. But I don't have a machine, usually. And I don't have time to stitch by hand. Why?"

"I was just wondering. I'm moving myself up to Hartville. And tips would be better there if I had Amish clothes. Instead of Mennonite."

"I'm sure I could get to a machine," Fannie said.

"You're not staying with friends?"

"Oh, people put us up, but they're not usually friends."

"Hey, Fannie. If I waited tables in Hartville, maybe you could visit me. I'd serve your table."

"I suppose," Fannie said. "That would be easy enough. But why are you moving to Hartville?"

"I need to tell you something, Fannie."

"What?"

"It's Teresa Molina. She found my mother.

She went there and threatened her. Mom told her I was in Columbus, so I have to move on. I can't even tell my own mother where I'm going. She can't know."

"That's terrible, Jodie. I mean, that's really awful."

"Fannie, what if Teresa Molina learns where your brother lives? She's really dangerous."

"I don't know. What are we going to do?"

"I'm moving up to Hartville. To work in the restaurant."

"That's such a well-known place, Jodie. What if she knows to look for you there?"

"She won't."

"But what if she does?"

"I can't think about that, Fannie. But I'm tired. I can't stand much more of this."

"Maybe you should get farther away. Maybe go out west somewhere."

"I've already started driving, Fannie. To Hartville. I'm on 62, headed north for Massillon."

"That runs right through Millersburg, Jodie."

"I'll be careful."

"I'm worried."

"Don't be. I can handle myself. Anyway, I was thinking. We might be safer together. At least I would be, hiding with you in Amish homes."

"I don't know."

"Just a suggestion."

"OK, but I'd need to think about that."

"I'll be fine in Hartville, I guess. For a while."

"Do you still want me to make you some clothes? I could mail them to you. Size what? Eight petite?"

"Maybe six, but not unless I came to see you."

"I'll think about it, Jodie. I'll ask Howie what he thinks."

17

Thursday, August 18
2:55 P.M.

Pat Lance was the first to arrive for the sheriff's meeting. She came into his office wearing all black — jeans, a button-down blouse, and soft walking shoes. She set a plaid valise against the wall inside the office door, and she crossed to the Clay Street windows.

Robertson was seated. He rose from his desk chair and picked up the valise to gauge its weight. "Not too heavy," he remarked and set the valise back down.

Lance shook her head. "It doesn't take much, Sheriff. Dress, apron, bonnet, and a brown wig."

"How are you going to carry, wearing a dress?" Robertson asked as he sat back behind his desk.

"Thigh holster under the dress."

"Any backup?"

"An ankle holster."

"That should be adequate. Is the dress going to cover it all?"

Lance laughed. "Amish dresses cover everything, Sheriff."

Rachel Ramsayer arrived. She chose the low leather chair at the front corner of Robertson's desk. She pushed herself back to lounge with her feet off the floor, and she said, "Nothing on any of the reports, Sheriff."

"How many are you following?" Robertson asked.

"Pretty much everything. Arrest records and bookings, nationwide. If anyone finds Molina, we'll know about it as soon as the documentation is posted."

"Long shot," Robertson commented.

"Better than nothing, Sheriff."

Scowling a bit, Stan Armbruster entered and said, "I couldn't sleep, Sheriff." He was dressed in a new change of clothes, slacks and a knit shirt.

"Did you rest any?" Robertson asked.

"A little, I suppose," Armbruster said. He turned for the coffeepot.

When Bobby Newell arrived, he said, "I haven't been able to find any taxi or limo service that brought Howie Dent into town."

"He may have gotten a ride down from Middlefield," Robertson said. "Maybe on one of the private Amish-hauler vans."

"I've also been back to the county garage," Newell said. "To search the VW again. There's nothing there. Just what we already processed. An empty backpack, and the contents of the glove compartment and trunk. None of it is remarkable. There's nothing from the VW that can help us."

In uniform, Deputy Ryan Baker stepped in from the squad room adjacent to Robertson's office, and two more deputies came in behind him. Chief Deputy Wilsher followed them. He entered the office and leaned back against the wall beside Robertson's display of arm patches. "Is there coffee?" he asked, and beside the coffee credenza, Stan Armbruster said, "It's stale, Chief."

Wilsher came forward, switched off the brewer, and carried the carafe back to the squad room. When he returned with fresh water, Missy Taggert had arrived. She was seated in one of the wooden chairs in front of the sheriff's desk. "Make it strong, Dan," she said to Wilsher. Wearily, she pulled off her surgical cap and let her hair out of its bun. "Bruce," she said, "have you found her?"

Seated at his desk, the sheriff said, "Mike

Branden called. They're following a slow buggy to a farm north of Middlefield. The scribe intends to introduce them to Fannie, if she agrees to talk to them."

"Does she have a choice?" Cal Troyer asked as he entered.

Del Markely stepped in behind Troyer and said, "The professor called again. They've started for the scribe's house."

"Thanks," Robertson said, and Del returned to her station at the front counter.

As she left, the sheriff answered Cal Troyer's question. "She has a choice, Cal. It's her decision."

Robertson stood. "Some of you know parts of my plan, but none of you knows it all. We're going to go over most of it, but Pat and Stan need to leave for Middlefield soon, so I want Cal to talk to us first."

When the sheriff stepped out from behind his desk, he motioned for Cal to take his place. Cal stood behind the desk to speak. "You probably all know more about Amish people than you realize. We're surrounded by their culture. You know that Amish people are more conservative than Mennonites. What Bruce wants me to explain in some detail, I think, is Fannie's particular sect. That requires a little history. So, Sheriff, how much detail do you want?"

Standing at the side of his desk, the sheriff spoke first to the others. "Dan has made fresh coffee. Take what you want. But Cal, we need to know specifics about Fannie and her immediate family. Also about relatives who may still live in the county. We know her brother moved his family to Kentucky, but maybe there are others."

"I don't think there are that many living here anymore," Cal said. "Most have moved away, to find cheaper farmland."

"Then whatever you think is relevant," Robertson said. "She's been traveling between settlements in Indiana, Michigan, and Ohio. Will that have caused her to cross lines between different Amish sects? Or would she always have stayed only with her own kind?"

"She's not extreme conservative Old Order," Cal said. "Not Schwartzentruber, anyway. So she would have been willing to cross between sects. Her ride to someplace new would have been more important to her than the destination, as long as that was Amish or Mennonite of some sort. Almost any Amish or Mennonite group would have taken her in."

"OK," Robertson said. "Start with her family history."

Cal pulled Robertson's desk chair out and

sat down. "First time in the big chair," he chuckled.

Robertson laughed, and some tension eased in the room. The sheriff took the last chair in front of his desk, and the others drew nearer to listen. The coffeepot stopped chattering, and Dan Wilsher poured a mug for Cal and set it on the sheriff's desk. Others got coffee for themselves as Cal began to speak.

"First," Cal said, "you should understand the origins of the Beachy Fellowship. Most people don't consider them to be Amish anymore, because around 1958 they agreed to own and drive cars. They call traditional Amish people the 'Horse and Buggy People.'

"Anyway, after they realized they held similar opinions on car transportation, seven families broke away from their Old Order district. They organized a new congregation and asked Uria Shetler to move to Ohio from Virginia, to lead their fellowship. Well, rather they asked him to give ministerial leadership. It was David Miller from Oklahoma who served as their first bishop.

"They held their first worship service at an old schoolhouse north and west of Berlin. They weren't popular with former Amish friends and neighbors, and during the service, someone let the air out of all

185

their tires.

"Soon after that, some more families from Sugarcreek joined the congregation. Then they drew lots to see who would serve as minister, and the lot fell to Roman Mullet.

"They built a church building, and Amish people didn't like that, either. Amish people are supposed to worship at the farm of one of their congregants. Mostly they still worship in barns. Anyway, the church building is east of Berlin, out on SR 39. Roman Beachy was made a deacon in 1960. By then, there were other congregations like this one. Maybe not perfect replicas, but they were similar regarding modern machines like cars. These types of congregations are called the New Order Amish, generally."

Robertson asked, "Is the Bethel Fellowship one of these? That's the one on 39, right?"

"Yes," Cal said. "But the New Order Amish are not always identical. The Bethel Fellowship is just one. The congregations vary in what they allow. They have it in common only that they permit certain types of modern machines."

"Cars," Robertson said, "but what else?"

"Bicycles early on," Cal said.

"But," Pat Lance said, "almost any kind

of Amish person rides a bike these days."

"Yes, now they do," Cal said. "But they don't always use power lawn mowers, for instance. Or garden tillers, or chain saws, or hay balers that pick up the bales."

"Some use balers?" Robertson asked. "But not the kind that will pick up the bales?"

"Right," Cal said. "Another example. Some New Order Amish have decided to use milking machines, but others don't permit them."

"It's endless," Armbruster said. "The differences, I mean."

"Yes," Cal said, "but they all know the differences. They know who is who, and they know who they should tolerate and who they should 'hold off.' "

"Over garden tillers?" Captain Newell asked.

"Yes. And phones. And storm fronts on buggies."

Wilsher asked, "The ones who drive cars, Cal. Are these the Black Bumper Amish?"

Cal smiled. "If they paint all the shiny parts black, then yes, they're called Black Bumper Amish. Other New Order Amish people just buy the plainest car they can find, and they don't worry about any shiny parts. They don't paint the chrome and silver parts to be flat black."

187

"OK," Armbruster said, "but Fannie's brother Jonas didn't have any kind of car at all, so they can't be New Order."

"Right," Cal said. "That's my point. The Helmuths stayed with the Old Order. They never went modern."

"I remember they had a lawn mower," Armbruster said. "A power mower."

Cal shrugged at the inconsistency.

"So, are they Old Order?" Armbruster asked.

"One particular kind of Old Order," Cal said. "They're the kind of Old Order who still won't have any fellowship with the New Order, but who have accepted some modern conveniences, nonetheless."

"Nobody could sort this all out," Wilsher said at the coffeepot. He poured himself another cup and added, "They can't possibly keep track of it all."

Cal stood up and stretched his arms and shoulders. "But they do keep it all sorted out, Dan. They keep track of it all. They watch each other. Some of them will use a gasoline weed whacker, and others, right next door, won't allow it. But they all know who does, and it makes a distinction for them."

Robertson joined Wilsher at the coffee credenza to pour himself a cup. "What you're saying, Cal, is that Fannie is Old Order, but not the extremely backward Schwartzentruber type."

Cal moved aside to let Robertson reclaim his place at the desk. Robertson sat in his chair, sipped his hot brew, and asked, "Would any of this have had an influence on her travel destinations over the last four months?"

"She'll have accepted rides with New Order Amish families," Cal said. "If they could take her where she wanted to go."

"But she won't let herself own a car?" Lance asked.

"Right. She won't own one, and she won't drive one. But her rules don't say that she can't *ride* in one. And she will probably accept a ride from anyone in a congregation who is going her way."

"Would she fly in an airplane?" Captain Newell asked.

"Probably not."

Missy asked, "Will she testify for the FBI against Teresa Molina?"

"Probably not."

"Does the FBI know that, Bruce?" Missy asked her husband.

Robertson shook his head. "I'm not going to tell them that, Missy. It's just Cal's opinion."

Newell asked, "Does Fannie know that Howie Dent is dead?"

"Mike and Caroline are going to tell her, Bobby," Robertson said. "Maybe they already have."

Wilsher asked Newell, "Bobby, have you found anything more at the Helmuth farm?"

"No," Newell said. "But, like what? Fingerprints?"

"Or trace evidence," Wilsher said. "Fibers or hairs."

Newell shook his head, and Wilsher asked Missy, "How about something on the body?"

"Nothing that we can use, Dan. Nothing definitive."

"What is the FBI doing?" Rachel asked. "How much do they know?"

Robertson answered. "They're waiting at a hotel west of Middlefield, for me to call. To tell them where Fannie is."

"Is that where they'll guard her?" Rachel asked.

"That's the agreement I have with them," Robertson said. "They've agreed to my terms for a transfer of custody."

Cal had moved to the door. "Does the rest of this involve me?"

"No, but thanks, Cal," Robertson said. "Can you think of anything else that we need to know?"

Cal took a moment and then said, "I've been thinking about your plan."

"And?" Robertson asked.

"And she may be Old Order, Bruce, but that doesn't mean that she's backward or hesitant."

"What do you mean?" Robertson asked.

Cal arched his brows. "It means, I think, that if you've told her enough in your letter, you can depend on her to do the best thing."

"I hope so, Cal. If she doesn't, she'll never be safe again."

After Cal had left, people stirred in the room, pouring coffee for themselves, changing to different seats or positions, and waiting for the sheriff to start again. Dan Wilsher excused himself so that he could manage his afternoon patrols. Rachel left to check on her searches for Teresa Molina in criminal arrest databases.

When the sheriff returned from a brief visit with Del Markely at the front counter, he stood just inside his office door and reviewed, with the remaining people, the details of the plan he had devised for Pat Lance and Fannie Helmuth. When he had finished, he asked, "Do you all know what to do?"

Bobby Newell answered first. "When Dan's ready, he and I will take deputies over to the hotel. I've gone over most of the preliminaries with hotel management. Some doors to corridors will be locked, and some will remain open. We'll decide where we need to post our guards. We should be ready by early evening."

"Good," Robertson said. "And Pat? Are you and Stan ready to leave?"

"We are," Lance answered.

"I don't have any details yet," Armbruster said.

"Pat can fill you in," Robertson said. "But you two should get started. I don't want to call the FBI until you're ready to start back to Millersburg."

Armbruster headed out the door without further comment. Lance followed with her valise.

Deputy Ryan Baker asked, "Sheriff, are you really going to give Fannie to the FBI?"

"Ryan," Robertson said, "I'd rather frolic in a minefield. But for the time being, yes I am."

"What about Teresa Molina?" Missy asked her husband.

"That's going to have to be the FBI's problem, Missy. Our focus has to be local."

"That could take a while," Missy said,

standing to leave.

"We're gonna give it three or four days," the sheriff said. "We won't be able to keep up the charade much longer than that."

18

At the somber pace of a dirge, the Brandens drove north out of Middlefield, following Abel and Irma Mast's black buggy. In the lead, the Masts' dappled mare was not encouraged to hurry. Rather, the pace was torturously slow. So at first, Branden rode the brakes. After a mile, he devised the method of bringing his car to a complete stop to let the buggy advance a hundred yards before he shifted into gear to close the distance without leapfrogging the buggy.

The road ran straight north. The berm was only modestly wide, and Mast kept his rig on the blacktop. Cars and trucks came up behind the Brandens and passed as soon as possible, some punching their horns impatiently. Still Mast held to an unhurried pace, and clouds began to gather on the horizon.

Everywhere north of Middlefield, the Brandens saw sprawling and prosperous farms, the evidence of a capable and industrious people. At one farm, a matched trio of brothers was offloading slab wood from an old wagon hitched to draft horses. At the next farm, a grandfather was scooping manure out of a barn using a gasoline-powered front loader with large tractor wheels. There were men chopping firewood for winter, mothers or daughters mowing expansive front lawns, and older children trimming the weeds in the ditches beside the road. At many of the farms, laundry hung in the breeze under second-story porches, or from clotheslines strung beside the houses. At each of the farms, there was something for the kids. Teeter-totters, swing sets, tetherball poles, sandboxes, or trampolines were set on the lawns.

Eventually, the Brandens turned right onto a lesser road, following the Mast buggy past the one-room Pleasant Valley School. Just east of the school, on the other side of the road, they pulled into a long gravel drive. The professor followed Mast around to the back of a two-and-a-half-story white frame house, and he parked his sedan on the gravel patch between the back of the house and a tall white barn. At the corner of the barn, a pair of concrete silos rose nearly fifty feet high. In front of the silos, an old green tractor was parked on blocks, with its wheels taken off, and the power drive at the back of the tractor was engaged with a belted conveyor that Mast apparently used to loft grain and hay into either the silos or the barn.

As he climbed out, Professor Branden noted the immovable tractor and said, "They're using engines, Caroline. So they're not conservative Old Order. But they're not New Order, either."

Standing on the stoop, Abel Mast waved the Brandens forward toward the back porch. They followed him inside, crossed a screened porch to a spacious kitchen, and took seats on a bench at a long kitchen table made of polished pine planks. Mast then spoke in Dietsch dialect to his wife, and she went back out through the porch and down the steps to cross the gravel to a Daadihaus that was situated to the back of the yard. Through the kitchen windows, the Brandens watched her knock on the Daadihaus door and enter directly. When Abel Mast spoke, they turned back to face him in the kitchen.

"My wife will tell her," Mast said as he stepped to the sink. He took two glasses out of an overhead cupboard, pumped water at the sink, and handed full glasses of cloudy brown water to the Brandens.

"You'll be thirsty," he said. He sat across from them at the pine table. "A buggy ride makes for thirsty work."

"So does delivering bad news, Abel," the professor said. "You didn't seem hurried. We took our time getting here."

"We were talking," Mast replied. "We were trying to find a gentle way to tell Fannie about Howie."

"I don't think there is a gentle way," Branden said. He drank the silted water that Mast had offered him. "Thanks for the water."

Mast lingered with his thoughts. Eventually he noticed that Caroline had sipped her water to be polite, but had not finished it. Mast attempted a smile, and he pushed up wearily from the table, saying, "Well water is disagreeable to some folk."

Caroline replied softly, "It's OK, Mr. Mast."

"Would you prefer bottled?" Mast asked as he returned to the sink. He opened the cupboard under the sink and produced a plastic bottle of Dasani. "We get it at Walmart," he said, and he sat back down at the table. He handed the bottle across to

Caroline. "That's the only thing my wife will drink."

Caroline opened the Dasani and drank gratefully. Mast took up her glass of well water and finished it himself. When he was carrying the empty glass back to the sink, Mrs. Mast came in from the back porch with Fannie Helmuth.

Caroline and the professor rose and stepped out over the low bench to greet Fannie. Mrs. Mast cast them a glance of caution. Fannie took one step into the large kitchen and stood wringing her fingers into a white handkerchief.

In her mid-twenties, Fannie Helmuth was a round and stocky woman. Her large brown eyes, set wide over a thin nose, carried a tearful sheen of distress. Her small mouth curved down at the corners, and her lips were quivering. Her gold wire spectacles seemed to have been dislodged by the news Irma Mast had brought her, and they sat low on her nose. She peered at the Brandens over the tops of the lenses, and she seemed disinclined to bother with the triviality of adjusting them. The spectacles hung from her ears like frames for a crestfallen soul.

As she tried to gather herself to speak, Fannie searched back and forth between the Masts standing at the sink and the Brandens standing at the table. She seemed to be looking for some gentle assurance that their cruel joke about Howie Dent had played out long enough to suit them. That they would surely now relieve her sorrow with a laugh or a smile. When she realized that they could not relieve her, Fannie began to cry.

Fixed wordlessly to her place inside the kitchen door, without raising her handkerchief to her eyes, Fannie let her tears stream down her cheeks. She dropped her handkerchief to the floorboards and stood motionless, blinking at tears that she was unable to dry. Lost in her grief, Fannie appeared also to have lost her place in the world. She seemed unaware of where she was. She began to waver on her feet. She closed her eyes and held out a hand as if she were reaching for a railing on which to lean. As if she were searching for a support that would stop her fall.

Caroline reached out for Fannie's hand and took it. With her other hand, she steadied Fannie's elbow and guided her forward to the bench at the kitchen table. Carefully, Caroline turned Fannie around to sit on the bench with her back to the table. With her eyes still closed, Fannie accepted Caroline's help to sit on the bench. Once seated, she clung to Caroline's hand and wept.

When Fannie at last opened her eyes, she whispered. "He promised he would be careful. He promised he would just get his car. Then come back."

"He did get his car, Fannie," the professor said. He sat on the end of the bench and took Fannie's other hand. "Someone must have been watching for him," he said. "We don't think he had much of a chance."

Fannie seemed to notice the professor for the first time. "I don't know you," she said, and she pulled her hands free.

"I have a letter for you, Fannie," Branden said. "From Sheriff Robertson. He has been trying to find you."

"You're not a deputy."

"A reserve deputy," Branden said, and he displayed his wallet badge.

Fannie glanced at the badge and asked, "Why are you dressed like that? You're not Amish." She indicated Caroline. "And she's not Mennonite."

"No," Branden said. "We thought it might take a long time to find you. We were worried that people here wouldn't trust us."

"But how did you find me?"

Branden explained about searching the

200

letters in the *Budget,* and Fannie began to cry again. Stammering, she said, "Howie wanted our families to know we were safe. It probably didn't work."

"It worked, Fannie," Caroline said. "Howie's mother saw the letters."

Fannie seemed puzzled by Caroline's presence, so the professor explained. "Fannie, this is my wife, Caroline. We want to help you move to a safer place."

Fannie shook her head. "Tell me how he died."

"He was murdered," the professor said. "At your brother's house."

Crying again, Fannie said, "He wasn't supposed to go there. He promised me he wouldn't go there."

Suddenly, Fannie stood. "She can't have been waiting there for him! Not all this time. Nobody could be that angry."

Caroline stood to embrace her, but Fannie jerked away. Turning to the Masts at the kitchen sink, she demanded, "Why did you bring them here, Abel? We would have been safe!"

Mast took a step toward Fannie. "They found you, Fannie. They found you easily enough, and it's a good thing it was the sheriff. Someone else could do the same thing."

"We don't even know them, Abel!" Fannie cried angrily.

Mast shook his head. "They have a letter for you from the sheriff. And this man has a badge. You need their help, now, Fannie. You are too easy to find."

"I'm not!" Fannie shouted back at him. "And I have Reuben."

Gently, Mast asked, "How is he going to be able to keep you any safer than Howie did?"

Fannie wrenched her shoulders as if she were caught in a net. As if she wanted to flee, but something unseen was preventing her escape. She stumbled backward and braced herself at the table's bench. She pulled her organdy *Kapp* away from her hair and balled it up in her fist to hurl it across the room. She cocked her arm and swung. But she did not release the Kapp. Instead, she pressed her fists angrily to her temples and shook side to side, trembling with tension and grief. Her hair fell loose from its bun, and it spilled down her back. She dropped her Kapp and tangled her fingers into her hair, pulling fiercely at its roots. Keening a pitched wail, she began to shout, "No! No! No!"

Caroline reached out to try to calm her, but Fannie turned and bolted through the kitchen door. She crossed the back porch, ran down the back steps, and stumbled toward the Daadihaus. Irma Mast hurried after her.

Fannie stumbled in the gravel before she got to the Daadihaus. Down on her knees, she screamed, "Howie!"

Irma tried to pull Fannie to her feet, but Fannie pushed her off, stood, and paced a tight circle of frustration and rage, pulling wildly at her hair. From a barn far to the back of the property, Fannie's fiancé Reuben ran to her and wrapped his arms over hers, to pin them at her sides. Thrashing in his arms, Fannie struggled to free herself. Gradually, she tired. Then Reuben embraced her and stroked her long brown hair. But Fannie's legs folded under her, and she fell slowly to the gravel, pulling Reuben down with her. Time and again, Fannie cried out, "Howie!" first and then, "Reuben!" as Irma and Reuben struggled to lift her back to her feet.

Abel and Caroline went out to help with Fannie, but the professor remained in the kitchen to call Stan Armbruster's cell phone. Armbruster answered on the second ring. "We're on our way, Professor. We're on the 271 outer belt, coming up to Solon."

"OK," Branden said. "You should be here in about forty minutes. The mailbox out front says number 15901 on the Burton-Windsor Road, north of Middlefield. We're near a school, but across the street."

"So, did you find her?" Armbruster asked.

"Yes, but she's losing it, Stan. You need to hurry. This is the Mast farm. It's Abel and Irma Mast. But there's another Amish man here, too. She's calling him Reuben."

"Pat's driving," Armbruster said. "We'll run with flashers. Is that address going to register on our GPS?"

"It should."

"Forty minutes?"

"Less, if you hurry. You have to come into town on 87 and then turn north on 608. A right turn puts you on Burton-Windsor, headed east."

"Should I call the sheriff?" Armbruster asked. "To tell him where Fannie is?"

"Not yet, Stan. Wait until you've talked with her."

"OK, but he's supposed to call the FBI after we've found her."

"Right now, Stan, I couldn't tell you what Fannie is going to decide. She's crying out for Howie, and she's completely lost in grief. She's not taking it well that we found her. She's in shock, and she's angry. So if she's going to trust anyone English like us, it'll have to be Robertson's letter that convinces her to do it."

19

Reuben helped Fannie to a seat in the Masts' parlor. He spoke briefly to her in dialect and turned to the professor to offer his hand. "I am Reuben Gingerich," he said. "I am Fannie's fiancé. We were posted with the church in Michigan. Just a few weeks after we met."

Branden took Reuben's hand. "Professor Mike Branden. And this is my wife, Caroline."

Reuben seemed surprised. "I thought you were a deputy."

"I am, Mr. Gingerich. A reserve deputy. I am also a college professor."

"That seems an odd mix."

"I suppose it is," Branden said. He sat across from Fannie on a diminutive Shaker sofa made of cherrywood. The seat was upholstered with plain, powder-blue fabric.

Caroline sat next to her husband.

The parlor was plain and simple, with straight lines in an unadorned style. The furniture was all of the Shaker variety — polished red cherry with blue fabrics matching the sofa. The heavy purple curtains on the windows had long pleats and fell straight to the red oak flooring. The baseboard trim and crown molding were made of polished cherry, matching the furniture, as if it all had been made by the same custom craftsman. The walls were stark white and unadorned. On two end tables and on one corner stand, there were lamps with white-ash silk mantles. These were piped for natural gas.

Outside, dark clouds were piling in from the west on a strong summer breeze. Thunder was cannonading in the northern distance. Cooler temperatures were riding through, ahead of a summer storm.

From the kitchen doorway, Abel Mast asked if a lamp should be lit, and Reuben replied briefly, "We'll be fine, Abel," focusing most of his attention on Fannie. He pulled a Shaker chair out of a corner and set it next to Fannie. Sitting beside her, he asked, "Are you going to be OK, Fannie?"

Fannie still appeared shaken. She reached a trembling hand out to Reuben. When he took her hand, she clasped her fingers over his.

From the kitchen, Irma Mast came forward with a tray of drinks. "I have bottled water and lemonade," she said. She served the drinks from the tray and returned to the kitchen. When she came back into the parlor, her husband, Abel, was with her. They pulled an old deacon's bench away from the wall and sat down to join the conversation.

Fannie looked at her fiancé and then at the Brandens. Angrily, she said, "It's not fair about Howie. He didn't do anything wrong."

Reuben spoke a few soft words in Dietsch to Fannie, and she smiled tragically and explained for the Brandens, "Howie loved that stupid yellow VW." Then she began to cry again. Reuben pulled her hand into his lap and cradled her fingers.

Fannie took her hand away from Reuben, pressed her handkerchief to her eyes, and said, "I'm not doing anybody any good, here."

"It's OK," Irma said. "Take your time."

As she dried her eyes, Fannie said to the professor, "I don't know why you are here. I don't know why the sheriff didn't come himself. Or Deputy Lance could have come.

I know her."

"Pat will be here in about half an hour," Branden said. "She's coming with Deputy Armbruster."

"Why?" Fannie asked. "Why so many people, just for me?"

"You're important, Fannie," Branden answered. "The government is going to want you to testify against Teresa Molina."

"But I only met her once," Fannie complained. "What does anybody think I could say?"

"Well, she did take the suitcase from you," Branden said. "And there's the Florida end of things, too. You can testify that Jodie Tapp gave you the suitcase to carry home on the bus."

"But I did that just once," Fannie asserted. "And I didn't know it was drugs. Jodie didn't know it was drugs, either. It's just not possible. She's my friend."

"Perhaps she didn't know, Fannie," Branden said. "But Ruth Zook did the same thing, and it got her murdered."

"The sheriff told me that," Fannie said. "It's why we ran."

"OK, but now," Branden said, "the sheriff wants you to let the FBI put you into protective custody. To keep you safe, while they look for Teresa Molina and Jodie Tapp."

Inside the pocket of her dress, Fannie's cell phone rang like a bell. She stood up startled and checked the display. She seemed at first embarrassed, and then she seemed apologetic. "This is my friend," she said with an awkward smile. "I have to take this outside."

When Fannie returned to the parlor, the professor asked her, "Fannie, is someone other than Teresa Molina trying to find you?"

Fannie sat down beside Reuben again and said, "Just a friend."

"Will you tell us who that was?" Branden asked.

"I don't want to. It was just a friend."

"There may be a lot of bad people looking for you," Branden said. "More than just Teresa Molina."

"This was a good friend," Fannie said. She passed an annoyed glance to Reuben. "She just calls to chat, so I don't think it's anything you should take an interest in."

Branden looked to Caroline, arched a brow, and turned back to Fannie. Careful not to upset her further with his tone, Branden said gently, "OK, Fannie, but now perhaps you could think about the FBI. The sheriff wants you to go into their protective custody, and they will probably be getting here in the next couple of hours."

Broadcasting nervous anxiety, Fannie popped off her Shaker chair and paced in the center of the room. The professor stood, too, and held out Sheriff Robertson's letter. "Please, Fannie," he said. "At least read what the sheriff wrote to you. Then if you don't like any of this, we can talk about it."

"And what?" Fannie demanded in place. "Do it my way? Do what I want? Well, I want Howie back! Tell that to the sheriff!"

Caroline and Irma rose together. Reuben Gingerich stood and tried to embrace Fannie. With her hands raised, palms out, Fannie held them off. "Just tell me what's in the letter!" she shouted into the room. "What in the world does he want from me, now that Howie is dead?"

Softly, Irma said, "Fannie, at least you could read what he has written to you. Maybe that's not asking too much."

"Why can't anybody just tell me what's in the stupid letter?" Fannie argued, clenching her fists. "What's so hard about that?"

Caroline answered, "None of us has read it, Fannie."

Irma reached out for Fannie's elbow. "Please sit down. You're angry."

Reuben sat back on his chair and said,

" 'Be ye not angry,' Fannie. You know this as well as anyone."

Startled, Fannie spun around to Reuben. She formed a reply with the leanings of a snarl, but she did not speak it. She looked to Irma, and Irma nodded her agreement with Reuben as she sat back down next to her husband. Abel had held to his seat on the deacon's bench, staring sadly at the floorboards while Fannie fumed.

Caroline reclaimed her seat, and the professor sat again, too. In the middle of the room, Fannie stood alone with soft tears spilling from her eyes. She looked long at her fiancé, wrestling with a tangle of anxieties that showed plainly in the mix of her expressions. She struggled for a moment and then seemed to acquire some degree of resolution. When she sat next to Reuben, she said simply and serenely, "I am sorry, Reuben."

He took her hand into his lap without replying.

Fannie sat with her head bowed and said, "May I have the letter, Professor?"

Branden rose and handed the sealed envelope across to her. He sat back beside his wife. Fannie tore the edge of the envelope open and took out several folded

212

pages of white paper covered with bold writing.

Fannie began reading. She progressed slowly through the first page and turned to the second. Before she had finished the second page, she turned back to read the first again. She finished the second page and turned to the third. Then she turned to read the fourth page. When she had finished reading the entire letter, she read it all again slowly, carefully, pausing often to think.

As Fannie was folding the letter to put it back into its envelope, Branden asked, "Fannie, do you want one of us to read it, too?"

"No."

"Do you understand what the sheriff has told you?" Branden asked further.

"Yes."

"Then have you decided what you wish to do?"

"I wish to be protected by the FBI," Fannie said. "I want to go to the hotel that Sheriff Robertson has decided is best for me."

Reuben asked, "Are you certain, Fannie?"

"Yes, Reuben, I am. Can you wait for me here?"

Reuben looked to Abel Mast for an answer. Abel nodded his consent.

To Fannie, Reuben said earnestly, "As long as it takes, Fannie. I'll wait for you as long as it takes."

20

At the jail's radio consoles, Del Markely handed her headset off to Ed Hollings, the night-shift dispatcher. She gathered up personal items from the desks and counter, tossed them into her heavy canvas purse, and stalked down the hallway to the sheriff's door. There she knocked and entered without waiting for an invitation.

The sheriff was standing beside his desk, staring thoughtfully at his display of law enforcement arm patches. Del marched in dramatically, clanked her heavy purse onto the old cherry desktop, and took a seat in one of the straight chairs in front of the desk.

Robertson turned around slowly and drawled, "Are you just visiting, Adele, or do you need a place to stay?"

"Sheriff, my mother used to call me

215

Adele. I haven't tolerated that name for twenty-five years."

Robertson moved to his chair and sat behind his desk. "What can I do for you, Del?"

"Some of the deputies are talking."

"About me?"

"About the situation."

"And what is that?"

"You're flummoxed, and they're worried."

"Flummoxed?"

"Hesitant, Sheriff, like you don't know what to do next. They think you're being too tentative. So they're talking. Some of them, anyway."

"Well, that didn't take long, did it."

"It's been building since April," Del said. "Double shifts, extra pressure, the hunt for Fannie Helmuth. At any rate, they're talking now, some of them, saying that you're considering whether or not you can still handle the job."

"Is anyone actually saying that I cannot handle the job?"

"No. They're saying that *you* don't think you can handle the job. Or they wonder if you're hesitating because you don't *want* to do it anymore. So, that's a problem you've gotta fix. I just thought you should know."

"Anything more, Del, that I should fix?"

"Well, it's maybe going around town that this Fannie Helmuth case has you more rattled than it should. Like maybe you've been pushin' your people too hard, for too long, but you haven't explained to anyone why it's got you so rattled. Why you're takin' it so hard that Fannie ran off with Howie Dent."

Robertson leaned his chair back on its springs. He held a brief and unconvincing smile and said, "That's just it, Del. She walked away from my protection."

"Then are you maybe takin' this too personally?"

"No," Robertson huffed. He rocked his chair forward and stood behind his desk. With a frown that seemed to crease every worry line in his face, he said, "It's not personal, Del. It's professional. I take it as a professional indictment. An Amish girl chose not to trust us to keep her safe. She thought she'd be safer out there on her own than she would be here with us. And I consider that to be a professional vote of no confidence. It's a negative judgment about our abilities to do our jobs. She might as well have stuck posters up around town. 'Robertson can't handle the job.' Or 'You can't trust Robertson with your life.' That's much more than just personal to me, Del.

It cuts to the core of who I have always demanded myself to be. It cuts at what I've always expected myself to do. And if Fannie gets killed because she figured that she couldn't trust me, then that's on my shoulders, isn't it?"

After Markely left, the sheriff pulled a folded page from his shirt pocket and read Bobby Newell's list of items found with the yellow VW. Simple items from the glove compartment. The normal contents of a trunk. An empty red backpack.

Robertson pocketed the list, took out his cell phone, and tapped in Armbruster's number. When Armbruster answered, Robertson said, "You should be almost there."

"We're just pulling into the drive, Sheriff."

"OK, look, Stan." Robertson hesitated. "I need you to remember that I do have a plan."

"I remember."

"And I need you to see this through, Stan, just like I laid it out in our meeting."

"I know, Sheriff."

"Then there's one other thing I need from you, Stan. There's one last thing to check."

"Sheriff?"

"Examine all of our original assumptions, Stan."

"OK."

"Start with the day Howie and Fannie got off that bus in Charlotte. The day they caught a Greyhound bus to Memphis."

"Are you asking why they did that?"

"Yes. And I'm asking *how* they did that."

"You want me to question Fannie about this?"

"Yes. Ask her how that bus pulled into the restaurant parking lot for their breakfast stop. Ask her if they actually got any breakfast that day."

"Do you want to know about that whole day, Sheriff, or just what happened at the breakfast stop?"

"The whole day, Stan, but especially everything at the breakfast stop. I want her to tell you everything she can recall. From the moment their bus pulled out of Sugarcreek, until she and Howie were in downtown Charlotte, seated on a Greyhound bus for Memphis. Then I want you to examine the assumptions you made when you first discovered the yellow VW and Dent's body."

"That was just yesterday morning, Sheriff."

"I know. But we all made assumptions

when we processed the scene. And we all missed something."

"What am I looking for, Sheriff?"

"That's just it, Stan. I don't want you to be looking for anything at all. Nothing in particular. Because when you first saw the VW, you had already started making assumptions. And when I questioned the Dents about Howie's VW, I had already started making my own assumptions. Assumptions that must have been false."

"OK, Sheriff," Armbruster said. "I'll ask Fannie about the bus stop in Charlotte."

"Without making any assumptions," Robertson answered.

Fannie took Sheriff Robertson's letter back from Reuben and asked, "Does that mean what I think it means?"

They were in the front room of the Daadihaus, behind the Masts' main residence. Fannie was at the window, watching Pat Lance park her patrol car on the wet gravel pad in front of the barn. It was raining steadily, drearily, like the cold drizzles of April. Skies as gray as cemetery granite.

"I think so," Reuben replied cautiously. "I think it means just what it says. And I've seen that hotel. It's big."

Looking out at the arriving car, Fannie

said, "That's Deputy Lance."

Reuben joined her at the window. "Do you trust her?" he asked.

"I think so. As much as any English, I suppose. Really, it's the sheriff who I trust the most."

"Because of his letter?"

"Yes." Fannie nodded. She watched Pat Lance and Stan Armbruster as they climbed out of the patrol car and hurried in the rain to the back steps. "I never expected that kind of honesty from a lawman."

As Lance and Armbruster huddled under an umbrella and knocked on the back porch door of the main house, Reuben asked, "Do you know both of these English?"

"Just Deputy Lance. But she's *Detective* Lance. I spent most of a day with her."

"And the other? The man?"

"I saw him at the jail that day. I think he's a detective, too."

Turning Fannie gently to face him, Reuben asked, "Will I be able to see you at the hotel?"

"I don't know, Reuben."

Reuben handed the pages of the letter back to Fannie. "Are you certain that you understand the sheriff's message?"

Using the gray light at the window, Fannie read the letter a last time.

221

Sheriff Bruce Robertson
August 18th
Millersburg

Dear Fannie,

By now you know of Howie Dent's murder. I am very sorry for your loss.

By now you also know that I cannot protect you in Holmes County. I know that, too, Fannie, so I won't ask you to come back here.

Most people will think, however, that you have come home, and that I am endeavoring to protect you. That is precisely what I want them all to think.

The FBI has insisted on protective custody for you, and I cannot oppose them on this point. I have, however, set the terms of your protective custody, and I have arranged the details so that they will be advantageous to you.

Once Teresa Molina has been captured, she will be prosecuted for the murder last April of Ruth Zook. I want you to know, however, that nobody can force you to testify in that trial. You can decide for yourself whether or not you want to do that.

But if you don't agree to testify, the

FBI will not be willing to keep you in protective custody any longer. I expect that soon after your surrender to them, they will ask that you sign an agreement to testify. I advise you not to sign any such agreement until you are certain that you want to do it. Hold them off until you have decided.

But even if you do testify for them, or conversely if Teresa Molina is never captured, please understand that the FBI cannot really keep you safe. Not for certain, and not forever.

In custody, you will have a few familiar types of people around you — Amish and Mennonite maids, for instance. And you will be in a part of the state that most Amish people know well, at a large tourist hotel on 87, west of Middlefield. I hope this makes a difference for you.

My guess is that your FBI handlers will not be able to distinguish one Amish sect from another. They probably won't even know the differences between Amish people and Mennonites.

I suspect that you are alarmed that we found you. Really, it was a lucky guess on our part, aside from the fact that I have very capable detectives and deputies working for me. My point is that I very much doubt that anyone like Teresa Molina could ever do something similar. You would have been safe among your people, if only there hadn't been regular news of you in the *Budget*.

So now, Fannie, you have to be very cautious about who you trust. You have to be cautious about who you trust with your life. I advise you to assume that everyone and anyone is suspect. I need you to realize that Teresa Molina will search for you relentlessly, and that she will employ any and all resources necessary while hunting for you.

Have I told you enough? I pray that I have. Do you understand what I am telling you? I pray that you do.

Sincerely,
Bruce Robertson
Holmes County
Sheriff

When she had finished reading, Fannie took the letter to the wood stove in the corner of the room. She laid the folded pages inside, on top of the old ash left over from winter. As she touched a lighted match to the corners of the pages, Fannie answered, "I understand the letter, Reuben.

I'm just not sure I have the courage to do it."

21

With the stony gaze and austere judgment
of cold granite, the soldier atop Millersburg's Civil War monument kept watch as
Sheriff Robertson and Captain Newell
crossed Jackson at Clay and then crossed
Clay with the light, heading purposefully
west under a misting of rain. Once across
Clay, Robertson stopped under an awning
on the corner, and he turned back to survey
Holmes County's Courthouse Square,
dominated by the three stories of ornate
brown and tan sandstone that constituted
the court building, and on the adjacent
corner of the square, the imposing red-brick
jail, with its elaborately painted yellow
cornices and lintels, the black iron bars over
windows on the back half of the structure
marking the wing where the sheriff's cells
held their charges. It was all solid, Robert-

son mused. The rock heart of Holmes County's law enforcement soul. Stone, granite, brick and mortar. Built to last centuries, and as certain and sure as justice itself. From this central Millersburg edifice of stubborn stone and immovable brick, Robertson had always drawn strength. From this imposing Courthouse Square he had always drawn resolve.

So as the rain fell harder, Sheriff Robertson stood under the awning at the diagonal corner and surveyed the institutions of justice that these old buildings represented. OK, he thought — resolve, determination, and strength. Unfaltering dedication to duty. Steadfast dedication to the ploy that would avenge the murder of Howie Dent.

Newell tapped the sheriff on his shoulder. "Bruce, the hotel?"

Robertson shook himself loose from his ponderings. "Right, Bobby. Hotel St. James."

Robertson turned around, started down the sidewalk, and led Newell past several of the businesses in old Millersburg — a music store, a drugstore, antique shops, and a used-clothing store — and then in the middle of the next block, Robertson turned with Newell into the front entrance of the new boutique Hotel St. James, slotted between an attorney's office to the right and a take-out pizza shop to the left.

Inside the lobby, the reception counter along the right wall was made of polished black marble. On the left wall, there was a white marble fireplace, with modern seating in front of it — chairs and loungers of brushed steel and royal-blue leather. High overhead, the restored wooden ceiling boards were made of red oak two-by-fours laid on edge. The boards had been given a light oak stain to reveal the rich grain in the wood, a sturdy badge of honor from a bygone era.

The contrast couldn't have been greater, Robertson thought. An interior decorator's nod at the past, with its main design anchored firmly in the present. Oak planks from the old world, mixed with modern steel, polished marble, and soft leather. A curious metaphor for his Fannie Helmuth gambit.

Past the reception counter, there was a white door on the right marked OFFICE in red block letters. Next along the narrow lobby, there was a new elevator with pastel lights and an insistent bell. Beyond the brass elevator doors, there were vending machines with fruit drinks in boxes and snacks in bags. A stairwell door led to rooms on the upper two floors. At the very back, the rear entrance to the lobby opened through a heavy metal door onto the alley behind the hotel.

Robertson punched the lighted button to call the elevator. Standing beside him, Newell asked, "Only the two entrances, then?"

"Right," Robertson confirmed. "Only two doors into the lobby. But there are fire escapes at each floor, on the front and back of the building. Plus the roofs of these three buildings are all contiguous. You can climb to this roof from the adjacent ones."

On the second floor, Robertson stepped out into the hallway, turned around, and showed Newell the stairwell to the left of the elevator and a maid's closet to the right. Past the maid's closet, along the length of the narrow hallway, there were three doors to guest rooms.

"These three rooms are the larger ones," Robertson said. "They're all booked through the weekend." Newell pulled a spiral notebook out of his jacket pocket, and he sketched the second floor layout, with rooms 1, 2, and 3.

On the third floor, Robertson led Newell down the hall past the maid's closet to four smaller rooms marked 4, 5, 6, and 7. At the door to 6, Robertson used an electronic key card to open the lock. Inside the room, there was a standard hotel arrangement of dressers, tables, chairs, and a desk, with a closet and the bathroom just inside the door. There was no window in the room. Instead, there was a large LED television mounted on the far wall over a low dresser.

At the back of the room, Robertson used a traditional metal key to open a door that gave access to the adjoining room number 7. This room was laid out as a mirror image to 6, except that a front window in room 7 gave a view down onto West Jackson Street. "You can make a suite of the two rooms," Robertson said as he relocked the door. "We have them booked for the next five days."

"Pat will be in 6?" Newell asked.

"Yes, and we'll set up in 7."

In the hallway, Newell sketched the configuration of the third floor. Back on the first floor, Robertson opened the rear entrance and showed Newell the alley. Crossing back through the lobby to the front entrance, Newell said, "We'll use Baker, Johnson, and two more deputies here in the lobby, one at a time, rotating in shifts. They'll all have photos of Teresa Molina and Jodie Tapp."

Robertson agreed and said, "I want to use

Armbruster as much as we can on the third floor, in the hallway outside the elevator and staircase."

"You don't want Armbruster to stay with Pat?"

"No. He needs to get some sleep at night. But when she's out in the daytime, it'll be you or me who goes with her, Bobby. Plus the professor as her escort. That'll give Armbruster a chance to trail behind us."

They exited the main entrance onto the Jackson Street sidewalk, and Robertson turned right. At the adjacent door to a take-out pizza shop, Robertson pushed inside, and Newell followed. A teenage girl in a white chef's apron came forward from the back ovens with an order pad in her hand.

Robertson introduced himself as sheriff, and he introduced Captain Newell. Then he said, "We'll have an Amish guest for a number of days, next door at the St. James. Room number six, on the third floor. She likes pizza, and I want to pay her bills. Whatever she orders, would you please send the bills to me at the jail?"

The girl wrote on her pad and said, "I can do that."

"OK now, who are your delivery people?" Robertson asked. "I want to screen them for security ahead of time."

231

"Weeknights, it's usually a couple of high school seniors. Ones who have their own cars." She wrote several names on the back of an order page and handed that to the sheriff.

Robertson handed the page to Newell. "And on the weekends?"

"Then it's almost always old Ernie."

"Short fellow?" Robertson asked. "About a hundred years old, with a wrinkled face?"

The girl in the apron laughed. "Old Ernie."

"He works for the bus company, in Sugarcreek," Robertson said.

"The buses don't run so often in summer," the girl explained. "He fills in for us on weekends, to make extra money."

"Is it just him?" Newell asked. "Just one guy?"

"No, he has a crew. From the bus company."

Robertson laughed. "They must not pay very much at the bus company."

"We don't pay them very much either, Sheriff. I think he just likes making deliveries. It keeps him out and meeting people. You know, moving around. He doesn't seem to mind the pay."

"OK, it's Ernie and his bus crew on the weekends," Robertson confirmed. He took several bills from his wallet and handed them to the girl. "I'll pay ahead some, if you don't mind. She should be arriving this evening."

"She?"

"Our guest."

"Have a name?"

"No. She's just our department's guest."

Out on the sidewalk, Newell said, "That wasn't very subtle, Sheriff."

Robertson stopped in front of the Hotel St. James. The rain had abated for the moment. "I'm not trying for anything subtle, Bobby. This is just the start of our showing her around. Pizza is just the first thing."

"You know this Ernie?"

"I interviewed him once, when Fannie first disappeared. Armbruster talked with him, too. He handles the northern terminus for the bus company in Sugarcreek. Mostly I think he just cleans the buses when they come back from Florida."

"OK, where else are you going to send her?" Newell asked as they walked back toward the square.

"I've made a list for tomorrow," Robertson said. "It's in your e-mail. Tonight, all I want her to do is have dinner in Hotel Millersburg. They don't have a restaurant at the St. James. And she can walk the block for some air after dinner. The professor and I will go with her."

"You want her to be seen, Bruce?"

"By as many people as possible."

Jodie Tapp was crying when Fannie answered her call. "Oh Fannie! They've got my new phone number!"

Fannie was alone in the Masts' Daadihaus. "Who, Jodie?"

"Teresa Molina. She's gotten my new phone number from my mother. And unless I give them five thousand dollars by Saturday at noon, they're going to tell Sheriff Robertson that I was part of their drug gang."

"Jodie, they've killed Howie."

"What?"

"He was murdered yesterday. At my brother's farmhouse near Charm."

"How do you know, Fannie? How can you possibly know that?"

"The sheriff's people are here, now, Jodie. They told me."

"It's not possible! I just drove through Millersburg. I had lunch there. The way people talk, I would have heard something."

Fannie began to weep. "It's true, Jodie. I have a letter from the sheriff."

Jodie gasped. "Does he know where you are?"

"His detectives are here. I'm sure they have told him."

"Fannie, what about your brother? If Teresa Molina found my mother, she could find him, too. You've got to warn him."

Fannie was still crying. "I've already called him. To tell him about Howie."

"Fannie, I need five thousand dollars by noon on Saturday. I have to give it to them at a rest stop north of Akron."

"What are you going to do?"

"I don't have that kind of money, Fannie. I've been living out of my car. I need to see you. I need a loan."

"You shouldn't come here, Jodie. These detectives are here. But don't you remember? We always said that we could never see each other."

"There has to be a way."

"I could mail the money to you. They can't stop me from mailing a letter."

"They'll inspect your mail, Fannie. And I need the money by Saturday morning."

"Can't you get the money some other way?"

"You're the only person I know with that kind of cash money, Fannie. You said that Reuben has money."

"They'll never let me see you, Jodie."

"There has to be a way. You must be close by. You said Michigan, right? And you said that it's been raining there. That has to be northern Ohio."

"What?"

"That's the only place the weather radar shows any rain around here, Fannie. I checked with an app on my phone. So I must be close to you. You have to be somewhere close to Akron, and I need to see you."

"We can't risk it, Jodie. Howie always said that we can't risk seeing each other."

"Then I'm lost, Fannie. I have nowhere to turn."

"You should go to Sheriff Robertson. You should go to him and tell him your side of the story, before Teresa Molina does."

"He'll never believe me."

"I trust him, Jodie."

"Well, you shouldn't!"

"Reuben thinks I should trust him."

"And the FBI? Does Reuben think you should trust them?"

"Well, not as much."

"Fannie, you have to help me. You have to think of some way to help me. If you can't, I'll have to be a thousand miles away from here by Saturday noon."

22

On the second floor of the Masts' main house, the bedroom had plain plaster walls painted stark white and accented with dark, rich-grained walnut trim along the baseboards, around the crown molding, and around the framing of the doors. Covering tall wooden windows on two walls in the corner room, there were long and plain purple curtains reaching full-length to the floorboards, which were painted a nondescript flat gray. The furniture, consisting of a headboard, dressers, and nightstands, was of a classic Shaker style, with clean lines and simple round knobs. Everywhere in the room, it seemed, a determined effort had been made at simple, unadorned functionality. Everywhere, that is, except the bedspread.

On the king bed, the Masts had displayed

an ornate quilt that had been elaborately hand-stitched to make an intricate, repeating six-point star pattern in green, rose, and periwinkle fabrics. To Pat Lance it seemed curious that the room was purposefully plain and simple, as all Amish no doubt would have it, whereas the quilt, from conception and design to construction, was an artful expression of unrestrained creativity. She laid her suitcase on the quilt and thought it a shame to cover so beautiful an object. In contrast to the rich colors of the quilt, outside the bedroom windows a drab and misty rain continued to spill from a dull and leaden sky.

Irma shook her head and stepped to the windows to close each of the long drapes. "No point letting all of the gloom inside," she remarked. Then for a gaslight in the ceiling, Irma opened the valve in the wall pipe. She lit the lamp with a wooden match and carefully adjusted the flame on the silk mantle to a white-hot glow. This she repeated at a lamp stand in the corner of the bedroom. When she turned to Lance, she asked, "Your dress?"

Lance opened her suitcase on the bed and took out a pale green Mennonite dress. "It reaches to the floor," she said, holding the plain dress to her neck. "I also have a white apron." She pulled the second garment from her suitcase. "It has some lace, but I thought it might do."

Beside the dress and apron, Lance also set out a white organdy prayer Kapp with string ties. "I got this at the dry goods store in Mt. Hope," she said, and she looked to the Amish women for their opinions.

Fannie shook her head and pressed her fingertips to her lips to mask a frown. In solemn Dietsch dialect, she spoke at considerable length to Irma.

Once Fannie had finished, Irma said to Lance, "Maybe only in the bedroom, Detective. We think it's much too fancy for public attire."

Distracted while fumbling with her cell phone, Fannie asked Lance, "You bought the dress in a store?"

Lance nodded earnestly. "At Walmart, in Millersburg. I bought the plainest, simplest dress I could find. I saw other women in Walmart wearing the same thing."

Fannie slipped her phone into a side pocket of her dress. "This would do for a Mennonite woman," she said, "but never for Amish."

Irma held the dress to herself, with the apron displayed in front, and again the Amish women spoke dialect. Lance understood only that they were asking questions of each other about the dress.

"I gather this won't do," Lance said, embarrassed. "It seems that I've missed the mark."

"It's a little too short," Irma said. "And the stitching is much too fancy."

"And there aren't the proper number of pleats," Fannie added, checking the display on her phone. "Plus it's not gathered at the shoulders correctly."

"According to whom?" Lance asked, smiling now, aware that the women had made mild sport of her. "Who decides about dresses?"

"The bishop decides, of course," Irma said. "Each district has its own way. It's the bishop who decides."

"The number of pleats in a dress?" Lance asked, curious now more than embarrassed.

"Pleats in front," Fannie said, phone tumbling in her agile fingers.

"And on the rump," Irma added. "They'll be different."

"The rump?"

"In back," Irma said. "The rump. What do you call it?"

Still wrestling with the notion of the bishop's actually approving dress styles, Lance asked, "Are you saying that a bishop decides how many pleats are to be sewn into a woman's dress?"

"Who else?" Fannie asked. She punched several buttons on her phone, seeming distracted by worrisome thoughts.

Detective Lance took note of Fannie's detachment, but she was more concerned at the moment with what the two Amish women had been saying about fashion. She arched a brow and shook her head disbelievingly. "And the stitching is also *approved*?"

"Of course," Fannie said. She put her phone in her pocket and seemed to gain some focus on Lance's questions. She advanced a step toward Lance. "The style of a hem, Detective Lance. And the length of a dress, the cut of a sleeve, and the colors, too. The bishop decides what is approved and what is not. We can tell a lot about your bishop by the way your clothes are made."

Irma came forward to stand beside Fannie, and both women moved closer to Lance, as if to encourage the detective. Irma reached out delicately to take Lance's hand. In her other hand, she held a measuring tape and a thimble, which she had drawn from the pocket in her apron. "We make our own dresses," she said with a smile. She released Lance's hand and explained, "No proper Amish woman would wear a store-bought dress."

"How would I have known that?"

Together the Amish women shrugged.

"Then do you have something I can borrow?" Lance asked. "I really need to wear a proper outfit."

Irma held up her tape measure. "We'll make a dress for you, Detective Lance. It shouldn't take any time at all."

"OK, but I guess I'll need an apron, too."

"We have some of those already," Fannie said. "And your Kapp is fine. It's just that your dress would never work outside the bedroom."

Irma paused with a thought, and a soft blush appeared in her cheeks. Delicately, she stepped into the adjoining bathroom. With the door closed behind her, she called softly to Fannie in Dietsch, and Fannie smiled. It was the first unguarded and genuine smile Lance had seen on Fannie since she had arrived that afternoon.

"What now?" Lance asked, expecting that she had overlooked some additional arcane trifle in proper Amish attire.

Fannie continued to smile as she turned her gaze to the floorboards. "Detective Lance, Irma has asked if you will be expecting to return your dress to Walmart."

Not understanding the intent of the question, Lance answered, "I gave the receipt to my sheriff. I thought I'd be reimbursed for the expense."

Fannie brought her eyes up to Lance and cocked a brow, with a hint of guile giving soft curvature to her smile. "I don't think Irma wants the dress to be returned, Detective Lance. Perhaps, she is thinking, you will not have need to keep it?"

In the Daadihaus, Professor Branden was on the phone with the sheriff. While he talked, Caroline sat with Reuben Gingerich and Abel Mast in the corner of the open room, at a round dining table near the kitchen door. Watching for the arrival of the FBI, Branden talked into his phone while standing on the other side of the room near the front window. The three at the table listened to his end of the call until it ended.

"It shouldn't be too much longer," Branden said, closing his phone. "The FBI knows where we are."

Gingerich stood and paced in the large room, ignoring the professor. He was lost in thought, his concern for Fannie showing in the troubled creases around his eyes.

Abel Mast, from his seat at the table, asked the professor, "Will they let her have any visitors?"

"I don't know, Abel," Branden said. He crossed the room and took the chair that Gingerich had vacated. "Really, I doubt it. They probably should not permit her to have any visitors."

"But we are all Amish," Abel argued.

"I know," Branden said. "I'll speak to them about it."

As Gingerich paced in front of the window, Caroline asked him, "Reuben, are you prepared to wait? It might be weeks. And they might move her around a lot."

Reuben answered a simple, "Yes," and paused to stare out the front window at the gray weather. A steady and cool rain was spattering puddles on the gravel drive, where the Brandens' sedan and the detectives' patrol cruiser were both nosed up against the back porch. Through the pane, Reuben could hear the rain pinging insistently on the metal roofs of the cars. It was a tinny racket to which he was not accustomed.

Reuben turned to stare out over the fields beyond the gravel drive. A cover of fog was starting to collect over the pastures beyond, as the cool rain was lifted as vapor from the rich earth and the sun-warmed crops, producing damp aromas that held the hint of autumn weather, despite the fact that it was still only August.

Worried about Fannie, Reuben let his gaze wander to the back corner window of the main house. A lantern had been lit there, in the sewing room adjacent to the kitchen. Through the gray mist of the rain, Reuben could see Fannie and Irma both at work in the sewing room, Irma seated at the treadle machine, Fannie cutting fabric from a bolt of cloth in the standard color of dusty rose.

Reuben turned away from the window to address the professor. "Is Fannie just supposed to sit by herself in some lonely hotel room?"

"It's the best thing for now," Branden said.

"Will she have books? Her sewing? Anything that is hers?"

"A television, I suppose."

Reuben snorted disgust. "Television is a hideous circus spectacle," he declared with rare heat. "Americans are addicted to circus spectacles. They indulge themselves in grotesque spectacles of the most insidious kind, and they don't even have to leave their living rooms to do it."

"I wouldn't argue with you," Branden said. "Maybe some of the TV channels are not so bad as that, but really Reuben, I wouldn't argue with you at all."

Tires crunched the gravel outside

Reuben's window. He turned back to peer out and saw a black panel van with no markings turn in at the corner of the main house. The van rolled to a stop behind the cars, and two men in dark suits got out of the front seats and opened large black umbrellas. The sliding door opened, and two more men got out at the side of the van. One of the black umbrellas was handed to the second pair of men, and together the four men crowded under the two umbrellas to confer. The men were dressed so similarly that they might have been wearing uniforms.

"They're here," Reuben said disdainfully. "I'm going out to talk to them about books. They've at least got to let her have some books."

While Fannie cut fabric, Stan Armbruster crowded into the corner of the small sewing room and pressed in against a stack of a dozen upright bolts of fabric. In the corner near the window, Irma was vigorously working the foot pedals of her sewing machine, feeding dusty-rose cloth under her needle. With her back turned to Armbruster, Fannie was bent over the cutting table using hand shears, cutting cloth from a bolt of the same fabric.

While the women worked, Armbruster

asked Fannie about the April bus trip to Florida, and about the morning when she and Howie Dent had stopped with their fellow passengers for breakfast in Charlotte. Fannie described the ride south on I-77 from Sugarcreek as uneventful and unremarkable, the small hills of the southern Ohio countryside blending gradually into the stately mountains of West Virginia, Virginia, and North Carolina. She recalled the curviness of the route as it wound its way between rivers and mountains in Charleston. She remembered the high mountain pass beyond Wytheville, where the fog that night had been dense. Together, she and Howie had been seated near the back of the bus, and they had talked through the night.

Then Fannie described the two stops the bus had made before arriving in Charlotte the next morning. Some of the passengers had finished their trips at these early destinations, and more passengers had joined the trip, heading for Florida like the others. Fannie remembered that she got off briefly at the second stop to use the bathroom. When the bus arrived in Charlotte for breakfast at a restaurant near the highway, she and Howie had gotten off with the others, and the bus had circled around to a nearby gas station for fuel.

"The restaurant was already crowded," Fannie said. "So I waited with Howie in line, so he could use the men's room. It was at the back of a hallway that led to the kitchen."

"He did that?" Armbruster asked. "He got a turn in the restroom?"

"Yes, and when he came out, we turned in the long hallway to go get breakfast. But we saw some pushy men circling among the tables, looking at faces. They were rough-looking men, and Howie didn't like the way they were staring at people."

"Did you think they were looking for you, Fannie?"

"No, but Howie did."

"Then what? No breakfast?"

"No breakfast. He pulled me into the kitchen at the back of the hallway. We went out the back door, between two Dumpsters."

"How did you get to downtown Charlotte?"

"Howie pushed me into a cab. He wanted me to scrunch down beneath the windows."

"He chose downtown?"

"No. He told the cabdriver to get us to the Greyhound station. That just turned out to be downtown."

Fannie hesitated with a memory. "I'm lucky I had my purse. I paid the cabdriver. All Howie had was his phone."

"But why did he think those men were trouble? Because they seemed to be looking for someone?"

"I think so," Fannie said. She measured a length of fabric, chalked it, and took up her scissors. As she cut, she said, "Really, it was Howie who was nervous about them. I wouldn't even have noticed."

"Did he say anything about them, or did he just lead you out through the kitchen?"

"No, he said, 'That's not right,' or something like that. Maybe 'They're not right.' "

"Do you remember how many there were?"

"I only saw two, but Howie said four."

"When did he say that?"

"In the cab."

"Did he recognize any of the men?"

Fannie thought, remembered, and said, "He said he recognized the *type.* He said he really did not like the *type* of men they were."

"That doesn't seem like much," Armbruster said.

"Well, he had been talking on the bus all the way down to Charlotte. About how those people would be looking for me."

"Which people, Fannie? Did he say? Did he mean someone in particular? Or someone he actually knew?"

"He just meant the people who killed Ruth Zook," Fannie said. "And that woman in the gray Buick who came looking for me at my brother's house."

"Teresa Molina."

Tears welled in Fannie's eyes, and she whispered, "They must be the same people who killed Howie." She laid her scissors down and dried her eyes with the hem of her apron. "That must mean that Howie saved my life in Charlotte."

"Yes, Fannie," Armbruster said. "In Charlotte that morning, I think he did save your life."

23

Thursday, August 18
6:30 P.M.

Sheriff Robertson drove his Crown Vic northeast through Millersburg on SR 241, angling around the curves and hills of town, headed for Ricky Niell's home in a new development that had been carved out of pastureland a mile beyond the city limit. It was a neighborhood of new ranch homes with uniform design and construction, where the curbs and sidewalks were new and white, and the mailboxes were matched in style. Unlike the rest of Millersburg, which seemed to sprawl haphazardly across the patchwork of steep hills east of the Killbuck marshlands, Ricky and Ellie's neighborhood was a planned community where few trees had made a start and where several homes were still under construction. The lawns were newly sodded, and most of the fences were only partially finished. Ricky and Ellie lived in the second house beyond the main gate. It had been one of the first model homes the developer had constructed, and Ricky and Ellie had bought the home furnished. While Robertson was parking his Crown Vic at the curb in front of their house, a call rang in from Mike Branden.

When he finished with the professor's call, Robertson got out, locked up, and walked along the gentle slope of the drive, up to the brick path that led to the Niells' front door. The sheriff rang the bell, and he heard Ellie sing out from inside, "It's open."

The sheriff stepped inside and found Ellie stretched out on the living room couch, propped on several bedroom pillows, with her feet up and shoes off, obviously pregnant and shifting uncomfortably on her stacked pillows. By way of a greeting, Ellie said, "Hello, Sheriff. I shouldn't get up."

"Stay right there," Robertson said. He sat on the front edge of a soft recliner across from Ellie, and his weight compressed the cushion uncomfortably low to the floor, pinching his legs to an acute angle at the knees. He pushed himself farther back into the seat and said to Ellie, "You don't look very comfortable on those pillows."

"Sheriff," Ellie said with her eyes closed,

"if only I could tell you."

"That bad?"

"Worse. The doctor says it has to be either the couch or the bed, and I'm not to get up by myself."

"But you look good, otherwise," the sheriff said, trying again for a more agreeable position on the seat of the low recliner. "I mean you look healthy."

Ellie laughed out a challenge. "A *happy glow,* Sheriff? That's what my father calls it."

Robertson gave the best smile he could manage and defended himself. "I just mean it's good to see you, Ellie. And I hope you're going to be OK."

Ellie pushed up on her pillows. "I'll be fine as soon as I can walk by myself and get out of the house. And wear decent shoes again."

"Can you ride in a chair? Have Ricky wheel you around the neighborhood?"

Ellie laughed with apparent good cheer and wriggled into a better position on her pillows. "Not really," she said and laughed again. "Picture that, if you can, Sheriff. Wheeling me around on the sidewalks. Anyway, the doctor says no."

"That's rough."

"I'll get there," Ellie answered. "In the

meantime, Caroline has been coming to help me every day, and Del Markely has been keeping me up to date."

Robertson scratched his chin with narrowed eyes. "I'm not sure Del Markely's gonna work out as dispatcher."

Ellie laid her head back. "You just need to give her time, Bruce. You know you don't like change."

Robertson shook his head and growled a little to clear his throat. "When can you come back to work, Ellie?"

"We'll see."

"But you are coming back, right?"

"We'll see."

The big sheriff found it impossible to make himself comfortable on the recliner. He also found it impossible to mask his concern for Ellie. So he held to his seat and said softly, "I can't imagine running my department without you." Then to dispel his embarrassment, he turned awkwardly in his chair to study the room. "Is Ricky doing the housework? Because it looks like he needs some help."

"Yes, Ricky's doing all the housework. And all the shopping."

"That where he's at, now?"

"Yes. Are you offering to help with any of this?"

Robertson cleared his throat with difficulty. "Whatever you need, Ellie. You know that."

"I know, Bruce. Don't worry. We've got it covered."

To camouflage his unexpected sensitivities, the sheriff said brusquely, "OK, but when can I have Ricky back? I need everyone I can get, Ellie. You know that as well as anyone."

"Not for a while, Sheriff. Maybe when the doctor says I've stabilized."

Robertson nodded with an unhappy frown. "I'm really not sure about Del, Ellie. I mean really. She's not anything like you."

"Ricky says the deputies like her, Bruce. You need to let her settle in."

"I had hoped you would be back to work before I had to do that."

"I won't, Bruce. You need to give her a chance."

"Whatever." Robertson rubbed anxiously at the top bristles of his gray hair. "Anyway, the Dent murder has us tied in knots."

Ellie rearranged her pillows to lie back more. She knew that nothing more she might say on the topic of Del Markely would prove effective with the sheriff, so instead of pressing her case, she asked,

"How are Stan and Pat doing in Middle-field?"

"Well, they're still up there. With Mike and Caroline. Mike just called."

"What'd he have for you?"

"Well, Fannie has a fiancé, from Michigan."

"So, Fannie and Howie weren't in love?"

"Either that or she figured she had to marry Amish."

"Could be."

"Mike also said he's going to try to get details from the fiancé, Reuben Gingerich. About how Fannie and Howie moved around this summer. And how they chose their next destinations."

"What about the yellow VW?" Ellie asked. "Anything there?" She struggled to adjust her pillows.

Robertson popped off his chair. "What can I do?"

Ellie pulled at the corner of one of her pillows. "Just raise this one up. More behind my head."

Robertson worked with the pillows and felt foolish for being so clumsy. He mumbled, "I'm sorry," but he persisted. Eventually, Ellie gave him a thumbs-up, and Robertson returned to his chair, asking, "Is that any better?"

Ellie was breathing heavily from her exertions. "A little bit, Sheriff. Caroline or Ricky usually helps me with this sort of thing. So tell me what was in Howie Dent's VW."

Robertson scratched nervously at his chin. "Ellie, did you know that Caroline Branden suffered a number of miscarriages early in their marriage?"

Ellie answered softly. "Yes, Bruce. She's told me. It's horrible."

"Does she come here every day?"

"Yes. I've tried to tell her that it isn't necessary."

"Don't, Ellie. Don't tell her that. She needs to help you. It's good for her. She's always been fragile on this topic. If she's coming here every day, it means that she needs to be here every day."

"OK, Sheriff. Now tell me about the yellow VW. What was in it?"

"His killers took most of Dent's belongings, Ellie. There's nothing in the car that can help us."

"Maybe Dent wasn't going back to Middlefield," Ellie said. "Maybe he was going to leave Fannie with this Gingerich."

"Then why not just return home to his farm? The Teresa Molina crew has no reason to harm him, because he was never involved in any of the drug smuggling. So, why would he take the car in the night?"

"I suppose."

"Really, Ellie, I don't think he'd stay with Fannie all summer and then not go back to her with his car. He could have driven her anywhere. It's just what she and Gingerich would need — a ride to anywhere in America. So I can't imagine he wasn't going back to help her."

"OK," Ellie asked, "so what did he do in Millersburg to get himself abducted?"

"Right. That's the question. I've been trying to figure where he'd go, once he had retrieved his VW."

"There has to be something that answers that, Bruce."

The sheriff's phone rang. He pulled it from his coat pocket and checked the display. "Armbruster," he said to Ellie, and he answered the call. "What have you got for me, Stan?"

The sheriff listened a bit and then said, "Wait, I'll put you on speaker phone."

He set the phone on the coffee table, switched to speaker, and said, "I'm with Ellie, Stan. Say that again."

Armbruster repeated, "I said, Dent was concerned about some men at the bus's breakfast stop last April in Charlotte. That's why he pushed Fannie into a cab. It's why they took a Greyhound to Memphis."

"Did he think those were Molina's people?" Robertson asked.

"I think so," Armbruster said, and he recounted for Robertson and Ellie the details of the scene in the Charlotte restaurant, just as Fannie had described it, with the men searching for her. Then the cab ride to the Greyhound station downtown. Paying the cabbie. Buying the tickets for Memphis.

"At least that's what Fannie says," Armbruster finished. "But I'll get more if I can. In the meantime, the FBI has arrived here. They want to get Fannie into custody as soon as possible."

"Then you won't have any more time with her," Robertson said. "That's a problem."

"We'll get everything we need from Fannie," Armbruster chuckled. "The FBI won't be a problem. Caroline and Reuben Gingerich are right up in their faces, and if you want information from Fannie, all you'll have to do is call Caroline."

"What's going on?"

"Gingerich insists on a proper chaperone for Fannie. He says she's not going to a hotel with four strange men without a woman to chaperone her."

Ellie leaned from her pillows toward the

phone. "Stan, it's Ellie. Caroline could do that. Chaperone."

"I know," Armbruster said, laughing. "She's telling them right now that Fannie's not going anywhere without her. It's a showdown out of some classic western movie. You ought to see this. A professor's wife haranguing the FBI."

As Reuben Gingerich argued with lead agent Parker, Caroline paced behind him, kicking at the gravel beside the FBI's black panel van. Her hands were hanging like stiff cudgels at her sides, and uselessly, her fingers were begging her to make claws. A hoarse rattle had built a nest in her throat, and she felt as if it were hatching chicks there. She growled to clear the tangle in her throat, and Reuben turned momentarily to smile appreciation at her before he resumed his arguments with the agent.

Caroline kicked up a stone and paced. Fannie's protests had counted for nothing. She had retreated to the Daadihaus with Irma. Caroline spun in place and then paced again.

Her husband's credentials as a reserve Holmes County deputy had counted for nothing. He had gone into the kitchen for water. Or so he had said.

Reuben's arguments about the impropriety of an engaged Amish woman staying in a hotel room with four strange men had counted for nothing. The agents, it seemed, cared not a whit for Fannie's sensitivities.

So Caroline was pacing and growling. She felt as if she would not be able to work through her tension unless she could claw something loose from the FBI's wall of intransigence. Unless she could claw something loose from their barricade of practiced indifference.

As Caroline scored the gravel with the toe of her shoe, the professor stepped off the back porch with a bottle of water and said, "Here, Caroline. Drink this."

Caroline snatched the bottle from his hand and took a single long drink. When she handed the bottle back, she whirled around and pulled gently at Gingerich's sleeve to press forward to the FBI's lead agent. With her index finger punctuating the vacant space in front of the agent's nose, she snapped, "You said it was a suite, Parker. You said it yourself. A suite with two bedrooms. So that puts Fannie and me in one bedroom, and you with all of your roughies in the other. We share the middle space. And we're gonna use the kitchen."

"It's not big enough for all of us," Agent Parker said. "And it's not proper procedure."

"I don't care," Caroline said more temperately. "It's a suite, and I'm going with Fannie."

"Not possible," Parker insisted.

Reuben pressed forward again. "Then Fannie's not going."

"She has to go," Parker said. "We need her testimony."

"Does she have to testify?" Reuben asked. "I mean, does she really *have* to testify?"

"No, Reuben," Caroline answered authoritatively. "Her testimony is voluntary."

"Is that right?" Reuben demanded of Parker. "Is it really her decision?"

Parker ignored the question and said to Caroline, "Mrs. Branden, are you prepared to sit indefinitely in a hotel room? Are you prepared to play chaperone until Teresa Molina is caught?"

"I don't *play* at anything," Caroline said. Her index finger reappeared in front of Parker's nose. "And don't you try to intimidate me."

"I'm not, Mrs. Branden. But really, have you thought this through?"

"Don't you try to patronize me, either, Agent Parker. I'm going to spend my nights here with Fannie. During the day, I'll be going back and forth to Millersburg. I have a friend there whose pregnancy is not going well, and I'll have to split my time between here and there."

"You can't be coming and going like that, Mrs. Branden. It'll upset our routines."

"I'm coming with Fannie, Parker. That's just how it is."

From behind them, at the open door of the little Daadihaus, Fannie called out, "Stop! Stop arguing, all of you." She stepped forward on the drive. "It doesn't matter, Agent Parker. If Caroline is not going, then neither am I."

24

Thursday, August 18
7:15 P.M.

Standing out at the curb in front of Ellie's house, Sheriff Robertson called the professor on his cell. When Branden answered, Robertson asked, "Where are you with things, Mike?"

"Caroline is going to go with Fannie to the hotel," Branden said. "They've decided on that much. Now Gingerich is haranguing them about books, knitting, and Fannie's liberties while in custody."

Robertson pulled the door open on his Crown Vic. "Would I like this Gingerich?"

"Quite a lot, Bruce," Branden answered. "You'd like this Gingerich quite a lot. Anyway, I estimate it'll be another half hour. Then Caroline and Fannie will be headed to the hotel, and I'll be riding home with Lance and Armbruster."

"You won't drive your car?" Robertson asked.

"No. Caroline is going to follow Fannie in our car. She wants to be able to drive home to check on Ellie during the day."

"Good. Ellie can use the help."

"You've seen her?"

"Just now. She's struggling, Mike. But how is Caroline going to handle all of this? It's too much."

"It's Caroline, Bruce. If she doesn't think she can take care of Ellie, she'll hire a nursing service or something."

"Mike, she's worried about a miscarriage."

"Can you blame her? Given our history?"

"No. I suppose not. Look, Mike, are you still dressed Amish?"

"Yes, but they tell me here that it's more like conservative Mennonite attire. It'll do, they assure me, since Gingerich is from a Michigan congregation, and dress is not always similar. So nobody would expect Gingerich to dress exactly like a man from Holmes County, anyway. They assure me that the outfit will do the job."

"OK, then is Lance dressed like Fannie? That'd be more critical."

"Yes, only they had to make her an outfit. And I gather they gave her some lessons on how an Amish woman should behave."

"Like what, exactly?"

"Mostly it's aspects of proper public behavior. Being demure and submissive. Reserved. That sort of thing."

"How did that go over with Lance?"

"You can guess. But look, Bruce, I've been thinking. Whatever Dent's killers got out of his VW, it didn't help them find Fannie."

"Or she'd already be dead," Robertson said in agreement.

"Precisely," Branden said. "And whatever they left behind at the Helmuth farm, we have to understand that those are things that they thought they didn't need."

"Yeah, Mike, but I've been trying to guess what they might have taken away with them."

"Items from his backpack," Branden said. "Among other things."

"I suppose. If so, when we catch them, they'll have something of Dent's in their possession."

"They wouldn't be that stupid."

"But maybe they are stupid, Mike. I mean, think about it. It was a mistake to leave anything at all in the VW."

"Or even to leave the VW sitting right there in the open," Branden said.

"OK, Dent must have wanted his car for some reason. Otherwise, why would he risk

266

coming home for it?"

"I think Fannie expected that he'd come back here to Middlefield," Branden said. "He could have driven Fannie and Reuben anywhere they wanted to go."

"Do you know where they were going next?"

"Not yet. I'll ask. But Fannie said that Howie loved that VW. Maybe he just wanted it, and they really hadn't figured out where they'd go next."

Robertson climbed in behind the wheel. "Call me if you get more, Mike. And call when you are actually leaving Middlefield."

"OK. It might take more time than I thought. The FBI doesn't understand a single thing about Amish ways."

"I'm counting on it, Mike. And with Caroline there to help her, it'll be even better for Fannie."

"What do you mean?"

"Has either you or Caroline read the letter I wrote to Fannie?"

"No, should we?"

"Caroline should."

"Right now?"

"Once she settles in at that hotel."

"What's in the letter, Bruce?"

Robertson started his engine. "Mike, I just

told her where I thought she'd be the safest."

When the professor punched out of the call, Fannie had already climbed into the side door of the panel van with her suitcase. Reuben Gingerich was standing in the rain at the open door, speaking to her. A line of rainwater was spilling off the back rim of his straw fedora. He seemed focused on Fannie, oblivious to the rain, and he stood immobile there beside the open door of the van, talking softly. Branden could see Fannie nodding, as if she were reassured by Reuben's words.

Branden crossed the gravel to his wife, who was opening the driver's door of their sedan. "Are you ready for this?" he asked as he came up to her. "You didn't bring anything for an overnight stay."

Caroline covered him with her umbrella, embraced him with her free arm, and said, "As soon as I have her settled, I'll go out shopping somewhere, Michael. To buy clothes, groceries, and toiletries."

"OK," the professor said. "I'm riding back with Stan and Pat."

"Right."

"There might be some trouble."

"I know, Michael," Caroline said. "I trust you."

"And how about the FBI, Caroline? Do you trust them? You going to give them a break?"

"Not likely."

"Good. I don't think they get it."

"Get what?"

"Anything, really, and Bruce says you should read the letter he wrote to Fannie. Once you get to the hotel."

"Fannie has it?"

"I presume so."

Twenty yards away, Reuben turned from the panel van's sliding door to address Agent Parker again. His voice was only a whisper, but his posture was stern. Caroline watched Reuben and said to her husband, "That's fun to see. A plain Amish man confronting the exalted FBI."

"Right now, I don't think Agent Parker could tell you who he's dealing with."

"Right now," Caroline smirked, "I don't think Agent Parker could tell you Peter Pan's first name."

"That bad?"

"Worse. Are you going to carry a gun, Michael?"

"Always. Under my vest."

"The three-eighty?" Caroline asked. "Or

the nine?"

"The little three-eighty."

"It's not big enough, Michael."

"It's easy to conceal."

"Take the nine-millimeter," Caroline insisted.

"I'll be with plenty of people who have guns."

"Take the nine-millimeter in an ankle holster."

"OK, but I'll have to get it from home."

"So get it, Michael. Before you turn in tonight. Before you do anything else."

The professor agreed, and then a wide grin stretched across his face. "Peter Pan's first name?"

Caroline returned his smile and kissed him under her umbrella. "I'm just saying, Michael. They really don't know who they're dealing with."

25

When Stan Armbruster pulled to the curb in front of the Hotel St. James in Millersburg, Sheriff Robertson was waiting at the front entrance with an umbrella. Dressed in the clothes that Irma and Fannie had made for her, Pat Lance got out of the backseat of Armbruster's cruiser, carrying her suitcase. The professor, still dressed Amish, slid over on the backseat and got out behind Lance. Robertson held the umbrella for them as they hurried into the hotel lobby, and then the sheriff stood guard while Lance and Branden registered at the black marble counter for their rooms. In uniform, Deputy Ryan Baker was posted at the back alley door, at the far end of the hotel's narrow lobby. When Stan Armbruster knocked on the outside of the alley door, Baker opened it for him. Armbruster had parked his car in the lot behind the hotel. Another deputy was already at his post outside the elevator on the third floor, and he was also in uniform.

Once Professor Branden and Detective Lance had the keys to their rooms, Robertson and Armbruster rode with them in the elevator to the third floor. As Armbruster watched from the end of the hall near the elevator, Branden, Lance, and Robertson headed for their rooms at the other end of the hall. Branden entered room 5 briefly, dropped the satchel he had brought from home on the bed, and came out directly to the door to room 6. There, Pat Lance had already opened her door and entered, and Branden found her at the back of the room with Robertson, inspecting the lock on the suite door to Robertson's room, number 7. Branden came forward to say to Robertson and Lance, "There's not a door between five and six. Is that how you want it? Because, five can make a suite with four, but not with six."

"I know," Robertson said. "I doubt you'll spend much time in five."

"I'll need to sleep," Branden said. "Some, anyway."

"There'll be at least one of us in room seven, Mike. Probably more than that at any

272

given time. If you need to get some rest, that's going to be enough, I think."

"I suppose." Branden shrugged. "I just dropped my bag. Left a light on."

At a corner table, Robertson switched on a light for Lance and said, "We need to get some dinner across the street. They're going to close at ten."

Armbruster appeared at the door to room 6 and asked, "Am I going to dinner, Sheriff?"

"Negative, Stan," Robertson said. "Get some sleep. Be back here at six thirty in the morning."

Armbruster acknowledged his orders and left.

Once Lance had set out some toiletries in her bathroom and laid some clothes in a dresser drawer, she locked up and allowed Robertson and the professor to escort her to the elevator. Then she allowed them to escort her through the first-floor lobby. She was wearing the white organdy prayer Kapp over a bun she had made of her brown wig. Her own short blond hair was hidden under the wig.

Taking Fannie's instructions, Lance wore no makeup and no jewelry other than a copper wristband she had borrowed from Irma, which everyone in Holmes County would recognize as the bracelet favored by the Amish for its benefits in alleviating joint pain and arthritis. Otherwise, Lance was dressed as plainly and as demurely as any proper Amish maiden, in a long Amish dress in the approved color of dusty rose. The dress was pleated seven times in front and four times over the rump. It was gathered correctly over the shoulders, and its sleeves reached beyond Lance's elbows. The hem of her dress reached past her ankles to brush the tops of her soft black walking shoes. Lance's white day apron was entirely plain. It covered her bodice and front, falling to within precisely two inches of her dress's hem. The apron draped broadly back over her shoulders and across her shoulder blades, to tie in back at her waist. Properly, the ties were hidden in back, under a roll of the apron's back hem. Finally, though no one would see it unless she was seated, Lance also wore a suitable pair of modest black hose under her dress.

Altogether, very little of Lance's skin was exposed. Only her hands, her wrists, and her face. She was plain and unadorned. Apart from those who already knew her, she would be indistinguishable from any other Amish woman of Fannie's sect.

Lance understood that this was just as it

should be. That was the whole point, wasn't it? She reminded herself of the oddity of plainness as she crossed the lobby, and she reminded herself again as she crossed Jackson Street under the professor's umbrella. She needed to appear plain, simple, and unremarkable. She needed this strange and unremarkable quality of similitude, Fannie had assured her, and she needed demure behavior to match.

As she crossed the street in her Amish attire, Lance could hear the rain pelting the fabric of the umbrella over her head, but she thought her hearing seemed strangely muffled. She could see the streetlights shimmering in the dark rain water at her feet, but she thought her sight seemed strangely tunneled, as if anyone seeing her would recognize her not as an individual, but only as an indistinguishable representative of her sect. She wondered as she walked in the rain between the professor and the sheriff whether, if people could not see her as a person, would she similarly lose sight and recognition of others? She wondered how her attire would cause others to treat her differently. She wondered if she could treat others as she was now supposed to do. Clearly, Lance thought, the coaching that Fannie and Irma had given her would be wholly inadequate for so strange a charade as this.

Her behavior beside the professor — her fiancé — needed to be perfect. It needed to be restrained and respectful. Demure and submissive. Let him open the heavy wooden door at the Hotel Millersburg. Now let him take your elbow to guide you down the carpet to the hotel's restaurant. Stand beside him quietly as he chooses the table. Pull your own chair at the table? No. That was a mistake. He'll pull it out, but you can sit yourself down.

In this state of indeterminate confusion, Lance's meal at the Hotel Millersburg passed like an irretrievable dream, as she focused so intently, and worried so much, about doing everything properly. Fannie and Irma had told her what to do. They had coached her carefully on how to do it. But it seemed so foreign to Lance. So distant. So utterly impersonal.

"Fannie," she heard someone say at the edge of her awareness.

Again, someone said, "Fannie."

A light touch on her arm brought her some focus. "Fannie," the professor was saying. "Aren't you going to eat something?"

Slowly she turned her head to face the professor to her right. "I'm sorry?"

276

"Aren't you going to eat something, Fannie? You look like you've been thinking about something."

"I guess I have been," Lance said. "It's a strange way to live."

To her left, Robertson said, "Fannie, I really think you should eat something."

Lance looked down at her plate. She had ordered a chicken Alfredo, with some sautéed vegetables. Someone had brought the meal to her. She took up her fork and began to eat. "Sorry, Reuben," she said. "I think I was dreaming."

As a waiter filled water glasses at their table, Robertson made a point of speaking out. "Fannie, eat something while you can. Then we'll get you back over to the St. James."

Lance looked with curiosity at each of her dinner partners, and she wondered what they were thinking. The sheriff, in his gray suit and red power tie, probably thinking about tomorrow's schedule. The professor, in his suit of Amish clothes, probably thinking about his wife. Ryan Baker across the table from her, in his deputy's uniform, probably wondering about Lance's costume.

There were waiters circling among the other tables in the dim, carpeted room. All around her, the hotel's patrons were *English.*

She and the professor were the only Amish people there.

She gave the room a quick study and realized it was easy to spot the tourists. They were the ones staring at her and at her Amish-dressed fiancé. The locals were paying her scant attention. But the tourists in the corner booth were staring at her. They were staring at the professor, too.

These were prying, intrusive stares that objectified her more than Lance had realized was possible. It was worse than the stares the boys had given her at college. Worse than the stares of strange men in malls. These stares came with whispers of curiosity. As if she were on display for their entertainment, rather than a person who wanted decent privacy during a meal.

Lance groaned, shook her head, and began again to eat her pasta.

Robertson asked, "What, Fannie? Your meal's not good?"

"My meal is fine, Sheriff," Lance whispered as she ate. "Can't say that I appreciate the tourists."

Lance entered her room at the St. James and waited for Robertson to enter behind her and close the door. The professor had already retired to the adjacent room. Once

278

Robertson had some lights on, Lance pulled her Kapp off and then her brown wig. Standing in her Amish dress and apron, with her blond English hair exposed like a punctuating anachronism, Lance sputtered, "I don't think I can do this."

Robertson sat in a corner chair. "What, Lance? The outfit or the attitude?"

"Either one!" Lance answered. She sat heavily on the bed and began to untie the back laces of her apron. Abruptly she stopped and took up her Kapp and brown wig. "It's too much to remember, Sheriff. Like my hair. I'm allowed to take my hair down only for my husband. And this Kapp? I can never take it off in public. Or even most of the time at home. So really, Bruce, I can't do any of it. Not convincingly. Nobody's going to believe that I'm an Amish woman."

"You did fine, Lance."

"I don't know how they do it," Lance complained. "They're all bottled up, worried every minute that they'll do something wrong."

"That's not how it is, Lance. They grow up like this. It's second nature to them."

"Well, it's not second nature to me!"

"You'll get the hang of it."

"I don't think so."

"Look, Lance," Robertson argued. "You don't have to say much. And you don't have to talk to everyone. It's showing you around that's the important thing here."

"Who will I need to talk to?"

"A banker and a pharmacist. A real estate agent, and maybe a clerk at a convenience store. Maybe someone in a restaurant."

"Oh, is that all!"

"It'll be OK, Lance. You halfway looked Amish to start with."

"Oh, I look Amish, that's for certain. I had tourists staring at me during dinner."

"Tourists always stare at the Amish, Lance. You've known that for years."

"Yeah, well, it's the first time they've stared like this at me."

26

Thursday, August 18
9:35 P.M.

Almost as soon as they slid the door closed on the FBI's black panel van, Fannie suspected that she had made a grave mistake. By the time they were rolling silently into the center of Middlefield, she was nearly certain of it. As the van turned at the Middlefield city square to roll west out of town on 87, she was contemplating a jump from the sliding door. She was contemplating a run. An escape.

Feeling so completely alone inside the dark van, with four armed men as escorts, Fannie wondered if perhaps she had not foolishly forfeited her one best chance for freedom. She wondered if she had not lost her chance to walk away from the perverse legalisms of federal law enforcement. To walk free of the legalisms that demanded that she be held in isolation against the

281

improbable eventuality that the leaders of a violent drug cartel might one day be captured and brought to trial.

But Reuben had been so confident. So she would be confident, too. Tonight was not the night to run. That day would come soon, but it was not tonight. And remember, Reuben had said. Sheriff Robertson has given us the key. When it is time, it requires only courage. It requires only faith to see it through.

So Fannie rode with her escorts as the van pushed westward into the night, toward the hotel that Robertson himself had chosen. She rode silently as her escorts switched on a small roof light and checked their weapons. The black pistols made ugly clacking sounds as the agents worked the top gun parts back to peer inside. They made clicking sounds as the bullets slid into place. From a single overhead cabin light, Fannie could see the menacing triggers. She could smell the gun oil. She could imagine the muzzles spitting fire and death, and she regretted that she had ever left Reuben's side. She knew that she should have run when the Brandens first arrived.

Wordlessly, Fannie watched as the van circled into the wide parking lot of the hotel and rolled toward the rear corner of the four-story brick building. There it seemed to her that an unnatural darkness had descended where the lights of the parking lot should normally have been shining. She realized that the lights had been shut off for her arrival, and she groaned with the misery of her isolation.

As the van approached the building's corner, Fannie closed her eyes to pray. She felt the van circle sharply toward a stop, and she heard Parker, riding beside the driver, speak into a radio handset. "On the rear door. Arriving now."

The van came to a full stop in the unnatural darkness, with its headlights illuminating the front of a loading platform with steep concrete steps. The driver switched off the headlights, and the men stirred inside the van. Parker got out first, followed by the driver. Fannie heard chatter on the radio as Parker slid the van door open beside her.

"Come out now, Fannie," Parker said. He reached in to take her arm and guide her out.

The two agents who had ridden in the back of the van also climbed out to the blacktop behind her. On either side of her, the men took her elbows and led her forward to the steps. As if she couldn't manage it on her own, they lifted roughly on her arms to escort her quickly up the steps. Parker and the driver already had the steel door open for her at the back of the hotel. They ushered her inside, and the steel door clanged into place behind her. Squeezed between her escorts, inside a small and dreary basement vestibule, Fannie felt that she now understood the isolation of imprisonment. That she understood the loneliness of a jail cell. And she tried to summon the words to protest.

But before she had a chance to speak, Parker barked into his handset, "Go," and the doors to a service elevator spread open in front of her. Two more agents stepped off the elevator toward her, and she found herself surrounded by six armed men.

Parker next said, "One of you at each of the entrances," and three of Parker's agents disappeared into a stairwell door. Then Parker checked his watch, and Fannie found herself being hustled forward into the elevator.

Once the elevator had started its rise, Parker spoke again on his handset. "On our way up. Secure the hallway on four."

Just as the elevator doors were about to open on the fourth floor, Parker used his handset again, "Stepping out."

On the fourth floor, Parker and his two agents took Fannie left down the hallway. As she made the turn, Fannie looked to her right and saw yet another agent standing guard near the end of the hall. Beyond him, she saw an Amish woman, with an Amish man holding a position beside her. The Amish woman was delivering pillows to the last room at the end of the hall.

As the agents hurried her down the hall, Fannie counted three rooms to her right and four rooms to her left. They were all labeled as suites. The agents stopped her at the last room on the right. It was marked Suite 416.

Inside, Parker immediately directed Fannie to the bedroom on the left. Fannie was given her suitcase, and she carried it into the bedroom, where she turned around and sat on the end of the nearest of two queen beds. Parker switched the lights on for her, and she felt as if she had been marooned in a foreign land. She felt alone, and she realized that she could depend on no one but herself right then. So she calmed herself by studying the layout of her bedroom.

There was a long dresser to her left, with a flat-panel TV parked on top. Also there was a nightstand between the two beds, with a lamp and the TV remote laid out on it. A soft chair sat in one corner, and a desk with a lamp was in another corner. The bathroom door was situated to her right, on the other side of the bedroom's entrance.

The second queen bed was set beside the bedroom's single window. The window was covered with heavy drapes. Fannie rose instinctively to move to the window, but Agent Parker said, "Please don't go near the windows, Fannie. And please do not open the drapes."

Once Parker had closed the bedroom door behind him, Fannie sat again on the bed, whispering to herself, "Reuben, what have we done?" As she whispered for her fiancé, Reuben's reassurances returned to her. The words he had spoken to her at the door to the van gave her a measure of peace. She remembered what Reuben had said, and she held fast to the words of Sheriff Robertson's letter. She held fast to the key that Sheriff Robertson had given them: *You would have been safe among your people . . .*

Fannie heard a mix of voices on the other side of the bedroom door. She got off her bed and stepped forward to put her ear to the door. She heard Parker's voice most distinctly. Authoritative, commanding, insistent. "Is there another way in?"

"No," he was answered. "There are emergency exits, but after nine o'clock, they do not open from the outside."

Next, Parker asked, "What was that business at the end of the hallway just now?"

"Room 401 requested pillows," an agent replied.

"Were they checked out?" Parker asked.

"Of course. Both the maid and her supervisor. Also the occupants of 401."

"Why does it take two people to deliver pillows?" Parker asked.

A second agent explained. "It's hotel policy. A supervisor always escorts the maids when they make deliveries at night."

"They were both Amish," Parker said.

"They all are."

"Who is, precisely?" Parker asked.

"Everyone who works here. Maids, room service, kitchen staff, clerks, even the concierge — all of them, really. It's Amish owned and Amish operated. The tourists like it that way. And Amish women don't make deliveries to rooms at night without a male supervisor to chaperone them."

Next, Parker said, "OK, we'll sleep in shifts. Two at a time, three hours apiece. And let's get some food and coffee up here. We're going to be here all night."

"When will the maintenance team arrive?"

an agent asked.

"Nine A.M.," Parker said.

"And they'll maintain this location until Monday?"

"Right. Three days only."

"Then Cleveland?" another agent asked.

"Of course," Parker answered. "This place suits my purposes for now, but if Robertson thinks I'm going to keep a key witness in a tourist hotel indefinitely, then he's even more stupid than I thought he was."

Fannie retreated to a chair in the far corner of her room. Shaken by the swiftness of Parker's plan, she was also stunned by the callousness of his duplicity. Reuben had warned her, but he hadn't anticipated how soon she would be betrayed. Really, the sheriff had warned her, too. But like Reuben, the sheriff could not have expected this level of deceitfulness. Clearly, Fannie realized now, it would be foolish to trust the FBI past the weekend. But it was more than that. No doubt, she had been foolish to have talked at all to the Brandens. Or to have waited with the Masts until Detective Lance had arrived with her partner. Or to have waited even longer for the FBI.

And if it was Parker's intention — if it had been his intention all along — to spirit her away to Cleveland, where she would see no more of her kind as long as her protective captivity lasted, then it meant only that Reuben would have to be ready that much sooner. It meant that they would all have to be that much bolder.

Fannie stayed in her bedroom thinking for an hour before she unpacked her suitcase. She had heard Parker giving instructions to his men, and then the middle room of the suite had been quiet on the other side of her door. Alone in her room, she eventually found herself unable to remain idle.

Fannie opened all the drawers in the bedroom and in the bathroom, and she tested all the lamps and light switches. She turned off most of the electric lights, leaving only the bathroom light switched on, with the door cracked open. Dim lights for dark thoughts, she told herself as she sat in the corner chair. A quiet place to think and to plan.

After a while, Fannie turned her thoughts to what comforts the room could offer her. She paced on the plush carpet with her shoes off, crinkling her toes into the unaccustomed softness. She laid her head on each of the pillows and chose a soft feather pillow for herself. She picked up the handset of the phone and listened briefly to the dial tone. She turned on the hot water in the shower, thinking that she would bathe.

But while the water ran, she decided against that. She turned off the water and watched it drain away. Caroline would be coming. There would be time for a shower once Caroline had arrived. Or maybe even later in the night. She could bathe after she had gauged Caroline's intentions. After she had gauged her capacity for truthfulness.

Restless and uninterested in sleep, Fannie opened her bedroom door and entered the middle room of the suite to check in the kitchen's refrigerator. There she found only bottled water and a box of baking soda. She took out a bottle of water and carried it into the sitting area.

With a magazine in his lap, an agent was seated on a couch. He watched her cross the room. Fannie sat in a corner chair and the agent opened his magazine again. Curious to learn what he would do, Fannie returned to the kitchen and stepped around the small dining table to pull the cord on the blinds over the kitchen window. As she took the cord in hand, the agent appeared at her side and said, "Please stay away from the windows, Ms. Helmuth."

Fannie released the cord and smiled

demurely. "Can I go down for something to eat?"

"Sorry, but no. We're having food brought up."

"Where is Agent Parker?"

"Making his rounds, Ms. Helmuth."

"And the three agents who were with him when they picked me up at the farm?"

"Two are sleeping in the second bedroom. One is at his post."

"What can I do until my dinner arrives?"

"There's a TV in your bedroom, Ms. Helmuth."

"I don't like television."

"Sorry. We have a few magazines."

"May I stretch my legs out in the hall?"

"I'm sorry, but no."

"You could walk with me. And aren't there some stairs we could climb? For exercise?"

"There are two staircases, Ms. Helmuth, but you can't use them. You need to stay inside, here with us. It's for your protection."

"How are all of you going to get any rest?" Fannie asked, feigning concern for the agents. "There are eight of you, right?"

"There are seven, Ms. Helmuth. And we have sleep rotations in place."

"Are you the seven who will be my captors until the trial?"

"Well, we aren't captors, really."

"What would you call it, if I can't leave the suite?"

"We are the acquisition team, Ms. Helmuth."

"Does that mean I'll get a different team?"

"Yes, a maintenance team."

"When? Monday?"

"No. Probably tomorrow morning."

"Will they all be new people? Seven new people?"

"Yes, but there will only be four. Four new agents."

"Will these four new agents know who I am?"

"They will have been briefed, Ms. Helmuth. Really, wouldn't you rather get some rest? You've had a long day."

"I could sleep," Fannie said. "But isn't there something to read?"

"Only the magazines that are there on the coffee table."

Fannie turned to the center coffee table and took up the stack of magazines. She sorted through them and said, "Thank you, no."

"We can have some other magazines brought up."

"Is there a store in the lobby?"

"It's a newsstand and a small hotel store. There's also a souvenir shop and a bakery."

"I suppose Caroline could get something for me after she arrives," Fannie said.

"The hotel store is still open, but everything else is closed, Ms. Helmuth."

"Then in the morning?"

"That would be better, Ms. Helmuth."

"Thank you," Fannie said as she turned for her bedroom. "Would you please knock on my door when my dinner arrives? I might be asleep."

When Caroline entered the bedroom, Fannie was stretched out on the bed closest to the window. Eyes narrowed to slits, Fannie watched Caroline set her purse on the long dresser across from the foot of the beds. When Caroline switched on the bedroom lights, Fannie raised herself to sit on the side of her bed.

Caroline came into the room and asked, "Are you OK, Fannie?"

Fannie stood beside her bed and rubbed her eyes as if sleep had overtaken her. "Sleepy, I guess," she said. "And I'm hungry."

"There's food out there," Caroline said. "They had to check everything before they would let it come up to the room."

Fannie went out to the middle room, and Caroline followed her. On a cart inside the suite's front door, there was a stack of white dinner boxes. Two agents were sorting through them to select their meals. There was also a large white plastic carafe of coffee, and Agent Parker was pouring himself a cup. When Fannie appeared, he offered the cup of coffee to her, saying, "We were just about to knock on your door, Ms. Helmuth."

"Please, it's just Fannie."

"Fannie, then. Would you like some coffee?"

Fannie shook a sleepy "No" and took up a dinner box. Parker carried his coffee out into the hallway and closed the suite's door behind him.

Complaining, one of the agents grumbled, "They're all the same. Amish broasted chicken, mashed potatoes with gravy, and buttered green beans with bacon bits."

Fannie shrugged her condolences and said, "Typical tourist fare, I'm afraid. It will be food that was left over from the dinner buffet. Reheated in a microwave."

Once Caroline had taken a meal box, Fannie turned back into their bedroom. She sat on the edge of her bed. Caroline closed the door and sat on the other bed, knee to knee with Fannie. As they unwrapped their plastic dinnerware, Fannie began her series of questions.

"Is there a big lobby downstairs?"

"It's fairly big," Caroline said as she ate. "Most of the right half is restaurant. It's closed now, so I gather that's why we're eating out of Styrofoam boxes."

"Are they going to let me go see any of it?"

"I can ask, Fannie. Probably not."

"Why did it take so long for them to get dinner up to us?"

"Well, Parker had the agents check everything. And they've been asking to see everyone's ID."

Fannie laughed knowingly at Parker's mistake. "Amish people don't carry IDs."

"That's why it's taking so long."

"I recognized the maid with pillows," Fannie said.

"Who?"

"When I first came up. The maid at the end of the hall was Wanda Mast. She's Abel's sister-in-law. And her supervisor is Diener Miller."

"That's a deacon?"

"Yes. A diener is a deacon. A servant of the church. Ben Miller is a deacon in Abel's church."

"Then you may know some of the other people who work here," Caroline said. "Everyone is Amish."

Fannie nodded, forked loose a bite of broasted chicken, and smiled as if there was nothing that concerned her. "This is what most tourists think Amish 'home cooking' is like."

Caroline stirred her beans. "You can get the same meal in any restaurant in Holmes County."

"It's not really like home cooking at all, is it?" Fannie said, striving for sincerity in tone, troubled by her thoughts. "Too many additives for my taste. You know, chemicals." Was that chatty enough? Fannie wondered. Is this what will draw Caroline out?

"Like what, Fannie?"

"Oh, you know. Sugar, soy, preservatives. Chemicals. They're in all the baked goods they sell to the tourists. You ought to read the label of ingredients sometime."

"But it tastes good," Caroline said agreeably. "Most people think it's authentic."

"I suppose so. Are they going to let me go down to the restaurant at all?" Was that a reasonable question to have asked? Fannie wondered. Was she raising too many alarms with all of her questions?

Caroline set her box aside and stood

between the beds. "I can only ask, Fannie. Right now, they're pretty nervous about security. Maybe you could just give it a few days. Let everyone settle in, here."

"I suppose I can," Fannie said. *Three days until they move me to Cleveland. Three days to act. Fewer to test Caroline.*

As Fannie ate more of her dinner, Caroline took her box to the corner wastebasket, where she discarded the box and most of her food. Then she opened the bedroom door. An Amish maid was taking the dinner cart away. Her supervisor stood at her side.

Caroline asked, "Wanda Mast?"

Fannie heard the maid answer. "Yes, do I know you?"

Before Caroline could respond, Fannie stepped to the bedroom door and introduced the two women to each other. Then Fannie spoke Dietsch to Wanda, and she spoke with Wanda at considerable length. Eventually, the Amish supervisor, Ben Miller, responded to Fannie, too.

As the three talked, Fannie noted that the FBI agents were waiting to the side. Happily Fannie realized that they were uninterested in listening to a language they could not understand. They also seemed reluctant to interrupt. Fannie was able to explain herself thoroughly to Wanda Mast and Ben Miller.

When Agent Parker appeared again at the suite's door, he said, "Are we done here, folks? I need to move this along."

Fannie said a few parting words, and Wanda and Ben wheeled their cart away. Parker closed the suite's door, and Fannie returned to her bedroom with Caroline. Fannie sat again on the edge of her bed, with her dinner box in her lap. As Fannie finished her dinner, Caroline sat and asked, "What were you talking about with Wanda?"

"Oh, I just asked her to bring me some clothes," Fannie said, thinking, How much Dietsch does Caroline understand?

"Does she know your size and style?" Caroline asked. "For the clothes?"

"I told her my size. I can wear her style, I guess. For a while."

Fannie set her dinner box aside. "What am I supposed to do after the trial? If there ever is a trial." What honesty will Caroline give me now?

"I suppose you could go into the witness protection program."

"Wouldn't people still be able to find me?"

"Not really. They change your name in witness protection. They give you a new identity."

"I'd rather just stay me."

"If you did that, Fannie, where would you go?"

"There are Amish settlements all across America now," Fannie said. "Wherever I go, I'll be safe. And I'll want to live Amish. After the trial, that is."

"Did Sheriff Robertson explain any of this to you in his letter, Fannie?"

Caroline's forthrightness is honorable, Fannie thought. "He said I would be safe among my people." Could she trust her with more? She turned her attention to her dinner, took another bite of chicken, and looked back to Caroline.

Smiling enigmatically, Caroline said, "Fannie, I'd bet any amount of money that the sheriff told you not to trust the FBI very much. I know Robertson, Fannie, and I'd bet that he gave you options. That he's letting you make decisions, now, for yourself. That's just how he is."

Fannie returned Caroline's smile, thinking, She understands. It is unspoken, but Caroline understands. If so, has she guessed my intentions? Will she keep it to herself?

"I like him," Fannie said aloud. "Sheriff Robertson. I like it that he told me the truth."

"I do, too, Fannie," Caroline said. "But you should understand, if the sheriff hasn't already told you, that they might never capture Teresa Molina."

"I know," Fannie said, thinking, There is Caroline's honesty on display.

In the pocket of her apron, Fannie's cell phone buzzed. She drew it from her apron pocket and checked the display. "This is my friend," she said to Caroline. "I need to take this call."

Leaving her dinner unfinished, Fannie entered the bathroom and closed the door to whisper to Jodie Tapp.

Jodie was crying when Fannie answered her call. "Oh Fannie! I can't go to jail. I just can't do it. I'll die in jail."

"Wait, Jodie. Slow down. Tell me what's wrong."

"Teresa Molina called me back. She's really going to tell them that I was in her drug gang. And I don't have the money. Not five thousand dollars, I don't. Fannie, I'd just die in jail."

"Jodie, I'm sorry. I really can't get away right now."

"Then let me come to you. I've got until noon on Saturday. And I know you have to be close by."

"Where are you?"

"I'm at a little motel in Akron. I can get

300

to you, Fannie. Sometime tomorrow."

"You need to get far away, Jodie. You need to run away."

"I can't, Fannie. They said they would hurt my mother."

"You talked to them again?"

"Yes, Fannie! Don't you understand? Teresa Molina is going to kill my mother!"

"I have to think."

"I'm just going to kill myself. I'm going to jump off a building or something."

"You can't do that, Jodie."

"Why not? People die every day, jumping off buildings."

"Let me think, Jodie. Let me think about this."

"What if the police find me? I'd have to tell them about you, Fannie."

"Tell them what?"

"That you carried a suitcase for Teresa Molina."

"They already know that, Jodie."

"I'm sorry. I don't know what I'm saying. I've lost my mind or something. Please, Fannie. You've got to help me. If I don't have their five thousand dollars by noon on Saturday, they'll kill my mother. Teresa Molina told me that."

"But why? Why would they kill your mother?"

"These are really bad people, Fannie. You just don't get it. Do you know the girl who was killed in a buggy accident yesterday in Indiana?"

"No. I don't know anything about that."

"They ran her over, Fannie! Don't you get it? They killed her. They'll kill me."

"Why would they kill a girl in Indiana?"

"Oh Fannie. You're so naive. I knew her in Pinecraft. Just like I knew you. And they killed her just because she knew too much. They're cleaning up loose ends, and I'm next. Then they'll come for you, too."

"They'll never find me, Jodie."

"Well, they're gonna find me, Fannie. If you can't help me, they're going to find me, and they're going to kill me and my mother."

"I need to think, Jodie. I need to figure out how I can get the money to you."

"I can come to you. Really, Fannie, I can drive all night if I have to."

"OK, let me ask Reuben."

"Thank you, Fannie! You're saving my life."

"It will take some time, Jodie. Reuben doesn't carry that kind of cash. He'll have to talk to the bishop to get such a large sum."

"OK, Fannie. I can wait. I can wait until

Saturday morning. Then I've got to get back here to Akron. To give them their money."

"Just give us some time, Jodie. There are a few things I have to do first."

"Are you close by? Will I be able to get to you in time?"

"Yes. I'm only a little bit northeast of Akron. We've got time. Just let me think about this."

"Will you call me?"

"Yes. But I have to make some arrangements."

"To get the money?"

"Yes, Jodie. That, and a little bit more."

27

Friday, August 19
5:15 A.M.

It was the clang of a ricochet that broke Stan Armbruster out of his early-morning dream. It was the resonant clang of a bullet striking a bell. A note that couldn't be unrung. The arresting transfixation of an alarm.

The content of Armbruster's dream vaporized as soon as he opened his eyes. But the ringing tone of the ricochet lingered in his consciousness like a threat.

In his bathroom, Armbruster splashed cold water on his face, trying to refocus the dream. In his kitchen, he put up a pot of coffee, endeavoring to understand the warning. In his shower, he relinquished his efforts to recall the dream and struggled instead to scrub the bell's insistent note from his mind. In this he failed. So as he dressed, he again made the effort to recall his dream. But it was gone. He could decipher only that it had been a nightmare that had woken him with the startling awareness of peril.

Now he knew that something yesterday should have alarmed him. He understood this because of the bell of his dream. Something at the Mast farm? Something on the drive home with Lance and the professor? Perhaps something at the St. James.

But Armbruster could neither reach it nor grasp it. It had been only a resonance lodged in a vanishing dreamscape. It had been an audible warning without the clarity of specificity. An echo from memories he could not identify.

Armbruster finished his coffee and clipped his holster to his belt. He went out into the steamy August morning, locked his trailer home's door, and drove down the farmer's lane. It was a long gravel drive, potted with muddy holes. He rolled down the windows and heard the tires of his red Corolla splashing murky water to the sides as he advanced.

The hiss of the splashing called to Armbruster's mind the gravel drive at the Helmuth farm. That drive had been puddled, too. He remembered the rain that had fallen the morning when he had discovered Dent's body. That had been only two days ago — the day he had called in his location in the rain, sitting in a mud puddle beside his Corolla. *"The day,"* Armbruster muttered. The day that his new career as a Holmes County detective had skipped abruptly and irrevocably sideways. The day that his hopes of impressing Pat Lance had been dashed.

Armbruster stopped at the edge of the blacktop in the dark, and he anxiously considered the turn onto the county road toward Holmesville. His fingers clenched the steering wheel while his thumbs drummed against it. What had he overlooked yesterday? Why did it seem so important? Did he still have a chance with Lance?

Nervous with vague unease, Armbruster glanced left, then right. He studied the floodlight in his rearview mirror. His trailer sat two hundred yards behind him, at the end of the farmer's lane. It was parked in a glade beside the beagle run. Beside the hutches where he kept the farmer's rabbit dogs.

"Beagles," Armbruster groaned. He cranked his steering wheel and backed around on the lane. He drove slowly back toward his home. He had forgotten to tend to the dogs, and the urgent concerns of his dream were dissipated by the needful practicality of feeding the beagles.

Fannie Helmuth awoke in her hotel bed and lay for a moment with her eyes closed, thinking about last night's phone call from Jodie. Still troubled by the call, Fannie opened her eyes slowly, rolled onto her side, and saw that Caroline's bed was empty beside her. Slowly, Fannie became aware of water running in the shower, behind the closed door to the bathroom.

Had Caroline guessed last night who had called? Certainly she had been curious to know who it was. Was it a good sign that Caroline had not asked about the call? Perhaps. It did reveal her restraint. Did it also reveal her trustworthiness?

Jodie had always been so certain that nobody could ever know that they talked to each other on their phones. Jodie had been on the run, too — in hiding, just as she and Howie had been — and Jodie had always cautioned her not to tell anyone. Not to tell even Howie. They could talk, Jodie had said, but they could never tell. They could never meet. Jodie had said this from the very beginning, when Fannie had called her in April, on the new phone that she and Howie had bought at the Walmart in Memphis.

"Fannie," Jodie had cautioned her, "we can never try to see each other."

Quickly though, Howie had guessed who it was that Fannie was calling. And who it was that was calling Fannie back. Howie had known almost from the start that it was Jodie. He had known about the calls, and he had advised her not to continue. He had always suspected that Jodie was just as much an enemy as Teresa Molina was.

Still, hadn't Jodie said herself that Fannie should never tell her where she was? And Jodie in turn would never tell Fannie where she was. Their safety depended on this. That's what Jodie had always told her when they had started calling each other. It was to be a sign of trust that Jodie would never ask where she and Howie were.

And she hadn't asked. Jodie hadn't wanted to know. Through all of their weeks in hiding, Jodie had never wanted to know where they were. Until last night.

Last night, that had changed for each of them. Jodie knew that Howie had been murdered. And Fannie knew that Teresa Molina was threatening the life of Jodie's mother. Certainly these things changed everything. For Jodie and for Fannie. Now Jodie did want to see her. She had said that she urgently needed Fannie's help. Beyond the five thousand dollars, she was asking for the very thing she had promised she would never ask. She was asking, she had said, because of Teresa Molina's threat.

The bathroom door opened, and light and steam emptied into the bedroom. Caroline came out wrapped in a white bath towel. With a hand towel, she was drying her long auburn hair.

Fannie sat up in bed and said, "You were in Sarasota?"

Caroline spun the length of her auburn hair between the ends of her hand towel and answered, "Yes. We were there in April."

"Were you there because of me?"

"Partly," Caroline said. "We were there on vacation, and Bruce Robertson asked us to interview Jodie Tapp. Ruth Zook had been murdered. He knew Ruth had worked at the same restaurant where you and Jodie did. In Pinecraft."

"That's where I met her," Fannie whispered.

"Fannie," Caroline said, "how did you know I was in Sarasota? I never told you that."

"I have a friend who calls me," Fannie said. "Are you done in the shower?"

Caroline sat on the bed to face Fannie. She held her hand towel idle in her lap. "Is this the same person who called you last night? The one who called yesterday at the Mast farm?"

"Yes."

"Because, well, you went into the bathroom to talk last night. You didn't want me to listen."

Fannie pulled her covers off and stood up beside her bed. She walked into the bathroom, saying, "It was just a friend."

In room 7, on the third floor of the Hotel St. James in Millersburg, Bruce Robertson watched the red numerals of the digital alarm clock blink from 5:44 to 5:45. He was seated in a corner chair with the lights off. He had spent the night in the room, sometimes sitting in the dark, sometimes pacing with his thoughts. He had tried to rest at first, but he had found that impossible. Long after Pat Lance had closed her door and fallen silent in room 6 next door, Robertson had settled into the corner chair to watch the clock and to think.

The shades of the sheriff's Jackson Street window were tightly drawn. At no time had he turned on the lights in his room. When Lance and the professor had registered for their rooms, Robertson had already secured the key card for room 7 without putting it on record that he had taken the room for the night. In this he had secured the hotel management's cooperation. No calls would be put through to his room's phone. No deliveries would be made. None of the maids would knock on his door. He would leave and reenter, if he needed to, through the door to Lance's room, number 6.

Robertson rose in the dark and entered his bathroom by the dim glow from a nightlight he had installed near the floor. He ran cold water onto a washcloth and rubbed stiffness from his face. He rewetted the washcloth and brushed it several times back and forth over his bristly gray hair. He fingered the whiskers on his chin and took out his razor to shave. When he had finished, he came out and dressed without turning on the lights.

Lance would be waking, he thought. She's probably grumbling about the Amish clothes she'll have to wear today.

The professor will be up soon. If he managed to get any sleep. He had brought a small bag from home, but he, too, faced a day in Amish attire.

Once he had dressed, Robertson put his wallet in his hip pocket and swiped his keys from the dresser. The keys slipped from his grasp, and they clinked against each other when they landed on the carpet. He bent over to pick them up, and he gave them a shake. Again, they clinked against each other. They made a tiny cluster of notes, hanging from their ring on his index finger. He shook them again, and he found his thoughts roaming anxiously over the evidence that he had.

It wasn't much. There was the yellow car. And the red backpack.

28

Caroline finished dressing while Fannie was still in the shower. She had only the clothes she had been wearing the day before, so when she emerged from the bedroom, she appeared to be a traditional Mennonite woman in a turquoise dress and a white lace head covering. She closed the bedroom door and turned to the two agents seated around the middle room's coffee table. She was about to explain her intentions to go shopping for clothes and toiletries when there was a knock at the door to the suite. One of the two agents rose and went to the door, and when he opened it, there stood Wanda Mast with a male supervisor. Wanda held a stack of folded women's clothing, and she started to enter the suite. As she did so, the second of the two agents rose at the coffee table and came forward asking,

"What is that, please?"

"Clean clothes for Fannie Helmuth," Wanda said, stopping in the doorway. "She requested clean clothes yesterday."

"I'll need to see them," the agent said, and he took the clothes from Wanda.

Wanda attempted to enter farther into the suite with her supervisor close behind, but the first of the two agents remained at the door to bar their access. "Please wait there," he said, and he planted himself in front of the doorway.

Wanda spoke up as the second agent spread the Amish clothes across the surface of the kitchen's dining table. "It's just clothes. Fannie requested clean clothes."

On the dining table, the agent had spread out a long forest-green Amish dress that was identical in style to the blue one that Wanda was wearing. Beside it, there was a blue dress in the same shade and fabric as Wanda's. There was also a plain white day apron that matched Wanda's. There were undergarments and a pair of black hose. Finally, there was a pair of black cotton socks in a woman's size.

The agent refolded the clothes and carried the stack back to the doorway. He handed them to Wanda and said, "They're just like yours."

"They are Amish clothes," Wanda said. "Forest green is a popular color right now, and so is this blue. But our styles are all meant to be the same."

Caroline came forward to the doorway and took the clothes from Wanda. "Fannie's in the shower," she said. "I'll lay these out on her bed."

"I should have some more for her, tomorrow," Wanda said. "Today I just grabbed what was in my closet."

Caroline opened the bedroom door, carried the clothes inside, and came back out to find Wanda and her supervisor, who were still standing at the suite's door. "Fannie's in the shower," Caroline said again, and she gently closed the bedroom door. "I'll walk down with you, Wanda. I was just going out shopping."

As the two women turned down the hall, the Amish supervisor lingered at the suite's door to ask, "When may we make up the room?"

The agent who had remained at the door said, "Our two partners are down at breakfast, so our second bedroom is empty right now."

"Now, then," the supervisor confirmed. "I'll get a team and bring them up."

"They'll have to be checked," the agent

said. "And we'll have to search their cart."

"Of course," the supervisor replied as he turned to follow Wanda and Caroline down the hall. "You may search anything you like."

Caroline rode down in the service elevator with Wanda Mast and her supervisor. On the way, the elevator made a stop on the second floor, and two maids in forest-green dresses pushed their service cart onto the elevator to ride down. When the elevator reached the lower vestibule, the two maids pushed their cart off and turned for the laundry. Another team of maids was waiting in the vestibule to take the elevator back up. They, too, were in plain forest-green dresses with white aprons, soft black shoes, and white organdy Kapps.

Caroline, Wanda, and the supervisor stepped off the elevator, and the new team of maids rolled their cart onto the elevator. As the elevator doors closed in the vestibule, Caroline eyed Wanda suspiciously and asked, "Is forest green the color of the day, Wanda? Or did everybody just choose that color on their own?"

Wanda fingered the sleeve of her blue dress and said, "Forest green seems to be a popular color today, Mrs. Branden. I just happened to choose blue."

From the laundry room beside the elevator doors, another pair of maids in forest-green dresses emerged. One of them pushed the elevator button, and they both stood silently in front of the elevator doors to wait.

Caroline studied the dresses in front of her. Not only were they the same in color, they were also the same in style. The dresses were identical in the way they were hemmed and pleated. They were identical in the gathering at the shoulders, and in the length of the sleeves. The aprons were also identical in the front waist panel, the bodice, and the wrap over the shoulders. Caroline thought, remembered, understood, and smiled. The clothes that had been delivered to Fannie would be the same, she realized.

"I was going out shopping," Caroline said circumspectly to Wanda. "How long do you think I should take?"

Wanda returned Caroline's smile. "I should think a couple of hours would suffice," she answered.

The elevator doors opened. The two maids who had called the elevator stepped inside, and one of them held the doors open for Wanda and her supervisor.

Once the four Amish people were inside the elevator, Wanda said to Caroline as the doors closed, "It was nice meeting you, Mrs. Branden. Give our regards to the sheriff."

With the cart parked in the hall outside Fannie's suite 416, one of three maids in forest-green dresses knocked on the suite's door. She called out, "Room Service," and stepped back from the door, to stand with her partners.

The eyehole in the door darkened momentarily, and then an agent of the FBI's maintenance team opened the suite's door. He held an electronic wand. He stepped into the hall and closed the door behind him. Holding up his wand, he said, "I need to wand each of you, so please stand a little bit more apart. I will not touch you with the wand, but I do need to pass it over the entire length of you, front, back, and each side."

The maids stood still while they were wanded, and then the agent said, "Please step back while I check your cart."

The three women stepped to the side, and the agent sorted through the clean towels and linens. Next he opened several of the small bottles of shampoo and mouth wash to smell each of them. When he had finished his inspection, he said, "One moment," and he knocked on the suite's door.

Again the eyehole in the door darkened, and a man on the inside asked, "How many are there?"

"Three," he was answered. "They're cleared."

The suite's door opened, and the second of the two agents held the door to admit the maids. Two of the three maids carried stacks of clean towels, and as they entered, the agent stepped aside and said, "Please start in the bedroom on the right."

The two maids with towels turned right and started their work in the bathroom of the bedroom. The third maid went to the kitchen at the back of the suite's center room, and there she began to stack and wash dishes.

From the right bedroom, one maid carried out a bundle of wet towels and washcloths. She went to her cart in the hallway, dumped the wet towels in the cart's basket, and took up a stack of clean sheets and pillowcases. These she carried into the bedroom on the right.

When the maid in the kitchen had finished some of the dishes, she came forward to the bedroom on the right, to take a bundle of dirty sheets from one of the maids there. These she carried out to the basket on the cart. When she came back in, she carried bottles of shampoo and conditioner, plus a box of tissues. She took these into the bedroom on the right, and as she did so, one of the two maids who had started in the bedroom came out to work in the kitchen, to finish washing dishes.

Once this much of the work was finished, the kitchen maid stepped out into the hallway, where she remained. Spaced by an interval of about a minute, the two maids from the bedroom on the right emerged singly from the bedroom. The first of them walked back to the kitchen to dry dishes, and the other went out to the cart. When they reentered the suite, one maid carried towels and washcloths, and the other maid carried a stack of folded sheets and pillowcases. They entered the bedroom on the left.

After a while, a maid in a forest-green dress stepped out of the bedroom on the left carrying a tall bundle of sheets and pillowcases. She took them out to the cart and stepped aside. The maid who remained in the bedroom on the left turned on the television there, switched to a cartoon channel, and turned up the volume on a Tweety Bird cartoon. The sound played out into the suite's middle room.

Next, the maid in the kitchen finished drying the dishes and putting them up in the cabinets. She came forward from the kitchen and entered Fannie's bedroom on the left side of the suite. From there, a maid in a forest-green dress emerged with two small plastic liners from the wastebaskets in the bedroom. She took them out to her cart to toss them into a larger trash bag stretched across the push handles of the cart. There she waited alone for her partners to finish in the bedroom on the left.

When the last two maids came out to the center room, one of them said to the agents, "We have finished." She said this as she closed the door to Fannie's bedroom.

One of the two agents seated at the coffee table rose and carried a coffee cup into the kitchen. As he did so, a maid asked, "Can I wash that for you?"

The agent shook his head and said, "Thanks, but no."

The sound of the TV was plainly audible through the closed door of Fannie's bedroom. Tweety Bird was chirping in high form about a puddy tat, and thumping sounds accompanied the bird's antics.

The second agent rose from the sofa at the coffee table and asked the maids, "Is she watching TV?"

One of the maids shrugged. "We had no

idea she liked the Tweety so much."

Then the three maids in forest-green dresses said good-bye, and they wheeled their cart toward the service elevator.

29

Friday, August 19
9:30 A.M.

After breakfast at the Hotel Millersburg, across the street from the St. James, Professor Branden and Pat Lance walked on Jackson Street with the sheriff, heading east to the bank at the corner. Stan Armbruster and Captain Newell trailed several long yards behind them as a security detail.

As they approached the bank, people on the street took note of them. Most people recognized the big sheriff. Some recognized Bobby Newell. The attention was drawn by the fact that the lawmen were escorting an Amish couple.

An Amish man passed by, and he appeared to try to listen to the conversation between Lance and Robertson. Looking puzzled, he studied the professor's garb, and then he stopped in front of a window display and lingered there.

At the corner bank, Lance entered with Branden and Robertson. She used Fannie Helmuth's library card and one hundred dollars in cash to open a checking account in Fannie's name. Armbruster and Newell waited on the sidewalk in front of the bank, and when Lance and the professor came out, they made a show of passing the new checkbook around to admire it. The Amish man who had listened earlier on the sidewalk drew closer.

Two blocks west of the bank, Lance and Branden entered a pharmacy on Jackson Street with the sheriff, and Lance shopped the aisles for toiletries. These she took to the pharmacist's station at the rear of the store, and as she laid her items out on the sales counter, she presented Fannie Helmuth's checkbook. When asked for an ID, Lance answered that of course she had no photo ID, but she did have a library card. The pharmacist accepted the library credential, but she said to Lance, "There's no name on your checks."

Lance turned to Robertson behind her, and Robertson stepped forward to say to the pharmacist, "It's a new account. We just opened it at the bank down the street."

The pharmacist nodded her confirmation, and Lance paid with a check, signing it as

Fannie Helmuth.

Outside again on the sidewalk, Lance turned to Robertson. "Are you sure about writing these checks, Sheriff?"

Robertson smiled. "The check is good, Pat. The hundred dollars covers it, so you won't bounce a check."

"I mean about the forged *signature*," Lance answered.

Robertson acknowledged the concern, and he turned back into the pharmacy. He needed the signature to pass in front of the pharmacist's eyes, but he did not need a forged check issue tailing him into court, despite the fact that the bank would surely honor the check. So, at the pharmacist's counter, he handed across cash and asked for the check to be returned. The pharmacist drew the check out of the cash drawer and studied the check closely. "Is there a problem?" she asked.

Robertson took the check from her hand and said, "I don't want her to overdraw her account. She hasn't been keeping that checkbook for very long. Amish, right?"

Next, the group rounded the corner at the pharmacy and entered the alley parking lot behind the Hotel St. James. Lance and the professor got into the backseat of the Crown Vic, and Bobby Newell sat behind the wheel. Robertson stood beside the driver's window and said, "Walmart, Bobby. I'll ride with Stan."

At the Walmart south of town, Robertson pried himself out of the Corolla and came forward to the Crown Vic. There he took Lance's elbow chivalrously, as if to help her navigate the potted blacktop parking lot. Lance accepted the gesture for half of the distance and then pulled her arm loose, saying, "Really, Sheriff. Please."

As they entered the Walmart, Lance walked beside the professor. Captain Newell led the way inside. Robertson and Armbruster followed them into the cavernous store.

Using a cart, Lance and the professor walked the aisles in their Amish clothes, and they selected various items, shopping for light groceries. The professor picked out snack foods and sodas, and Lance carted some fruit. As they headed for the lines at the cash registers, Lance also took a box of tissues for the hotel room.

At the cash register, while Robertson and Armbruster watched, Lance paid with a check from Fannie's checkbook. As she did this, she frowned a measure of consternation at the sheriff. Robertson noticed, and he came forward with his wallet. The cashier was studying Lance's Fannie Helmuth check when Robertson reached out for it and handed over cash instead. As the cashier took the money, Robertson said, "Ms. Helmuth is a guest of the county," and the cashier gave a perfunctory nod as she muttered, "Cash or check. Suit yourselves."

Outside in the Walmart parking lot, Robertson drew his crew around him and said, "Next, the convenience store across the street. Lance, I want you to show Fannie's library card and ask if you can rent a DVD."

At the cars, the groceries were loaded into the trunk of Armbruster's Corolla. Robertson got into the Crown Vic on the passenger's side, and again Bobby Newell drove. Armbruster followed them out of the parking lot, and the rest of the morning passed for him pretty much in this same fashion. Follow the Crown Vic. Trail behind five paces at the stops. Drive behind them to the BMV. Wait outside while Lance inquires about a learner's permit. She wouldn't actually apply for one, Armbruster knew. She'd just inquire and take away literature.

After the BMV, Bobby Newell made a stop at a cell phone company. Armbruster went inside with the others. Acting as

Fannie Helmuth, Pat Lance inquired about getting a phone. She did not buy one, but she did leave with several brochures about the various plans.

The morning drifted along slowly for Armbruster. He felt like he was a chauffeur with no passenger, assigned to drive idly from place to place while shadowing a mirage, all of it to establish the identity of the sheriff's new "guest of the county." By the end of the day, nearly everyone in Holmes County would have concluded that Fannie Helmuth had come home. Also, it would appear to everyone who became aware of her that she intended to stay for more than just a day.

After lunch at the roadside restaurant in Charm, they headed for the more distant town of Baltic on the southern border of the county. Armbruster followed the sheriff's Crown Vic southeast on SR 557 to Ohio 93, and then south on 93 into Baltic. There Robertson had Bobby Newell stop at a real estate office beside the road, in the north end of town. The sheriff went inside with Lance and the professor, and Armbruster and Newell waited beside their parked cars.

When the three emerged from the office, a woman late in her years followed them out and turned back to lock the door.

Robertson directed Captain Newell to ride with Armbruster, and he let the real estate agent sit in the passenger's seat of his Crown Vic. Lance and Branden again got into the back of the Crown Vic as an Amish couple.

Robertson opened the driver's door of the Crown Vic and realized that Newell still had the keys. Across the roof of the car, he asked Newell for the keys, and Newell tossed them over to the sheriff. Robertson caught the keys, and they clinked in his hand. Startled, Robertson held the keys in the light and stared incredulously at them. He gave them a shake, and he tipped his head. He glanced over to Captain Newell, and Newell asked, "What, Sheriff?"

Robertson stood beside his sedan and thought about the keys. He turned his thoughts into an interior awareness, and a smile drifted across his face.

It took an hour and a half for Branden and Lance to show the Helmuth property to the real estate agent. As they did so, Robertson sat behind the wheel of his Crown Vic, distracted by his ruminations.

The real estate agent walked through each of the buildings, taking notes and snapping photographs. Standing between the barn and the main house, she marked the identities of the buildings on a Google Earth map of the property, and once she was done, she went back into the kitchen of the main house to spread surveyor's documents on the kitchen counter. She read through the papers and maps, and she appeared to be satisfied with what she had learned. As she left through the front door, however, she reminded Lance that she would need the deed holder, Fannie's brother Jonas in Kentucky, to send an affidavit that he did in fact wish to sell his property. A contract would be sent to him for his signature. When the real estate agent stepped onto the front porch, she asked Robertson to drive her back to Baltic.

Robertson, who was then standing with a troubled smile beside his sedan, replied, "Of course," and as the real estate agent took the passenger's seat, the sheriff gathered his team at the back of the Crown Vic. There Robertson opened his trunk and took out the red backpack that Armbruster had found beside the yellow VW two days earlier.

"I'll take her back to Baltic," Robertson said to the four. "It'll take half an hour. Then I want to meet you all at the Dent farm. Mike and Stan know the place, Bobby. While I'm down in Baltic, I want you to ask if this backpack does really belong to Howie Dent. His mother will know."

Lance spoke up. "She'll also know that I'm not Fannie Helmuth."

"Right," Robertson said. "So you just stay in the car. We've finished our travels today, anyway."

The sheriff closed the lid of his trunk. "Mike, I want you to show Stan and Bobby something at the Dents' house. They weren't there when you and I saw it."

Branden hesitated. "OK, Bruce, but what?"

"The nail," Robertson said as he stepped around to the driver's door. "The nail behind that hutch on their back porch. The nail where they kept their spare keys to the yellow VW."

At the Dent farm, it was Susan Dent who answered the door. She recognized Professor Branden. She appeared weary with grief, but she managed with effort to hold the screen door open for him, saying, "I didn't know you were Amish, Professor."

"Just today, Mrs. Dent," Branden said. He stepped inside. "You know Detective Stan Armbruster, and this is Captain Bobby Newell."

"Please come in," Susan said forlornly. "Is

it about my Howie?"

"It is, Mrs. Dent," Bobby Newell said. "And I'm sorry for your loss."

"Please, just Susan," Mrs. Dent said.

Branden asked, "Susan, is your husband home?"

Susan Dent appeared not to have understood the meaning of Branden's simple question. Her leaden feet stumbled along a path into the living room, where she turned and said, "Of course you're right to blame him, Professor. I begged him to let me call the sheriff."

Branden followed her into the living room. "Maybe we should talk with Richard," he said. "Really, Susan, maybe you should have something to drink."

"Didn't I tell you, Professor? I'm not talking to him today."

"OK," Branden said, "but can you tell us where he is?"

"Chopping wood," came Susan's vacant reply. "He's just been chopping wood all day."

Newell followed Branden into the living room and said, "I'm sure it's hard, Mrs. Dent. And again, I'm sorry."

Susan Dent brushed a tattered hankie across the surface of a dusty end table. She turned in place and selected her husband's brown recliner. She sat on the edge of its seat. While staring at the carpet, she said to the room, "Oh no. He wouldn't listen to me."

Branden mouthed "water" to Stan Armbruster, and Armbruster followed the hallway back into the kitchen. He returned with a glass of tap water, and he set it on the end table that Susan Dent had just dusted with her hankie. She looked at the glass of water and barked a strangled laugh. "I saw my Howie in the letters. Richard wouldn't listen."

Tears began to course her cheeks. "I begged him to call. That morning when we saw that the VW was gone? And I tried for weeks to tell him about the newspaper's letters."

With her wrinkled and tattered hankie, Susan dried her eyes. Branden pulled his handkerchief from the side pocket of his denim pants, and he held it out for her. "This one is clean, Susan. Please take it."

Susan dropped the soiled hankie from her fingers and left it lying at her feet. She took the professor's handkerchief and glared an accusation at him. "I don't see how he can blame me!" she shrieked. "I wish he'd chop that ax right through his foot!"

Again Susan wept, this time with the

professor's handkerchief to her eyes. Branden knelt beside her and held her shoulders to draw her close. She leaned toward him as if starved for human touch, and Branden held her while she sobbed.

Bobby Newell and Stan Armbruster stood nearby and waited for her anguish to pass. Eventually she stopped crying. She dried her eyes and blew her nose. She slipped the professor's handkerchief into the pocket of her dress. When she eased herself away from Branden, she appeared to have gained enough clarity to be both relieved and embarrassed. She stood and asked Captain Newell, "Why have you come? Do you know who killed my Howie?"

"No, Mrs. Dent," Newell said. "We don't know yet. But the sheriff wants us to look at something. Is that all right with you?"

Susan seemed to slip back into puzzlement. Her eyes seemed to drift along an invisible plane of nonreality. "Howie hasn't been home for weeks. I don't know where he is."

"It's the back porch," Branden said. "Where you kept the keys behind the hutch."

"OK," Susan said. "It's just beyond the kitchen. We keep spare keys there for Howie."

"I remember," Branden said. "May we?"

"What?" Susan asked. "May you what?"

Branden said, "We would like to have a look behind your hutch, Susan."

"Of course," Susan chimed. "Can I get you boys something to drink?"

Branden lifted the glass of water that Armbruster had brought out of the kitchen. "Here, Susan," he said. "We've already had some water."

Susan took the glass and sank back into the recliner. A question appeared in her eyes. She looked up at Branden and asked, "Do you have news of my Howie?"

On the back porch, Branden showed Armbruster and Newell where the nail was positioned behind the hutch. Newell came forward and felt behind the hutch, and then Armbruster did the same. Branden said, "That's the nail where they kept the VW's spare keys."

Saying this startled the professor. His eyes tracked several thoughts at once. He brushed his fingers through his hair. Astonished by new insight, he said, "It's the keys. It has always been the keys."

Armbruster stepped forward again to feel the nail. After he had done so, he took hold of the corner of the tall hutch and pulled it

335

out from the wall. There he saw the nail, and a carillon of bells pealed away in his mind. His thoughts raced back through the questions he had asked Fannie Helmuth just yesterday. When he saw there what the professor was talking about, he practically jumped in place. "It's the backpack," he said, and he turned back immediately to dash into the living room and out through the front door.

When Armbruster returned, he had the red backpack that Robertson had given them at the Helmuth farm. It was the one Armbruster had found in the rain beside the yellow VW. He took it into the living room, and as Branden and Newell watched, he knelt in front of the seated Mrs. Dent to show it to her. "Mrs. Dent?" he asked. "Is this Howie's backpack? We've always assumed that it was, but I need you to look at it."

Susan shook her head as if to deny herself any solace. She shook her head as if she deserved no sympathy for her pain. But she did look at the backpack, and then she took it into her hands. "No," she said dismissively, handing the backpack to Armbruster. "He has his FFA badge pinned to the flap."

Armbruster handed it gently back to her,

but he retained his hold on the front flap. "Here in the flap, Mrs. Dent," he said. "Aren't these the holes that his badge would have made?"

Susan fingered the tattered holes where long ago her son had pinned his Future Farmers of America badge, and a sheen of tears appeared in her eyes. She turned the backpack over, and she examined the straps. Small holes were evident there, too. "Howie had other pins on these straps," she said, and she clasped the backpack violently to her breast. "Oh Howie!" she shrieked, and she began to rock on her seat.

Armbruster took her hands away from the straps, and he held them. He waited for her to realize that he was talking to her. He waited for her to stop rocking. When she looked back into his eyes, he asked, "Are you certain, Mrs. Dent? Are you certain that this is Howie's backpack?"

"He loved this bag," Susan sobbed. "He carried everything in here."

Armbruster stood and motioned for Branden and Newell to take charge of Mrs. Dent. Hurrying toward the front door, he said, "I need to make a call." He dashed out onto the front porch and found Robertson coming up the porch steps. Waving his hands with excitement, Armbruster blurted,

"It's the bus ticket, Sheriff!"

Robertson smiled knowingly. "And the backpack, Stan."

As the sheriff came up to the top of the porch steps, Professor Branden emerged from the house and stood beside Armbruster. With a satisfied smile, he said to Robertson and Armbruster, "It's the keys. It's the backpack and the bus tickets, but it has always been the keys, too. We've known this all along. We just didn't realize it was important."

Mrs. Dent appeared at the front door, and she came out ahead of Bobby Newell. "What? What can you tell me about my Howie?"

Behind her, Newell stepped out onto the porch. "Howie would have left his backpack on the bus in Charlotte," he said. "We should have guessed that. He had only his phone. He never used any credit cards, because he left his wallet in his backpack, on the bus when they went in to breakfast. His keys and his wallet were left on the bus, in his backpack. That's why he needed the spare set of keys."

Susan Dent smiled as though lost in a haze. She turned back to Newell and said, "Oh, I told you. Howie keeps everything in that backpack."

Armbruster stepped forward. "Fannie told me that she had to buy their bus tickets to Memphis."

"Right," Robertson said. "It's all of that. Howie had to get keys to the VW from the nail behind the hutch because he left his own keys on the bus. In his backpack. On the day they fled to Memphis."

Branden said to Robertson, "You know who killed him, don't you."

Robertson smiled. Then he frowned. "I should have known when Stan told me that Fannie had to pay for their cab fare and for their bus tickets to Memphis. She told Stan that Howie didn't have his wallet when they ducked into that cab. That's what I figured out there in Baltic. I wondered about the keys. Why wouldn't Howie have had his own set of keys? Well, we should have seen it right from the start. He needed the spare set of keys when he came home for his VW, because he left his own keys on the bus to Sarasota last April. In his red backpack, along with his wallet. We thought we didn't have any evidence, but we always knew that he did not have his own set of keys. That was the evidence we ignored."

Behind them, near the front corner of the house, the deep thud of an ax biting into the trunk of a tree turned all eyes to Richard Dent. With the muscles of his face bunched in rage, he screeched, "I'll kill him!"

Dent's hands jumped against the ax handle. With the fury of a madman, he wrenched the ax head free of the wood. He advanced toward the porch with the ax raised over his head.

But to his left, Pat Lance shouted, "Stop!" and when Dent looked at her, she was walking a straight line toward him in her Amish clothes, with her revolver drawn from her thigh holster.

Dent turned toward her with the ax, and he hesitated as he looked both at the gun and at the Amish woman approaching him.

Again Lance shouted, "Stop!"

Richard raised his ax to full height and glared at Lance's revolver, seeming to contemplate what speed he could manage with his blade.

The sheriff shouted, "Stop, Dent!" and Richard turned away from Lance to see Robertson coming down off the porch, pointing his gun at him, too.

With a scream of agony, Dent slowly turned himself toward the front corner of his house. His eyes closed tightly, and his ax arched around swiftly to sink its blade deep into the corner frame of the house. When he fell to his knees, Dent growled to Robertson, "I'm going with you to kill him."

Robertson motioned for Lance to lower her weapon. He came up to Dent and took his elbow to help the man to his feet. As he put his gun back into his belt holster, the sheriff said to Dent, "You don't have to go anywhere, Richard. He's going to come to us."

Then Robertson smiled at Lance. "Pat, I want you to order a pizza."

30

Friday, August 19
3:35 P.M.

Sheriff Robertson climbed the back staircase
at the jail that afternoon with his mind racing over details. He pushed open the metal
door to the second-floor hallway, and as he
passed Bobby Newell's office at the south
end of the hall, he stuck his head in and
said to his captain, "Twenty minutes,
Bobby."

Newell answered, "Twenty minutes,
Sheriff," with his hand cupped over his
phone, and Robertson continued along the
hallway as if he were racing the clock.
Newell returned to his call.

At the north end of the second-floor hall,
Robertson entered the office of Chief
Deputy Dan Wilsher. Wilsher was standing
at his north-facing window, gazing down
onto Courthouse Square. There the August
sun was shining brightly on the Civil War

monument, which was starting to cast its afternoon shadow toward the sandstone courthouse. Robertson joined Wilsher at the window. For a brief moment, the sheriff contented himself with watching the comings and goings on the lawn below them. Then Robertson gave vent to harsh self-judgment. "I should have seen it sooner, Dan."

Wilsher turned from the window to face the sheriff. "You didn't know until yesterday that Fannie had to pay for their cab ride into Charlotte. And even then you couldn't have guessed that it was because Howie left his backpack on the bus."

"It was the keys, Dan," Robertson answered. "We had that all along. Almost right from the start. Dent didn't have his own set of keys, and that should have told us more." Robertson moved himself to a seat in front of Wilsher's desk. "Dan, if we had figured this out Wednesday, we might still have had a chance at him."

Wilsher shook his head. "He has no idea that we're looking for him, Bruce."

"Is anyone watching his house in Sugarcreek?"

"No," Wilsher said. "There's no point in alerting him beforehand. And I don't like the idea of our trying to take him down in public. If he's still in Holmes County, we'll have our best shot at him in the St. James."

Robertson rose and stuffed his fists into the side pockets of his sport coat. "I agree, Dan. So, for tonight, I want to be set up before seven o'clock."

"Do you still want us to move the couple out of room four? They're exposed on the third floor."

"Yes, Dan. Do that now. I want the only people up there to be our people. And then Earnest Troyer, if he really delivers that pizza."

"Are we going to wand him in the lobby?"

"We aren't going to put anyone in the lobby, Dan."

"Why not?"

"If we really want Troyer to come up after Fannie, he needs to think that we're not guarding her that closely anymore. And I want him isolated. So that no civilian mixes into the play. I want him trapped on the third floor, where he has nowhere to run."

"What makes you think he'll show up, Bruce? If he's smart, he's a thousand miles away by now."

Robertson shrugged. "I don't know what he'll do. We showed Lance and Branden all around today. That was always the plan. If he thinks that she really is Fannie, I don't believe he'll be able to resist coming up to her room for a look at her."

Wilsher paused to think. "All we'll be able to do is take him in for questioning."

"That's better than just letting him disappear, Dan. What I really want is cause for a search warrant for his house and for the bus company."

"And if he doesn't give us cause?" Wilsher asked.

Robertson wrenched a frown into place and left Wilsher's office without giving a reply.

Down on the first floor, the sheriff waited out the rest of the twenty minutes alone in his office, wondering if Fannie had understood his letter. He was confident that he had laid it all out for her. He was certain that he had told her enough. The question was whether or not she understood what he had told her. And whether or not she had the courage to act on it.

A moment passed, and Robertson's thoughts drifted to his childhood nightmare. He struggled to shake himself loose from the memory of the lion, and he wondered where he had found the kind of courage that he now asked of Fannie. He wondered if he had asked too much of her. He wondered again why he couldn't recognize the face of the lion tamer who taunted him in his dream to put his face close to the bars, the lion tamer who tried to press him forward to feel the whiskers of the lion on his cheek.

When it was time for the meeting, Bobby Newell was the first to arrive. He entered without speaking and stood by Robertson's west windows to watch the traffic on Clay Street. Dan Wilsher entered next. He took a seat in front of Robertson's desk. Stan Armbruster and Mike Branden arrived at the same time. Armbruster sat beside Wilsher, and Branden took his customary place in the low leather chair at the front corner of Robertson's desk. Pat Lance arrived last. Like the professor, she was dressed in English clothes. As she entered the office, she said, "I'm glad to have gotten out of that long Amish dress."

The professor turned toward her to make a reply, but Robertson started his meeting directly. "OK, Stan. What did you learn?"

Armbruster consulted notes in his spiral book. "Dick Bruder is one of the bus drivers. I called him when we first started looking for Fannie last April, and he remembered me today. He says that all of the lost-and-found items from the Sugarcreek-Sarasota Bus Company are sent back to Sugarcreek on the very next run. They are kept there in case anyone inquires about lost property. So that's Earnest Troyer, Sheriff, just like you suspected. He's in charge of the lost and found. And he delivers pizzas in the bus company's slow months."

"I thought so," Robertson said. "I interviewed him back in April. I'd bet anything that he delivers more than pizza. I'd bet a month's pay that he's been a part of this drug outfit all along. He took possession of the drugs from Teresa Molina, and he had a natural route to make deliveries when he went out on the weekends with his pizzas."

"I interviewed him, too," Armbruster said. "He's the one who gave me Bruder's phone number."

Robertson shook his head with disgust, and he turned to Lance. "Pat, are you willing to wear your Fannie Helmuth outfit tonight? I expect Earnest Troyer will come looking for her."

"I wouldn't miss it, Sheriff."

"Mike?" Robertson asked Branden.

"Sure," the professor said. "But I'm going to stay in room six, with Pat."

"OK," Robertson said to conclude his meeting. "We'll send Pat and Mike into the

St. James at seven. The pizza delivery is supposed to be at eight, and I don't think old Ernie will be able to resist."

After his people had left, Sheriff Robertson remained alone in his office. Time passed, but he took no note of it. Plans had been made, and he had nothing to do but wait. He thought of dinner, and he turned for the light switch beside his office door. He switched the lights off, and he was about to open the door and leave when Del Markely knocked on the door and entered. She saw that the lights were out, so she turned them on. Behind her was FBI agent William Parker. Carrying a white envelope, Parker entered the office behind Markely. He dropped the envelope onto Robertson's desk, and Markely left without speaking.

Robertson returned to his desk. He turned the envelope so that he could read it. On the outside, it was addressed to him. The envelope had been sliced open on its short edge. Gray fingerprint dust shook loose from the paper inside when Robertson pulled several pages out. It was a handwritten letter with the salutation: "Dear Sheriff Robertson." The sheriff turned to the last of three pages and read the closing, "Gratefully, Fannie Helmuth."

"OK," Robertson said as he laid the pages on his desk. "What is this, Parker?"

Stiffly, Parker demanded, "What did you write to Fannie Helmuth?"

Evenly, Robertson returned, "Why do you want to know?"

"She thanks you in her letter, there, for helping her 'see her way free of this.' "

"So, you've already read my mail," Robertson said. "You know what's in Fannie's letter."

"Of course," Parker said. "Where is Fannie Helmuth?"

To suppress a smile, Robertson pressed his legs painfully against the edge of his desk, and he made a show of drumming his knuckles sharply on the desktop. "I don't know, Parker," he intoned. "Have you lost her?"

Parker seemed to deflate. His posture surrendered some rigidity. He sank onto a chair in front of the sheriff's desk. Robertson matched him by sitting at his desk, too.

"We think she slipped out with the maids," Parker said. "And I think she got the idea from you. I think that's what her letter means. We found it in her bedroom, laying out on a blue dress that one of the maids had given her this morning. Do you know that they all wear identical dresses?"

"Have you looked for her, Parker?"

"Of course."

"Then my guess is that you'll never find her," Robertson said, still working earnestly to suppress a smile.

"Look, Robertson. She could simply have said that she did not wish to testify for us against Teresa Molina."

Robertson laughed. "Really, Parker? Would you have settled for that?"

Parker studied Robertson's broad smile for signs of deceit, and then he asked authoritatively, "Do you, Sheriff, have any evidence that Fannie committed a crime? Because, if you do, you're obliged to tell me, and we could force her to testify."

Deliberately, Robertson said, "I know of no crime by Fannic Helmuth."

"I didn't figure you would," Parker said. "I wouldn't expect you to admit it, even if you did."

"Why is that, Agent Parker?"

Parker stood and moved to the door. "Read the letter, Sheriff. Fannie says it all."

"I will," Robertson said. "When I'm ready."

Parker hesitated with his hand on the doorknob. He thought, released the knob, and turned back to Robertson. "What kind of person is she, Sheriff? I mean, really."

Robertson folded Fannie's letter and slid it back into its envelope. Gently, he laid the letter on his desk and answered Parker by saying, "She's the kind of person who was brave enough to testify, and smart enough to change her mind."

"OK," Parker said as he moved back toward Robertson's desk. "What did you tell her to change her mind?"

"Nothing," Robertson said with a smile that put light in his eyes. "She made that decision on her own."

"She says in her letter that you told her something," Parker countered.

Robertson considered his answer for a long moment. "I told her, Parker, that I thought she'd be safe among her own people."

"That's all?"

"Pretty much."

"Well, she obviously changed her mind about testifying," Parker said as he turned again for the door.

"Maybe *you* told her something to change her mind," Robertson said. "Maybe *you* changed her mind, Parker."

"No way," Parker said. "No way at all. We were preparing to move her to Cleveland, but we never told her that."

"Anyway," Robertson led.

"No, really," Parker tried again. "What kind of person is she?"

"Evidently quite remarkable," Robertson said with a proud smile. "She's the kind of person who has the courage to live her life honestly. She's the kind of person who could inspire her friend Howie Dent to stand by her while she hid from Teresa Molina all summer long. And last, Agent Parker, she's the plain kind of local genius who can slip sideways through the FBI's security net, and never be noticed while doing it."

"I'm going to help you, Jodie," Fannie said. "I'll get the money for you."

"Thank you," Jodie said. "Thank you a thousand times."

"I still have to work out some details," Fannie said.

"You're not with the FBI anymore?"

"No," Fannie said. "I slipped away with the maids."

"So, can you tell me where you are now?"

"I still need some time," Fannie said. "It's going to take the rest of the day to track down your money."

"I'll meet you anywhere, Fannie. Just tell me where."

"I don't know yet. I'll call."

"Fannie, I've only got until noon tomorrow."

"I know."

"I have to save enough time to get back to Akron by noon."

"I know, Jodie. I'll call."

31

Professor Branden drove up the hill on Jackson Street to the college heights on the eastern cliffs of town. At their brick colonial, he parked in the garage and saw that Caroline's sedan was already there. She was in the kitchen slicing vegetables for the grill when the professor entered.

"Why are you home?" he asked as he embraced her. "And what are we having?"

"You're grilling chicken," Caroline said. "And vegetables."

"OK, but why are you home?"

Caroline laid her knife on the cutting board and dried her hands on her apron. She stepped around the counter and sat at the kitchen table. The professor sat across from her and said, "What? Tell me."

"She's no longer in FBI custody, Michael," Caroline said, grinning as if it were

354

Christmas and she was still a child. "While I was out shopping, she walked out with the maids."

Branden shook his head, and a chuckling smile broke across his lips. "When did they notice that she was gone?"

"Not until I returned," Caroline said. "The television was turned on in her bedroom, and I thought that was odd. It was cartoons. I opened the door expecting to find her stretched out on her bed, but she wasn't there. The agents went nuts."

Branden chortled, "I'd like to have seen that."

"I didn't stay," Caroline said. She rose from the table and went back to her cutting board. Over her shoulder, she said, "I stopped to see Ellie."

"She OK?"

"Not really. I convinced Ricky to call her doctor."

"Do we need to check on her?" the professor asked.

"Ricky said he'd call me as soon as they had talked with her doctor. If he hasn't called me in an hour, I'll call him. Or I'll go over there. But I'm really worried, Michael. Ellie didn't look good at all."

"Do you think she'll be able to see her doctor?"

"Yes. I was there when Ricky called about the appointment. They were going to work her in. That was about two this afternoon, and Ricky was going to take her right over. But she was struggling. She really was."

"Are you going to see her? Do you need to go now?"

"Yes, but not now. I'll wait until Ricky has called me."

"OK. I'll start the grill," the professor said. "I'm going back at seven."

Caroline laid her knife down and turned to face him. "Tell me why, Michael."

The professor sat again at the kitchen table. Caroline joined him. He told her about the sheriff's plan to capture and question Earnest Troyer. Then, with Caroline's further questions, he explained how they all had concluded that it was Earnest Troyer who had killed Howie Dent. Caroline listened to the logic of it, and she said, shaking her head judgmentally, "It was all there from the beginning."

"I know."

"Really, Michael."

"I know! But it was Stan Armbruster who put it together for us. He learned from Fannie that Howie Dent had left his wallet on the bus in Charlotte. And he left his keys there, too. In the red backpack."

"Still, it should have bothered you more — and sooner — that he didn't have his own set of keys when he came home for the car."

"I know, Caroline. I know."

Stan Armbruster stood in his boxers, in front of the mirror in his trailer home's bathroom. His old uniform was hanging in the closet behind him. His new detective's suit still lay soaked and crumpled on the floor where he had dropped it beside his bed two days previously.

"The uniform again," Armbruster grumbled. The sheriff had asked that he wear it for the Earnest Troyer arrest, so that as many people as possible would be in uniform. He wanted Troyer to have no doubt that he was being approached by officers of the law. Armbruster considered it to be a sure sign of the end of his new career as one of Robertson's detectives. The sheriff had assured him that it wasn't, but Armbruster could see the handwriting on the wall. And with the end of his career as a detective, Armbruster knew that he was also facing the end of any chance he might have had with Pat Lance.

Barefooted, Armbruster padded into his kitchen and took two paper grocery bags

357

out of the cupboard. These he carried back into his bedroom. He bagged his suit coat, pants, shirt, and tie for the trip to the dry cleaner. Unceremoniously, he dropped the heavy, wet bags into the corner beside his nightstand.

Then Armbruster dressed slowly and methodically in his deputy's uniform. He buckled on his wide and heavy black leather duty belt. From the top shelf of his closet, he took down his gun safe, and he opened it on his bed. He took out the big SIG Sauer 9 mm pistol, loaded it, and slid it into the holster on his belt. Back in front of his mirror, he snapped the safety strap in place over the hammer of the gun.

At least he had resolved the alarm of his dream, he told himself in the mirror. It had been grizzled Earnest Troyer all along. There had been good reason for the alarm, and good reason for the clanging bell. Only last April, he had stood alone in that monster's house, asking innocently for phone numbers of the bus drivers. Troyer had told him then that he was in charge of turning the buses around for another trip down to Sarasota. So of course, Earnest Troyer would have had Dent's backpack all along. He managed the lost and found. And when Dent knocked on Earnest Troyer's door to retrieve his lost backpack? Well, that had been all that Troyer needed. Howie Dent had come straight to him, and as Armbruster remembered what Earnest Troyer had done to Dent in the basement of the Helmuth farmhouse, it put a chill down his spine.

So the alarm bell of his dream had been resolved. He could forget it. He felt relieved over that, if nothing else.

Still, behind the frontal activity of his thoughts, the bell was always there. He knew, beneath whatever reasoning he could exercise in his consciousness, that the bell could clang again at any time. Any day could skip sideways in an instant.

Pat Lance had come home to put on her Amish dress, but she postponed it as long as possible. She fixed a microwave dinner and stared at the organdy Kapp as she ate rubbery chicken and soupy mashed potatoes. She watched one of Cleveland's local news programs on cable while she fingered the dusty-rose fabric of the dress that lay on the couch beside her. She waited until the last minute before she began to dress.

In front of her bathroom mirror, she pinned her brown wig into position and set it so that the bun was placed properly at the back of her head. She put on the black hose, the rose dress, the white apron, and the organdy Kapp. Then, over her hose, she strapped her thigh holster in place under her dress.

It was easy to *dress* the part, she realized. It was harder to actually *live* the part. The costume was only an outward superficiality. The behavior was the real trick. To be demure. Submissive. And to do it gracefully.

But they had good and sufficient reasons, Lance told herself. She understood that now. The Amish had good and sufficient reasons, both for their dress and for their behavior. The average American could never make it work, but the Amish did it every day. They did it purposefully. They did it peacefully.

Standing in front of her mirror, dressed as Fannie Helmuth, Pat Lance found that she could respect that. She could never do it herself, but with new insight, she found that she could respect it.

32

The stairwell where Armbruster was posted in the St. James was dimly lighted. He was on the landing, half a flight of steps above the third-floor door. Beyond him by another half a flight of steps was the exit to the roof. If Earnest Troyer came up the stairs from below, or if he came down from the roof, Armbruster would be there to arrest him.

It was a suitable posting, Armbruster thought. But it was not the best posting. He would have preferred to be in room 6, with Lance. Or in room 7 with the sheriff. Then again, considering his failure to find Howie Dent in time to save him, perhaps he was lucky to have any posting at all.

As he waited in the dark, a door below Armbruster opened in the stairwell. It was on the first or second floor. He heard steps coming slowly up the staircase.

Then another door opened and closed in the stairwell. That was the second floor, Armbruster realized. Someone had entered the stairwell on the first floor, climbed to the second floor, and opened the door there.

Then Armbruster heard the elevator starting up from the lobby. He listened to the motor in the elevator shaft, and the doors opened and closed on the second floor, below him.

Armbruster checked his watch. Eight twenty-five. Troyer? Had he really come?

The elevator continued to rise to the third floor. The sound of the doors parting brought Armbruster silently down the steps to the stairwell door that opened onto the third-floor hallway. He waited there with his hand on his pistol.

The elevator doors closed, and the elevator stayed on the third floor. Armbruster heard a shuffling of cardboard, as if boxes were rubbing together, and he leaned his shoulder softly against the door. The latch had been altered earlier, so he was able to push soundlessly on the door to see into the hallway.

Just in front of the elevator doors to Armbruster's left, Earnest Troyer stood still in the hallway, with his back to Armbruster. He appeared to be thinking. Perhaps he was listening. He held two pizza boxes, one larger than the other. Armbruster watched through the slim crack of the door's opening, and Troyer pulled loose the edge of the lid on the larger pizza box on the bottom. Then Troyer slipped his fingers into the slender opening and started walking toward room 6.

When Troyer had advanced halfway down the hall, Armbruster took out his phone and sent the capital T text message that he had earlier addressed to everyone: Robertson in room 7. Lance and Branden in room 6. Bobby Newell, with uniformed deputies in the alley. Two more uniformed deputies on the roof.

Simultaneously, Armbruster and Robertson pushed open their doors and stood like bookends at the opposite ends of the hall. Earnest Troyer was caught in the middle.

With his hand resting on the butt of his gun, Robertson stepped forward and said, "We want to ask you some questions, Troyer."

Earnest Troyer backed up immediately. Robertson came forward, and Troyer backed up more. Behind Troyer, Armbruster commanded, "Stop!" and Troyer brushed the top pizza box off his stack. The box landed on the carpet at Troyer's feet, and the pizza spilled out.

Now Troyer was five paces from Armbruster, who was behind him, and ten paces from Robertson, who was in front of him. His hand was still slipped inside the open edge of the large pizza box he held.

Behind Robertson, the professor came out of room 6, and then so did Pat Lance. Dressed Amish, they both had their guns in their hands, and the sight of them puzzled Troyer momentarily.

Robertson stood fast and said, "We're taking you in for questioning in the murder of Howard Dent."

Again, Troyer backed up a pace toward Armbruster. Now he was four steps away. Troyer stopped there and studied Robertson's position. Behind Robertson, Lance and Branden were advancing. Troyer cranked his head around to see Armbruster in uniform. Armbruster advanced a step toward Troyer.

Troyer's face went slack, and his eyes hardened as he turned to face Armbruster. Taking care to speak distinctly, Troyer stepped closer and said, "You can ask me anything you like, Deputy. I don't even know a Howie Dent."

Troyer had taken another step as he said this. Now he judged that Armbruster was only two steps away. He could see that Armbruster's hand was on his gun, and he could see that the hammer strap was loose, but Armbruster hadn't drawn the weapon.

It was a mistake. Troyer lunged swiftly at Armbruster, knowing that the sheriff would not have a clean shot if he moved in close to the detective. As he lunged, he tossed the pizza box in Armbruster's face. Simultaneously, from the open edge of the box, Troyer drew a green blade with a serrated edge, and Armbruster had time to raise his gun only partly from its holster before Troyer was on him.

With his left hand, Troyer knocked at Armbruster's pistol, and with his right hand, he stabbed at Armbruster's left shoulder. The sharp plastic knife struck bone and tendons, and Troyer twisted the blade viciously, snapping off the tip in Armbruster's shoulder.

Armbruster screamed and dropped his gun. He sank to his knees and saw Robertson rushing forward. Armbruster made an attempt to lunge with his right hand at the feet of Troyer, but Troyer jumped over him, and Armbruster lost consciousness.

Robertson pursued Troyer through the stairwell door. He heard footfalls below him, and he knew that Bobby Newell would be bringing men up the stairs from the alley. Robertson also heard footfalls above him, and he started slowly up the stairs after Troyer. Halfway to the landing between the third floor and the roof, Robertson stopped. Glass shattered, and the stairwell above him became instantly dark.

Instinctively, Robertson took a step upward in the dark, and his mind flashed with the image of the lion in the cage of his childhood nightmares. He saw the lion tamer beckoning him to draw closer to the cage. He saw the big sign mounted to the top of the cage:

Fear the Roar
Trust the Bite

In the next instant, in a nightmarish flash, Robertson saw the face of the lion tamer clearly for the first time in his life. The tamer was shouting for him to press near to the bars, to feel the whiskers of the beast on his cheek. And instinctively, as he had always done as a child, Robertson backed away. Then he backed down the steps in the dark. First one step and then another. Three steps, and now a little light in the stairwell was visible to him from the floors below.

A green blade flashed out in front of the

366

sheriff's face. It gashed into the line of his jaw and bit deeply into his cheek. Swiftly the blade arched forward again, and Robertson shot. Stumbling back on the landing, he shot again into the dark. With his back flattened against the wall beside the stairwell door, Robertson fired his weapon twice again, and Earnest Troyer toppled down the steps and lay tangled in a heap at Robertson's feet.

Robertson fumbled for the door, and he lost his orientation. Bobby Newell appeared at his side to support him in the stairwell, and then Newell knelt beside the body of Earnest Troyer.

The sheriff tasted blood. He put his hand to his face, and he felt the slippery stickiness of blood. Wanting light, he pushed the door open with his hand, and he fell into the third-floor hallway. There he slumped to the carpet.

Despite the pain, Robertson pressed his palm back against his cheek. Deliberately, he placed his revolver on the carpet and tried to pull his handkerchief out of the inside pocket of his sport coat.

That's when the sheriff began again to hear. Pat Lance was shouting into her radio, "Man down! Third floor, St. James!"

Next, Robertson saw Lance kneeling

beside the body of Stan Armbruster. Robertson tried to speak, but he choked on blood. Lance looked over to him, and instantly she keyed her mic again to report, "Two men down, Del! Two men down!"

Robertson watched Lance move away from Armbruster's body and come in slow motion toward him. She still had her gun in one hand, her radio in the other. She knelt beside Robertson, and she placed her palm over his hand, to help him press the bloody handkerchief against the ragged gash in his jaw and cheek.

Robertson grasped the sleeve of her dusty-rose dress and muttered, "Stan?"

Bobby Newell pushed through the stairwell door and came immediately past Robertson to help the professor tend to Armbruster. Over his shoulder, Newell shouted to Robertson, "He's dead, Sheriff! Troyer's dead."

Armbruster was unconscious on his back. The professor was trying to find a way to stop the flow of blood from Armbruster's shoulder, but the tip of a jagged green plastic blade protruded from the wound, and Branden was having no effect applying pressure.

Sheriff Robertson pushed Lance up and away from himself, and as he lost strength, he asked, "Where's my squads?"

Lance keyed her mic and shouted, "Del!"

The radio made a garish squawk as Markely answered, "Coming!" and Lance turned back to kneel with Branden and Newell, beside Armbruster.

When the sheriff lost consciousness, both Bobby Newell and Professor Branden were pressing their fingers into the wound in Stan Armbruster's shoulder. The wound was spurting blood past their fingers.

Pat Lance was on her feet, holding the tip of the plastic blade. She was shouting again into her handset, but Robertson couldn't hear her words. The sheriff got one last look at Armbruster, and then he passed out with the pasty, coppery taste of blood in his mouth.

33

Friday, August 19
9:35 P.M.

Paramedics were able to sedate the sheriff only because they established a viable IV port on the back of his hand while he still lay in shock on the third-floor carpet of the Hotel St. James. In Millersburg's Pomerene Hospital, the anesthesiologist was able to anesthetize the sheriff's jaw and face for surgery in an ER bay only because Robertson had earlier been sedated. Even then, despite the anesthesia, they were able to close the long arc of the knife wound on Robertson's face only because they were able to add Demerol to the cocktail of pain medications that he was receiving through the original IV port. Otherwise, the sheriff would have torn the ER apart trying to get down the hall to the surgery suites, to find out what progress was being made with Stan Armbruster's shoulder wound.

When all of the commotion had settled down, Robertson lay on his back in a semiconscious state of disgruntlement, in a recovery room between the ER and the surgical suites of the hospital. Over a span of about twenty minutes, he dozed on and off. Eventually, he became aware, while struggling out of an ensnaring hallucination, that a bearded Amish man was standing at the railing beside his hospital bed. It caused the sheriff a moment of confusion, because his struggle had not been with anything Amish. It had been a struggle with a morphine-induced hallucination of semi-human shapes writhing inside the translucent walls of his room. But the sight of a plain Amish man seemed incongruous enough to the sheriff to cause him to hold his eyes open and study the man more closely.

He wore a vest, Robertson could see. He was in denim. His hair was short. It was too short for an Amish cut. The long blue sleeves of the Amish man's shirt were stained with blood. The man's hands had been scrubbed, but Robertson could see a reddish grime under his fingernails.

Because of the pain, Robertson was able to turn his head only slowly. He looked more carefully at the man's face. It wasn't a face with a proper Amish beard. The beard was neatly trimmed, not full and bushy. It was a professor's beard. Only gradually, because his thoughts were muddled by the sedatives and the morphine, was Robertson able to recognize the man.

"Mike," Robertson whispered through lips he could barely move. The effort to speak nearly exhausted him, but he managed to add, "Armbruster?"

"Still in surgery, Sheriff."

"Earnest Troyer?"

"Dead, Bruce. Missy is taking his body to the morgue. I'm to tell you that she'll be up here as soon as she has logged her evidence."

Though his efforts to move were suffused with exhaustion and pain, Robertson grasped the professor's sleeve and said, "We should have wanded him, Mike."

"It was a lettuce knife, Bruce."

Robertson's eyes closed, but he waved his hand to encourage more from Branden.

The professor leaned in over the bed railing. "He sharpened a plastic lettuce knife, Sheriff. It wasn't metallic. We would have passed right over it with a metal detector."

Robertson's eyes remained closed. Branden gently shook the sheriff's shoulder, but Robertson did not wake. So the professor walked into the bathroom to scrub again at the dried blood under his fingernails. When he came out of the bathroom, Sheriff Robertson was fumbling with the ice in a pink plastic glass of water that had been placed on his bed's rolling tray. Branden held the cup steady so that Robertson could take out a chip of ice. On the tray, a plastic spoon was in its wrapper. The professor unwrapped the spoon and lifted another sliver of ice out of the cup. He offered it to the sheriff, but Robertson ignored the spoon. He looked back at the professor with weary lids and troubled eyes.

Robertson closed his eyes and drew several deep breaths to steady his mind. Slowly, he lifted his hand to his face, and he felt with the pads of his fingers along the ragged line of sutures that had been used to close his wound. As he felt the alarming length of the wound, which started on his jaw-line below his left ear and arced across his cheek nearly to his lips, the sheriff whispered to Branden, "I got too close to the lion cage, Mike."

"I know, Bruce. You were lucky."

"Instinct," Robertson said grimly.

"I know, Bruce."

"I saw his face, Mike. First time in my life. I saw the face of the lion tamer."

"It wasn't a lion, Bruce," Branden said.

"It was just a man with a lettuce knife."

Robertson shook his head, and as he lost consciousness, he said, "Face too close to the bars."

While Robertson slept, the professor held vigil in a chair beside his bed. Branden tried his wife's cell number, but Caroline didn't answer. When he looked up from the phone, Robertson was struggling again to grasp the small plastic glass of water.

Branden rose and held the spoon with a sliver of ice to Robertson's lips. The sheriff took the ice between his lips and then sank back onto his pillow, asking, "Missy?"

Branden held the glass of ice water ready and said, "Not yet. I can call her."

"No," Robertson said. "She has her hands full in the morgue."

At the door to Robertson's room, there was a knock. Pat Lance entered carrying a cell phone. She was still in her dusty-rose Amish dress and white apron. She wasn't wearing her wig or her Kapp. She asked the professor, "Can he talk?" and Branden answered, "Little bits at a time. He whispers."

Lance came up to the side of Robertson's bed. Before she said anything, Robertson asked, with his eyes held shut and his mind dreading bad news, "Armbruster? Anything?"

"He's critical, Sheriff," Lance answered. "He's still in surgery."

Robertson grasped the sleeve of the professor's shirt. "Mike. How long has it been?"

Branden turned to the wall clock, but Lance answered directly, "One hour and fifty-seven minutes, Sheriff. They're almost done."

Robertson turned to Lance and asked, "Is that his phone? He has a blue case like that."

"Yes, it's Stan's phone," Lance answered. "I've been going through it, to see who I should call. He has only two numbers listed I.C.E."

Robertson closed his eyes again. "He has a sister down in Chillicothe. And his mother is still alive."

"They're all listed as just names, Sheriff. There's no 'Mom' or 'Sis' like you'd expect."

Robertson waved Lance out of the room. "Call the I.C.E. numbers, Lance. Gotta be family."

As Lance left the room, the professor's phone announced a call. He recognized the strumming tone, and to Robertson he said, "It's Caroline." He stood by the bed to take the call.

Robertson pushed himself up on his pillow and waited. Branden listened for a moment and then said, "I'm with Bruce, Caroline. I'm going to put you on speaker phone. OK, say that again."

Muddled by road noises, Caroline's voice sounded from the phone. "I'm driving to Akron behind the ambulance. They're taking Ellie to Akron Children's Hospital. There's trouble with her pregnancy."

Robertson became instantly agitated. He struggled to clear his voice, but he managed only to whisper, "Be OK?"

"What's that?" Caroline came back.

"Is she going to be OK?" the professor asked for the sheriff.

"I don't know. But her doctor told Ricky that they have better neonatal facilities at Akron. For preemies, Michael."

Branden took Caroline's call off speaker phone, and he retreated to a chair in the corner to talk with her privately. Robertson sank back onto his pillow. His head and arms lay immobile with the heaviness of lead weights. His thoughts seemed to swim against currents of viscous oil. Vaguely, he recognized Pat Lance as she came again into the room. The sheriff waved her up to his bedside.

"I talked to his sister, Sheriff," Lance reported. "She's driving up from Chillicothe. His mother will have to fly up from Florida."

Next, a doctor entered the room. He inspected Robertson's long arc of sutures and wrote notes on a clipboard at the foot of Robertson's bed.

The sheriff fought mental sluggishness to frame a question. He pushed on Lance's elbow to start her toward the doctor, and he managed to say only, "Stan?"

Lance asked, "Doctor, can you tell us anything about Stan Armbruster?"

The doctor slid his clipboard back into the bed's charting slot. "He's critical," he said. "They had him in recovery, but his blood pressure dropped, and they're deciding now if they can go back in, to try again to stop the bleeding."

Branden appeared beside the doctor at the foot of the sheriff's bed. "Why wouldn't they do that, Doctor?"

The doctor shrugged. "They need more of his blood type, Professor. They've already used most of what we had on hand. They're making some calls."

Immediately, Lance drew her cell phone from the side pocket of her long rose dress. She jabbed her finger at Chief Wilsher's speed dial, and when Wilsher answered, she said, "Stan needs blood, Dan. He needs it right now, if it's to do him any good."

Lance listened to the chief's short reply, and she switched out of the call. Her eyes turned to the ceiling as if she had been listening to answered prayer. "They're sending everybody here, Sheriff," she said, turning back toward Robertson's bed. "Dan is calling them all. Everybody. Holmes County, Wayne County, everywhere. To donate blood."

When Bobby Newell entered the room, Professor Branden was standing again beside the railing of Bruce Robertson's hospital bed. The sheriff's eyes were closed, so Newell asked Branden, "Can he talk, Mike? He's going to want to hear this."

Branden pushed on Robertson's shoulder, but the sheriff did not open his eyes. Branden shook the sheriff a little harder, and still Robertson did not respond. Branden laid his hand on Robertson's chest, and the sheriff was breathing restfully. So Branden pulled Newell away from the bed and said, "I'll tell him, Bobby, once he wakes up."

Newell hesitated and roughed up the tuft of black hair over one ear. "I can come back, Mike."

"He's going to ask me who was here, Bobby. I should have something for him."

"OK, it's Earnest Troyer's house," Newell said. "In Sugarcreek. We went in to search it, and we found a cutting table for drugs in his basement. He's been bagging cocaine, and he's had a lot of help. We're working through a list of contacts and messages on his phone. There are going to be a lot of arrests. Maybe a dozen people were involved."

"He had to have had some help, Bobby. At the Helmuth farm. There had to be at least one accomplice to drive Earnest Troyer off the property."

"I don't know, Mike. Maybe Troyer followed Dent there. Maybe he had his own car. But on the drugs, he had plenty of help. Dozens of people, Mike. This is how most of the cocaine in Holmes County was being distributed."

Branden arched a brow. "He managed the northern terminus, Bobby. All of Molina's drug shipments eventually went to him."

"Right," Newell said. Nervous energy rippled through his muscles.

Branden shook his head and smiled as if he shouldn't have been surprised. "He delivered more than pizzas, Bobby. He had a ready-made delivery route for drugs."

"We've impounded his car," Newell said,

agreeing. "But we pulled out of his house."

"Why pull out?" Branden asked.

"I called in the BCI labs. This needs to be handled at the state level."

"Did you tell the FBI, too?"

"Yes. I think I had to, Mike. I think we should let the state and the feds handle this investigation. I'm down to one detective, and she's standing uselessly outside the surgical suites. Looks like she's been Tased."

"What about evidence of Howie Dent's murder?" Branden asked. "You'll find evidence in Troyer's house in Sugarcreek."

"I turned the house over to an FBI forensics team, Mike. We'll process the scene at the St. James. And we have Troyer's car. If the FBI finds evidence in Sugarcreek that Troyer killed Dent, then I'm willing to wait to let them tell us that."

"Sounds reasonable," Branden said.

"Maybe," Newell said with a vexed smile. "My question is whether the sheriff is going to think that it's reasonable, too."

Newell turned to leave, but his phone rang. He stopped in the room to take the call. He said, "Hello," and listened for several moments. Then he said, "Mike, I have to take this out in the hall. You'll never believe who it is."

As Newell left, Pat Lance returned with Armbruster's phone. On the display, she had found a picture of herself, taken by Armbruster when she was in the Mast home, wearing the dusty-rose dress that Fannie and Irma had made for her. Lance showed the photo to Branden and said, "Stan took this. I didn't know."

Branden looked at the phone and said, "That looks like it was taken at the Mast farmhouse."

"It was," Lance said with a smile so confused and crooked that it turned only one corner of her lips. "And there's more, Professor. He's taken other photos of me on the job."

Lance selected a second photo from the phone's light box, and she showed it to the professor. It was a picture of Lance working at a computer, while she and Armbruster had been searching the *Budget* newspaper for evidence of Fannie Helmuth's movements.

With puzzled chagrin, Lance asked the professor, "Has he been talking about me?"

To delay the obligation to answer, the professor gave a reluctant smile. But from his bed, the sheriff answered readily, "He likes you, Lance." Then as he struggled to rise up on his pillow, the sheriff added, "I can't believe you didn't know that."

Pat Lance stared back at the sheriff as if he had surrendered to insanity. She looked again at the photo on Armbruster's phone, and she switched it off. Her face flushed with pink heat, and she spun around and hurried out of the room.

Robertson watched her disappear through the door. To Branden, he said, "I can't believe she didn't know."

"Apparently she didn't," Branden said.

Robertson shook his head and reached out for his glass of ice water. He managed without help to get a chip of ice with the plastic spoon and slip it into his mouth. As he set the glass on the tray over his bed, the sheriff said, "Armbruster has to make it, Mike. He just has to. If he doesn't, I don't think Lance can handle it."

Then the sheriff said, "It was my father, Mike. All these years. In all those dreams."

"*Who* was your father?"

"I should have known, Mike," the sheriff said. His voice trailed into a whisper as sleep pressed in upon him. "But I never recognized him. Until tonight. In that stairwell, with Earnest Troyer coming at me in the dark."

Leaning in over the bed rail, Branden asked the sheriff, "Recognized who?"

"The lion tamer, Mike," Robertson said as his eyes closed. "In my childhood nightmares. My father is the lion tamer. Taunting me to step close to the bars."

34

Friday, August 19
10:55 P.M.

Fannie's cell phone rang just as she and Reuben were crossing the Denison–Ashtabula Road on State Route 87 in northeast Ohio. In the hours since Fannie had emerged from the hotel outside Middlefield, they had been pacing slowly east in their buggy. The buggy was loaded heavily with provisions stacked in the rear cargo bay. Fannie had sat all day beside Reuben on the sprung seat of the buggy.

Reuben had managed the reins and the horse since leaving Middlefield. He had been careful to keep the rig well to the right side of the pavement. There had been light traffic on the roads, but it had been dark for several hours, and Reuben had anxiously been watching for a suitable place to turn off for the night. The journey had been made harder by a vaporous drizzle that had overtaken them from the west as soon as they had crossed into Trumbull County.

As her phone began to ring, Fannie checked the display and said to Reuben, "It's Jodie, again."

Reuben gave the reins a slap, but he offered no comment.

Fannie answered Jodie's call. "Hi, Jodie, we're still out on the road."

"I'm worried, Fannie," Jodie said. "I'm anxious. I don't have much time, now."

"We'll meet you, Jodie. Early tomorrow morning. You'll have enough time to get back to Akron with your money."

On the buggy seat next to Fannie, Reuben said, "Whatever you think is best, Fannie. Tell her we have to stop for the night, but we'll see her tomorrow morning."

The rain came harder, and Reuben steered the horse into the little roadside town of Gustavus Center. He found a white-sided town hall on the right, and he pulled into its broad circular drive. To Fannie, he whispered, "We'll park here for the night. It's too dangerous to stay out on the road in this much rain."

Fannie held her phone in her lap while she considered her decision. The rain increased its thudding spatter on the canvas roof of the buggy. A lone car passed by them on the road. With a resigned sigh, Fannie said, "We have to meet her, Reuben."

Taking up her phone again, Fannie switched it from mute and said, "We're near the Pennsylvania border, Jodie. Reuben wants to stop now, because the rain is getting worse."

"I can be there by morning," Jodie said. "Maybe by eight."

Fannie whispered to Reuben, "Do you still think we should do this?"

Grimly, Reuben nodded a yes.

"OK, Jodie," Fannie said into her phone. "We'll meet you at eight tomorrow morning. On the Vernon Center Bridge. It's on Route 88, crossing the Pymatuning River into Pennsylvania."

35

It was pain that dragged Sheriff Robertson out of sleep early Saturday morning. It was pain in his jaw, pain in his cheek, and pain along the entire length of his wound. There was pain when he swallowed, and there was pain at the core, the kind of deep pain that arises from wounded bone. With his eyes closed against the challenge of enduring it, he fumbled for the call button that would summon a nurse.

His wife, Missy, had been waiting beside his bed. She grasped his hand and helped him push the button. When her husband opened his eyes, she leaned in close and kissed his forehead. She held his hand and laced her fingers into his. With her other hand, she brushed her fingertips across the bristly top of his hair.

The sheriff's eyes closed and then

reopened. "Missy," he said, looking at the ceiling to ride the pain. He wanted to pull her close to him, but he lacked the strength. His eyes closed again, and he dozed.

When the nurse arrived, Missy requested more pain medication for her husband. The nurse took up the sheriff's chart and inspected his medications log. "Another hour," she said. "We need to wait another hour."

When the sheriff next opened his eyes, it was only ten minutes later, and Missy was still holding his hand. He turned his head slowly to her and asked, "Nurse?"

"She was just here, Bruce. She'll be back as soon as she can."

Robertson drew a labored breath. "Rough," he said. "I hate hospitals."

"I do, too," Missy said. "But thank God for them."

"No doubt," the sheriff answered. "Anything about Stan?"

"He's in recovery, Bruce, but they're not very hopeful."

"Blood?"

"They have enough, Bruce. They're waiting to see if he can stabilize."

"Wake him up," Robertson growled. "Tell him to fight."

"You need to let his doctors manage this, Bruce."

Robertson appeared to sink into his pillow as if something there was pulling him into a nightmare. He seemed to retreat from a threatening vision. He rolled his head to the left and to the right, and he sounded like he was quoting Scripture when he recited, "Steadfast devotion to duty."

"That sounds like your father talking, Bruce," Missy said. "That's something he would have said."

"Heard it all my life," the sheriff answered. His eyes were open now. He was awake again with the pain. "I heard it every day, Missy. 'A man's honor derives from his relentless and steadfast devotion to duty. It derives from his steadfast devotion to justice.' "

"Father or not, that's all you, Bruce," Missy whispered in his ear. "That's you, Bruce, through and through."

"Well, I got it from my father. Right along with my worst nightmare."

"The lion cage," Missy said.

Slowly, the sheriff's chin tipped with a painful nod. He winced against the pain.

"It's just a dream, Bruce. A stupid childhood dream."

Robertson opened his eyes and turned

them to his wife. "Have I been wrong all my life, Missy? To insist on wearing duty like armor? Because I'll tell you, it requires the kind of self-assurance that I don't think I have anymore."

"Devotion to duty is not just your armor, Bruce. It's your core."

"Yeah? Well, maybe that's gotta change."

Missy pulled the sheriff's hand farther into hers. She leaned in close to his ear. "You could do a few things differently," she said. "But if you start doubting yourself, you'll lose it all. Your entire department leans on you. They do it because they trust you."

"I don't see why anyone would trust me, Missy."

"I'm not willing to listen to this, Sheriff. Even Fannie Helmuth trusts you. And she met you, what, maybe once? She met you once, and based on one letter you wrote to her, she trusts you enough to walk away from FBI protection."

"I didn't tell her anything, Missy."

"That's nonsense. I know what you wrote to her."

"What?"

"You wrote at least five versions of that letter, Bruce. I found them in the wastebasket. I know what you wrote to Fannie. And I'll tell you something else. I also read Fannie's letter to you."

Struggling inside the strictures of his medications, Robertson stared at the ceiling and considered what Missy had said. The letter. Fannie's letter. He hadn't read it. He had lost it. There had been so much to do, to set up for Earnest Troyer. Fannie's letter.

Robertson looked at Missy. He squeezed her hand. "I never read the letter," he said.

"I have it, Bruce. It was in your coat pocket when they brought you to the hospital."

"You have it?"

"Yes."

"What does it say?"

Missy laid her husband's hand gently on the sheet beside him, and she stepped away from his bed. Robertson misinterpreted the moment, and he closed his eyes, expecting no reply. But momentarily, Missy retrieved his hand, and the sheriff heard the rustle of paper. He held his eyes closed and waited. Missy began to read.

Friday, August 19
Hotel near Middlefield

Dear Sheriff Robertson,
    Thank you for your letter. I know what I have to do. I know that wherever I go,

391

I will be safe among my people.

I miss Howie so very much, but my fiancé is a fine and wonderful man. I will have a good life with him. But Howie wanted his car. He had it all through college. I told him to forget it, but I guess he just couldn't do that.

Thank you for helping me see my way free of this. I have courage because you trusted me with the truth.

I have always believed that the faith of a single person is more consequential than all the powers on earth. In this, I believe I will be proven right.

Sincerely and truly yours,
Fannie Helmuth

36

Saturday, August 20
4:10 A.M.

In the darkest hours before sunrise, when the nurse came into Armbruster's hospital room, Pat Lance was still sitting at his bedside, holding Armbruster's phone. The nurse hung a new dose of platelets on the IV stand and connected the tubing to the new bag. He adjusted the delivery rate, tossed the empty bag into the medical waste container, and came to the foot of the bed to take up the medical chart. As he recorded Armbruster's newest IV data, he said to Lance, "You've been here almost all night, Detective."

"I know," came a weary reply.

"Should you maybe get something from the cafeteria?" the nurse asked.

Lance shook her head. "He's going to wake up."

The nurse hesitated at the door. "It's still

a couple of hours before daylight, but it's warm outside. Maybe you could get some fresh air. Fresh air might do you a lot of good."

Lance clicked on another photo in Armbruster's phone and shook her head.

"Are you going to call someone?" the nurse asked as he came back to stand beside Lance.

Again, Lance shook her head, but did not speak. She held Armbruster's phone so that the nurse could see the photo of her in Irma Mast's parlor, and when she turned her face up to the nurse, there were tears in her eyes.

37

Saturday, August 20
6:20 A.M.

At Ellie Troyer-Niell's bedside, Caroline Branden held her vigil of prayer. The late-night Cesarean deliveries had been complicated. The babies had been so very small. The doctors spent a long time closing Ellie's incision. They had spent far too long, Caroline realized. But she tried to say encouraging things to Ricky. She tried to give him hope, both for his children and for his wife. She hid from him the fear for Ellie that had engulfed her. The fear she suffered for the babies.

Memories of her own miscarriages haunted Caroline through the night, and although she had lost her babies many years ago, she was powerless at Ellie's bedside to dispel the pain and sadness of those losses. She was powerless to hold out more than the frailest of hopes for Ellie and Ricky.

Ricky was standing in the neonatal unit down the hall, unable to decide whether Ellie needed him more, or whether their babies did. Caroline had promised him that if Ellie woke up, she would summon Ricky immediately. So far, Ellie had slept, and Caroline had sat alone with her. Because of her own heartache of loss, Caroline could not find a way to understand Ellie's sleeping as an encouraging sign. Ellie's breathing was shallow and labored. It would be weeks or months before she could hold her children. If they survived, Caroline thought, losing heart. If Ellie survived.

Caroline rose and stepped with her burdens to the window. A chaos of despondency and despair tumbled through her thoughts. The Akron skyline was emerging from shadow as the sun came up, but the elaborate play of architecture and form, and the chorus of morning traffic on the streets below, meant nothing to her. It was a city, Caroline thought bitterly. Just a stupid city. No one down there knows a thing about Ellie Troyer-Niell. Even if they knew, these were not the people who would care.

Behind her, Michael entered the room silently. As he crossed to stand beside her, he whispered, "She's going to be OK, Caroline."

Caroline turned to her husband with negativity and denial laced fiercely into her tears. "You don't know that, Michael!" she shouted, and then quickly she covered her mouth. Whispering, she accused her husband with her grief. "There's nothing we can do to make this right, Michael."

The professor reached out to embrace his wife, but she stiffened as he drew her close. He caressed her hair and kissed her forehead. "We lost children, Caroline. That doesn't mean Ellie and Ricky will. You're talking this way because of the pain of your memories."

"What if I am, Michael? I know what she faces. I know what is possible, here, better than anyone. I can't handle it, if her babies die like ours did. I can't handle it if Ellie dies."

"You're letting the pain talk, Caroline. You don't have any good reason to fear for Ellie. You don't have any good reason to fear for these babies."

Standing stiffly in her husband's arms and thinking only that her fear would never abate, Caroline said sternly, "I want you to call Cal, Michael. I want you to call Cal Troyer to pray."

The professor caressed Caroline's hair and pulled her tightly into his embrace. "He's already here, Caroline. I brought him with me. He's down the hall right now, with Ricky and the children."

38

Saturday, August 20
6:20 A.M.

Although Reuben and Fannie got an early start Saturday morning, the travel was slow because of weekend traffic on SR 87. Reuben held to the berm wherever possible, and this impeded their progress even more, because the overnight rains had made potholes in the gravel beside the road.

When they approached the wetlands bordering the Pymatuning River, they found that the rain had produced flooding. Standing water had risen nearly to the level of the pavement. This was low country. They passed swampland, marshes, creeks, and lily pads. Everywhere they saw the encroachment of brown river water.

In Kinsman, Reuben followed 5W/7S through town. First there came Saint Patrick's Catholic Church. Then the Kinsman Chapel of the Christian & Missionary

Alliance, plus the Dollar General, Marathon, and Main Drug. As they approached the gazebo at the center of town, they passed nineteenth-century homes set well back from the road. Brick-fronted businesses on the town square. Old buildings, with weathered and cracked bricks that had settled on their foundations.

Reuben paced his horse steadily south out of Kinsman on Route 7. At 88, he turned east, and the long low span of the Vernon Center Bridge came into view. The straight run of blacktop led from the intersection to the bridge, and Fannie could see a small blue pickup truck parked to the side, halfway across the bridge. Beside the pickup, Jodie Tapp was standing out on the pavement.

Reuben moved forward slowly. There were heavy metal guardrails on either side of the road. Over the guardrails, the land dropped steeply into the river bottoms. On the span of the bridge, low white walls guarded the edges. The lowlands bordering the Pymatuning River were flooded on each side of the road. The dirty brown water surged around marsh grasses, tall timber, and tangles of dense, bushy cover.

As Reuben started across the bridge, Fannie saw brown water rushing along at flood stage, only inches from the underside of the bridge. At the center of the bridge, Jodie stood smiling. She waved for Fannie to come to her. Fannie climbed down from the buggy's seat as Reuben set the hand brake. Fannie walked forward, and Reuben sat with the reins.

Over the swollen river, the two women met in the middle of the span. When Fannie held out her arms to embrace Jodie, Tapp stood stiffly in place, with her hands tucked into the front slit pocket of a gray hoodie.

Fannie released Jodie and stepped back. "What's wrong, Jodie? Is it your mother? Teresa Molina? What?"

Tapp answered, "I can't believe you are this naive."

"What are you talking about?" Fannie asked as she stood in front of Jodie.

Reuben climbed down from the seat of the buggy and came forward to stand beside Fannie. "Is there a problem here, Fannie?"

Tapp stepped back a pace. "I knew you'd come," she said flatly.

Reuben held Jodie's gaze. At his side, he took Fannie's hand in his.

Tapp's hand clutched at something inside the slit pocket of her hoodie. She snarled and said, "I can kill you both right here."

Reuben stared peacefulness back at Tapp.

"You can do nothing to harm us that God has not already allowed."

Fannie reached a hand out to Tapp, and Tapp shouted, "Stay back!"

Fannie put her hand back at her side. "Jodie," she said, "were you really part of the drug smuggling?"

"Oh, I cannot believe you naive and stupid Amish girls!" Tapp laughed. "Of course I was part of it."

"I don't believe you," Fannie said.

"I know you don't. That's why it was so easy to talk you Amish girls into carrying my suitcases home on the buses. Dozens, Fannie! It was dozens of Amish girls. Pennsylvania, Ohio, Indiana. And it worked, too. Until stupid Ruth Zook dumped my drugs into a farm pond."

"Did you kill Ruth?" Fannie asked.

Exasperated, Tapp shouted, "No, you moron! I was in Florida!"

"Then who killed her, Jodie, if you didn't?"

"Teresa's cousin. Dewey Molina. They tracked him down in Bradenton. I had to pretend to be his hostage."

"I grow weary of this," Reuben said. "Fannie, this cannot be a part of our lives."

Fannie took a step toward Tapp. "Are you really going to kill us, Jodie?"

With scorn, Tapp said, "You're too stupid to live, Fannie."

Fannie stood immobile. She studied the face of her friend and grew sad. She stepped back to stand beside her fiancé.

Tapp glared spitefulness into Fannie's eyes.

Fannie looked sadly back at Tapp, and then she closed her eyes. She beheld the oneness of creation, and she embraced the true and eternal testimony of her life, even if that required her death at the hands of a friend, on a deserted bridge over a swollen river.

"Take out your cell phone," Fannie heard Tapp command.

Fannie opened her eyes. She lifted the phone from the pocket of her dress, and she held it forward for Tapp.

"Throw it in the river," Tapp said.

Fannie turned around and threw the phone into the roiling brown water. Then she turned back to face Tapp.

Tapp turned to Reuben. "Do you have a phone, too?"

"No," Reuben answered flatly.

"Why not?"

"They are harmful."

"Oh," Jodie ridiculed. "Are we afraid of frequencies close to the brain?"

"No."

"Then explain why," Jodie insisted, stepping closer. "Because you people don't make any sense to me at all."

Reuben glanced right to smile at Fannie, and he turned back to Tapp. Slowly and deliberately, Reuben answered. "In your world with cell phones, Jodie, who among you deems a friend so precious that you would ride for half a day in a buggy, just to sit on a porch with a glass of tea and talk for an afternoon?"

"You're crazy," Tapp replied.

"I don't think I am," Reuben said evenly.

Jodie Tapp seemed to stall on a thought. She seemed to have caught a fleeting insight that she had never before considered. She realized that Fannie had spoken to her, and she said, "What?"

"Jodie," Fannie said, "aren't you afraid of Teresa Molina? Shouldn't you be hiding from her?"

Tapp laughed, and she laughed again, as if pleased by some hidden mystery or taken with some entertaining irony. Fannie and Reuben waited for her answer.

Tapp swallowed nervously and wetted her lips with the tip of her tongue. She appeared to be pressurized by bottled anxiety. It was apparent both to Fannie and to Reuben that she was not a woman at peace. She was not a woman who enjoyed simplicity of thought. The plain beauties of life would forever be inaccessible to her.

Fannie said to her, "Have you ever known any peace?"

As if addressing a simpleton, Tapp smiled with condescension. "Teresa Molina was running from her own cartel, Fannie. They don't tolerate failure. So I killed her for them. No one will ever find her body. I made sure of that."

Hoping that Jodie would talk a little more, Fannie asked, "How did you find us, Jodie?"

"I just kept calling you, Fannie. I knew you'd tell me where you were, eventually. Once you called me with that new phone of yours, I knew I'd find you, sooner or later. I have to admit, I didn't expect it would take four months."

"I mean, how did you get here so fast this morning?" Fannie said.

"Oh Fannie, really? Are you kidding? Each time I called you, I learned a little more about where you were. 'It's raining here,' you said once. I checked my radar. 'There's a fabric store here.' I checked the Internet for fabric stores near Amish communities. 'The Indians' games are on the radio all the time.' That meant near Cleveland. More and more, each time we talked, I drew closer to you. I moved every day. I was in Middlefield last night. I must have just missed you."

"You said you were down in Akron, Jodie."

"See? It was so easy to fool you."

With deep and genuine chagrin, Fannie said, "I'm sorry, Jodie." She pulled a wire loose from inside her apron, and she showed Jodie the microphone that had recorded their conversation.

Jodie stepped back, startled. She drew her hands out of the pocket of the hoodie, and she pointed a revolver at Fannie.

Immediately, three uniformed deputies dashed out of the bushes at the ends of the bridge. They were led by Captain Bobby Newell. They all rushed forward on the flat span of the bridge, and Newell shouted, "Drop your weapon, Tapp!"

Jodie stared slackjawed at Fannie. She turned her head to see Newell approaching, but she did not drop her weapon.

Again, Newell shouted, "Drop your weapon!"

Jodie leaned over at the waist, put her revolver on the pavement at her feet, and backed up slowly to the edge of the bridge. "How did you know?" she asked Fannie. "How did you figure it out?"

Fannie said, "Jodie, how did you know I

had been staying with the FBI?"

"You told me."

"No, I didn't."

"I'm sure you did."

"No, Jodie. I never told you that. So that's when I began to suspect you. When you first asked me about the FBI. Only then. Until then, I thought you really were my friend."

Jodie pressed back against the low wall at the edge of the bridge. Behind her, the brown flood waters rushed away under the pavement. Newell and his men surrounded Tapp with their guns pointed at her. Jodie looked a last time at Fannie, smiled as if lost in tragic irony, and threw herself backward into the surging river water.

The current drew Jodie immediately under the bridge. Fannie rushed to the other side and watched for Jodie to pass from under the bridge. She saw nothing at first. Then, some fifty yards downstream, Fannie saw the lifeless body of Jodie Tapp, snagged on a tree trunk, head down in the water, limbs twisting erratically in the current.

39

Thursday, September 29
7:40 A.M.

Six weeks after the stabbings, Detective Pat Lance drove down the farmer's lane to Stan Armbruster's old trailer. She parked beside a Dumpster where friends and family had thrown out what no one wanted of the brittle and broken household goods that Armbruster had left behind.

Slowly, Lance climbed the wooden steps to Armbruster's trailer door. She used a key his sister had given her to unlock the door, and once inside, she drifted from one empty room to another.

There was half a roll of paper towels left in the kitchen. Maybe a new tenant would want that, Lance thought. There was a stack of old magazines on the carpet where Armbruster's couch had sat with its back to the trailer's kitchen counter. No one would want them, Lance realized. She carried them outside to the Dumpster.

Back inside, she wandered from corner to corner in the musty rooms. It was all gone, she realized. Nothing left. But in the bedroom, in a corner behind the folding door to the bathroom, Lance found two brown paper grocery bags. Inside there was damp, musty clothing — a blue business suit, with subtle charcoal pinstripes. A white dress shirt and a red tie. It was all dirty, and it was all ruined by mold. Armbruster had dropped it there the day he had found the body of Howie Dent, and that had been the end of it, Lance realized.

Lance pulled the suit out of the bags and peered into the bottom of each sack. In the second one, there was a sparkle of silver, and Lance lifted out a sterling tie chain. She put it in her pocket.

The clothes went back into the sacks, and Lance carried them out to the Dumpster to toss them onto the top of the pile. She shook her head and thought how much she wished Stan had done better for himself. In the Dumpster, there was worn and broken furniture, much of it little more than family hand-me-downs. There was rusty kitchenware and dented pots and pans. Chipped plastic glasses. Dated foodstuffs. And now old magazines and a ruined suit.

"Stan," Lance said to the Dumpster, "you should have done better for yourself."

From farther back on the lane, Lance heard the barking of dogs. She wandered back to the cages and watched the farmer ladle dog food into bowls.

Lance said, "Hi," and the farmer returned her simple greeting. When he had set the bowls in the cages, he came out and said, "Armbruster was the best trainer my dogs ever had."

Sadly, Lance replied, "I know," and she turned for her car.

As she drove back to Millersburg, Lance thought of Armbruster's phone. She thought of his pictures of her, and she wondered again, as she had done many times since she discovered them in the hospital, why he hadn't ever shown them to her. Why he hadn't ever spoken to her, to tell her how he felt. Why he had never asked her out.

East of Millersburg on SR 62, Lance turned south on 557 to head toward Charm. Halfway there, she turned onto the lane for Miller's Bakery. She knew it had always been Armbruster's favorite. Inside, under the dim lights of the gas ceiling mantles, she bought a maple cinnamon bun and had it boxed to carry it out.

Back on 557, Lance turned right behind a lumber truck, and she followed it around the many curves of the road into Charm. She parked at the Roadside Amish Restaurant, and she carried the little box with the cinnamon roll inside.

Stan Armbruster was seated in a booth beside the front windows. His left arm was cradled in a sling. On the table in front of him was the farmer's special breakfast. Lance slid onto the bench seat beside him and pushed him gently sideways to make more room for herself. She gave him the box with the cinnamon roll and said, "Not that you need more food."

As he opened the box, Armbruster said, "Thanks. I'll save it for later."

Lance smiled and laughed and shook her head. "We can split it, Detective."

"Oh really?"

"Yes, and when I finally get you out of that sling, you can start running laps. If you keep eating breakfast here, you'll be as big as the sheriff."

When Armbruster had finished his breakfast and a last cup of coffee, Pat slid off the booth's seat and said to him, "Follow me back into town, Stan. I want to stop at the jail."

Armbruster slid out and carried his bill and his box to the cash register. "I'm not sure I'm ready," he said as he fished his wallet out of a back pocket. "I haven't been back there yet."

"I know, Stan," Pat said. "We're going to fix that today."

In the restaurant's lot beside Armbruster's red Corolla, Lance said, "Robertson figures that it's time for you to come off medical leave, Stan. And he's grousing about Ricky, too."

Armbruster unlocked his car and set the pastry box on the passenger's seat. He straightened up beside the car and asked, "What's with Ricky?"

"Half days. He goes up to Akron with Ellie every afternoon to see their babies. It's going to be two more weeks before they can bring the children home. So Robertson has been squawking about how he has only one detective."

Armbruster rolled his eyes and rapped the knuckles of his good hand against the window glass. "And has he needed more than one detective, lately? Has there been anything to detect?"

"Not really." Lance laughed. "There hasn't been a thing."

"So what's his problem?"

412

"He wants you back, Stan. At least for today. He wants me to bring you back to the jail today."

"Why?"

"I don't know. Maybe he's lonely."

"Right. I'm sure."

"No, Stan. Just follow me into town. I'll meet you on the front steps."

"If you say so."

"I do say so, Detective. I do."

Pat Lance opened the door into the jail's front counter lobby, and she nudged Stan Armbruster through the door. They were all standing there to greet him.

Applause broke out, and pink heat blushed into the fair skin of Stan's cheeks. As Pat steadied him with her arm looped into his, Stan stood inside the door and took it all in.

At the very front stood little Rachel Ramsayer, reaching up to shake Armbruster's hand. Behind her were Professor Branden and his wife, Caroline. To the left, Ricky Niell stood beside his wife, Ellie. Beside Ellie was Pastor Cal Troyer. To the right, close to the counter, stood Chief Deputy Dan Wilsher and Captain Bobby Newell, both in their dress uniforms. Also in their dress uniforms were several deputies clustered

413

behind the chief. Del Markely stood applauding behind her counter, and at the back corner of the counter, Melissa Taggert stood with her husband, the sheriff, who was sporting a new beard to mask the long pink scar on his face. Armbruster surveyed it all with a wide smile.

As the applause died away, Del's voice boomed out, "OK, OK, now everybody just stand aside. I have something to present."

She carried a paper sack out through the counter door, and she pulled the sheriff along with her. Robertson resisted at first, but Missy urged him forward with Del.

Once Del had Robertson and Armbruster positioned in the center of the lobby, and once the people had gathered around, she planted her feet wide and fluffed the bushy gray ponytail at the back of her head. She waved her arms for fanfare, and she bent over the sack. From it, she pulled a plaque, and she held it up to show it around. Framed behind glass were two service photographs, one of the old sheriff and one of young Armbruster.

"This is going on my wall," Del announced with pride. She pushed her way back through the crowd to stand behind her counter. There she took out a nail and a hammer, and she pounded the nail into the knotty pine paneling over her radio consoles.

"Sheriff," she declared loudly, "I hate this old pine paneling. You seriously need to remodel."

Again there was applause. The sheriff waved a surrendering palm in the air. "OK, Del. Whatever you say."

Del nodded and bowed with the flare of an accomplished magician. Then she hung the plaque on the nail and stood back to point to the inscription that was written underneath the photos of Robertson and Armbruster.

"STABBED IN THE LINE OF DUTY," she read aloud. "STABBED, BUT TOO ORNERY TO DIE."

ABOUT THE AUTHOR

Paul (P. L.) Gaus lives with his wife, Madonna, in Wooster, Ohio, just a few miles north of Holmes County, where the world's largest and most varied settlement of Amish and Mennonite people is found. His knowledge of the culture of the "Plain People" stems from nearly forty years of extensive exploration of this pastoral community, which includes several dozen sects of Anabaptists living closely among the so-called English or Yankee non-Amish people of the county. Paul lectures widely about the Amish people he has met and about the lifestyles, culture, and religion of this remarkable community of religious separatists. He is the author of the Amish-Country Mystery series.